ASHES

THE KINDRED SERIES, BOOK 2

ERICA STEVENS

ALSO FROM THE AUTHOR

Books written under the pen name

Erica Stevens

The Coven Series

Nightmares (Book 1)

The Maze (Book 2)

Dream Walker (Book 3)

The Captive Series

Captured (Book 1)

Renegade (Book 2)

Refugee (Book 3)

Salvation (Book 4)

Redemption (Book 5)

Broken (The Captive Series Prequel)

Vengeance (Book 6)

Unbound (Book 7)

The Kindred Series

Kindred (Book 1)

Ashes (Book 2)

Kindled (Book 3)

Inferno (Book 4)

Phoenix Rising (Book 5)

The Fire & Ice Series

Frost Burn (Book 1)

Arctic Fire (Book 2)

Scorched Ice (Book 3)

The Ravening Series

The Ravening (Book 1)

Taken Over (Book 2)

Reclamation (Book 3)

The Survivor Chronicles

The Upheaval (Book 1)

The Divide (Book 2)

The Forsaken (Book 3)

The Risen (Book 4)

Books written under the pen name

Brenda K. Davies

The Vampire Awakenings Series

Awakened (Book 1)

Destined (Book 2)

Untamed (Book 3)

Enraptured (Book 4)

Undone (Book 5)

Fractured (Book 6)

Ravaged (Book 7)

Consumed (Book 8)

Unforeseen (Book 9)

Forsaken (Book 10)

Relentless (Book 11)

Coming Fall 2020

The Alliance Series

Eternally Bound (Book 1)

Bound by Vengeance (Book 2)

Bound by Darkness (Book 3)

Bound by Passion (Book 4)

Bound by Torment (Book 5)

Coming Spring 2020

The Road to Hell Series

Good Intentions (Book 1)

Carved (Book 2)

The Road (Book 3)

Into Hell (Book 4)

Hell on Earth Series

Hell on Earth (Book 1)

Into the Abyss (Book 2)

Kiss of Death (Book 3)

The Edge of the Darkness

Coming Summer 2020

Historical Romance

A Stolen Heart

Special thanks to my husband for always being there,
my parents for raising some amazing children,
my siblings for being those children, and Leslie Mitchell at G2
Freelance Editing for all her hard work and encouragement.

CHAPTER ONE

"HELP! I NEED HELP HERE!"

Devon slammed through the hospital doors, shoving aside anyone in his way as he searched for someone in the identifying white lab coat. Panic hammered through him as he nearly barreled over a man on crutches. Cassie's limp head rested against his chest, her breathing had become shallow; the beat of her heart had slowed to an alarming rate.

"Now!" he bellowed when no lab coats appeared. "I need help *now*!"

A young man, in the much sought after white coat, appeared through another set of doors. "What happened?" the doctor demanded.

"An animal," Devon lied smoothly. "Some kind of animal attacked her."

The doctor rapidly assessed Cassie's prone form. "Someone bring a gurney!"

Devon's hand dug into the golden silk of her hair as nurses and orderlies bustled about. The doctor and a nurse came at him with their arms out to take her. His need to keep her close to him was almost overwhelming.

"Give her to us son, let us take care of her" the doctor commanded gruffly.

Devon took a steadying breath as he tried to quell the unstable beast lurking just beneath his surface. Finally, he managed to regain enough control to hand Cassie off to those best prepared to help her survive. His arms felt empty without her reassuring weight; his body instantly missed the physical connection between them. His mind brushed along the edge of hers to keep himself reassured she was still alive. That connection to her was keeping him sane right now.

The doctor focused on the tear marks and blood on Devon's shirt. "Are you injured?"

"No." Devon barely glanced at the jagged gashes in his chest. The bleeding had already stopped and he could feel the muscle knitting itself back together.

The doctor's shrewd eyes assessed him. "Did you two have a fight?"

Devon bristled as he took a step closer to the smaller man. "There was no fight, it was an animal, now save her," he barked.

The doctor swallowed loudly as he took a small step back. "We'll have to… ah, we have to alert the police. Procedure, you know," he stuttered out.

Devon's gaze burrowed into the doctor's as he thrust his power forward, and pushed into the doctor's mind. Latching onto the man's will, he bent it to his own, as he altered memories and forced him to bow to what Devon required of him. This was one of his abilities that he didn't relish using, but it did come in handy. The doctor's hazel eyes glazed over, he nodded quickly before turning away to hurry after Cassie. Devon silently followed, moving like a wraith through the stark halls.

They pushed her gurney into a bright room, where they hooked her up to a bunch of beeping, whirring machines. The dazzling light of the room was harsh against his sensitive eyes; he found the stringent, chemical smell abrasive. In the middle of the sterile room, Cassie was a warm beacon. Her golden hair, spread out like a fan around her, was the most vivid thing in the entire room.

The delicate blue veins in her neck, forehead, and around her eyes stood out against her abnormally ashen skin. His heart ached to hold her and save her from anymore pain as they stabbed her with needles and poked and prodded her. His hands fisted as he reminded himself they had to do this in order to save her life.

He turned away when they started to cut her shirt off; her modesty was forgotten in their rush to find the source of all the blood. He hadn't seen this much of her yet, and this was not the time or place, especially when she had no choice in the matter.

"Where did all of this blood come from?" Though Devon's saliva had mainly healed the life threatening injuries she'd sustained, there were still three small cuts in her neck.

It took a second for Devon to realize the doctor was speaking to him. He focused his gaze upon him, studiously avoiding Cassie's prone, half naked form. "The cuts on her neck."

The doctor furrowed his brow as he shook his head. "Those cuts aren't deep enough, they're superficial at best. I need the truth; if we're going to treat her, I have to know where all of the blood came from."

Devon's hands fisted as he took a step forward and pushed the smaller man back with his body. Drawing on his strong abilities, he opened his mind to everyone in the room. Snagging hold of the edges of their thoughts, he drew them all in. The hustle of the room crept to a stop as they turned toward him, their minds a blank slate for him to fill as he saw fit. "The blood loss is from the cuts on her neck, there are to be no more questions, now treat her," he commanded.

He left them dazed and glassy eyed when he withdrew from their minds. They blinked in surprise as their minds snapped back into place and the urgency of their jobs seized them once more. Devon focused on the back wall, so he wouldn't look at her again. He listened to the bustle of the people, the beep of the machines, the orders barked out and obeyed. It was taking all he had not to break something in an effort to ease his frustration.

The power of her blood still hummed through his veins, making him feel as if he could conquer the world. He had a strong ability for mind control and bending people to his will, but sometimes using the ability left him depleted and exhausted. He was neither now. If this was what a few drops of her blood could do, he could only imagine how a good dose would make him feel.

A shudder ran through him, the monster within was coiled just beneath the surface like a rattlesnake ready to strike. He ground his jaw, his hands clenched as the humans hurried past him. They were as inconsequential as gnats to him, gnats he was trying not to swat in order to ease some of his frustration.

"Do you need medical attention?"

Devon blinked in surprise at the nurse staring at him with concern in her eyes. "No."

Her eyes widened at his harsh tone, but he sensed a keen interest in him that had nothing to do with his possible injuries. He relentlessly stared at her until she took the hint and slunk away. Devon risked a glance back, his shoulders slumped as he realized they had Cassie mostly covered now. Bags of blood were brought in, more needles were inserted, dials and knobs checked, but the chaos of the room was easing as medical personnel filed away.

"Is she going to be ok?" he demanded of the hassled looking doctor.

The doctor took off his cap and ran his hands through his shaggy brown hair. "There was quite a bit of blood loss, but yes, she is young and healthy. I think she will be fine."

Devon nodded as the doctor swept past. Though the man had no recollection of what Devon had done to him, he was still very unnerved by his presence. Humans weren't stupid, and the doctor was instinctually fearful of him.

Devon cautiously moved toward Cassie, his chest constricted and his mouth went dry at the thought of touching her once more. The machines beeped, her chest rose and fell with the rhythm of her breath. The beat of her heart was strong in his ears. Relief filled him as he slid his hand into hers. Her silken skin was a salve to his soul.

Though she was stronger than any human, she was still vulnerable to death, and she had nearly succumbed to it tonight.

Grasping her hand within both of his, he struggled to retain control of his raging emotions. In all his seven hundred and fifty-two years, he'd never experienced the protective compulsion that drove him when it came to her. He wanted to take the frailty of her existence from her and make her *his*.

He knew what his possessive impulses meant for the both of them, but he wasn't ready to acknowledge that this wasn't going to end well for either of them.

Devon's head jerked away from her as loud voices filled the hospital hallway. He was appalled to realize while he'd been staring at Cassie, his veins had begun to burn, and his sharp fangs had lengthened. He'd been very close to biting her, draining her, *changing* her, and that was something he couldn't do. Cassie was too innocent and sweet to be condemned to a life of darkness and eternal thirst.

He would protect her from that at all costs.

Though it was an effort, he focused on the chaos outside of the room. Shouts and slapping feet bounced off of the tiled floors and cement walls. "Another animal attack!" a voice barked.

Questions bounced around the halls, loud voices demanding to be heard. Voices he recognized.

He rested Cassie's hand carefully on the bed so as not to disturb any of the tubes hooked to her. He made it two steps toward the door before Luther, Melissa, and Chris barged into the room. They froze for a moment, as their gazes darted between him and Cassie.

"You son of a bitch!" Chris charged across the room like a bull in a headlong rush at the red cape.

Devon braced himself for Chris's attack. Stepping to the side, his hand lashed out and encircled Chris's throat. Thrusting sideways, Devon lifted him up as he pinned him against the wall. Chris's feet dangled a good foot off the ground; his hands clawed at Devon's, his eyes bulged as his face turned red.

"You're not big enough to mess with me!" Devon snarled.

"Wait, wait! Stop!" Melissa rushed over and grasped hold of Devon's arm as she uselessly tried to tug him free. "Let *go* of him!"

Luther knocked Melissa's hand free as he pushed his way in. Though Devon was prepared for Luther to try and pull him away, he was surprised when the man simply rested a hand on his arm. His intense gray eyes met Devon's head on. Devon had questioned Cassie's strange relationship with Melissa's adoptive father, but he realized now Luther was the Guardian of the three of them.

Luther was the man who trained them, and helped to guide them in their journey as Hunter's. He now understood Cassie's words from the dream lake when she'd said, "Out there everything is hard. Out there, this cannot be." He'd intended to keep her sheltered from the dark realities of his life, but he hadn't realized she was already fully immersed in them.

"There wasn't any time for camp once Luther and Melissa came." She'd told him in the dream. Now he realized she wasn't able to attend camp afterwards because she was *not* a human child.

Luther was the reason Cassie had fought him so vehemently when he'd first arrived. Devon couldn't find it within himself to be resentful toward Luther though, not when he'd helped to keep Cassie alive. *He* may have been too blinded by his infatuation with Cassie to recognize what Chris, Melissa, and Cassie were upon his arrival, but other vampires would. Luther had helped to make sure they would be prepared for the monsters of the world, and able to defend themselves against them. Luther's training was the only thing that had saved her from Julian's attack.

"Cassie will be devastated if something happened to Chris. She would never forgive you Devon. Never," Luther said ardently.

Devon met Chris's bulging gaze once more. He'd actually grown to like Chris over the past couple of weeks, and the last thing he wanted was to hurt Cassie. Taking a step away from him, he released Chris with a small shove back. Chris stumbled a little before regaining his balance. He leveled Devon with a fierce glare as he rubbed his bruised throat, but he didn't attack again. Planting his body in between them and Cassie, he folded his arms firmly across his chest. He knew they wouldn't harm her, but he couldn't shake the insane compulsion to protect her from them.

Chris took another step toward him, but Luther grasped hold of his arm and held him in place. "What did you do to her?" Chris was shaking as his shoulders bunched beneath his shirt.

Devon glared at him, but to his credit, Chris didn't back down. "If *I* had done this to her, she wouldn't be here right now."

Chris tried to shake his arm free of Luther's grasp, but he wouldn't release him. "What does that mean?" Chris exploded.

Devon's arms fell back to his as he took a step closer to him. "It means I would have kept her for myself," Devon snarled.

"How is she?" Luther had apparently decided to ignore Devon's comment.

Devon's gaze returned to her pale, frail form. "The doctor said she will be fine."

Melissa began to cry. Devon blinked in surprise as the normally stoic girl burst into loud, heart wrenching sobs. Her tear filled eyes watched him warily as she hurried to the other side of the bed. "I was so scared," she whispered. "I thought she was dead, I thought we'd lost her. When I saw it…"

Her voice trailed off as tears choked her. "*Saw* it?" Devon inquired harshly. She'd seen something that could have prevented all this, and she'd done nothing to stop it?

Melissa didn't answer as she turned her full attention back to Cassie. "What is going on here?" Chris demanded. "He's a monster! We should be destroying him!"

"I'd like to see you try. You have *never* come up against the likes of me boy, you won't win this battle," Devon assured him.

Chris's eyes spit blue fury, but he didn't make another careless move toward Devon. Apparently he was a quick learner. "I think it's safe to say Devon isn't one of the bad guys." Luther's eyes were curious behind his glasses as he tilted his head to the side.

"Is that possible?" Melissa asked as she wiped the tears from her cheeks.

"Anything is possible, I suppose," Luther replied. "Though I've never heard of it before."

Devon bristled under Luther's scrutiny, but he remained where he was, mainly because he wasn't going to release Cassie's hand again. "Who did this to her then?" Chris demanded.

Devon was unsure how much he should tell them, but the tension in the room wouldn't be diffused if he refused to tell them anything. "Julian did."

They exchanged confused looks before focusing on him again. "Who is Julian?" Luther asked.

He wasn't ready to get into a detailed explanation of *that* just yet. "He's a monster," Devon answered simply.

"That's the pot calling the kettle black," Chris retorted.

Devon's head shot up as his upper lip curled in a snarl. "You don't know what I am or what I'm *not*! But you keep pushing me and you *will* find out!" he spat.

For the first time a bolt of apprehension flashed through Chris's eyes. "This is not the place for this conversation. I'm sure Devon will give us some answers later, but Cassie will also require them. Now, let's just calm down. Fighting won't solve anything, and he did save her life," Luther reasoned.

Chris folded his arms over his chest, but wisely kept his mouth shut for a change. "Have you called her grandmother?" Devon inquired.

Luther shook his head, pushed his glasses up his nose and glanced apprehensively at Cassie. "No, we had to get Marcy to the hospital first, and in all honesty, we thought she was dead. That's something better told in person."

They all studied him like he was an odd bug they didn't understand. Devon didn't take offense to the fact they'd thought her dead. It was the nature of most of his kind to kill after all, and at one time he'd been the same way. If it hadn't been for Annabelle, he would still be a monster, destroying and killing whenever the mood struck him.

"How is Marcy?" he inquired.

"She'll be ok," Melissa answered as she wiped the remaining tears from her cheeks. "She's lost a lot of blood, but she'll survive."

"Yeah, now we have to figure out how we're going to explain all of this to her," Chris muttered.

"I'll take care of it."

Their gazes flew back to him. "How do you plan on doing that?" Chris demanded.

Devon was unwilling to divulge any of his secrets before they agreed to divulge some of theirs. Hunters possessed some of the same abilities vampires did, and he couldn't leave himself vulnerable to them.

"I have my ways," Devon murmured.

Chris's eyes narrowed, his lip twisted into a sneer, but he didn't push it further. "I saw you coming, but I didn't see *you,*" Melissa whispered.

Devon's forehead furrowed as he turned back to her. She was studying him with a deep, penetrating stare that slightly unnerved him. "Excuse me?" he asked in confusion.

She blinked as she came out of her reverie and shook her head. Her raven hair fell forward to shield her pretty features as she turned back to Cassie. Luther rested his hand on Melissa's shoulder as he lifted the phone and punched in some numbers. Chris continued to watch him closely while he moved to Cassie's other side and rested his hand on her arm.

Devon fought the impulse to leap over the bed and knock Chris's hand away from her. Instead, somehow, he managed to keep control of himself. If he didn't keep himself tightly reigned in, someone could get injured, and that was something he couldn't allow to happen; especially not with Cassie's life hanging in the balance and her friends surrounding him. Friends who were trained to kill him.

He glanced back at Cassie's prone figure. If she survived this, would she hate him too? Would she also want him dead? A shiver raced through him at the thought. He wouldn't survive it if she condemned him and turned him away.

She held both of their destinies in her hands; he could only hope she didn't destroy his. Didn't destroy *him*. He returned Chris's glare with one of his own as he slid his hand back into hers. He required her warmth to keep him tethered and to soothe his riotously swaying emotions.

Pulling up a chair, he ignored the surprised looks Chris, Melissa, and Luther shot him as he sat next to her. He didn't care what they thought; he wasn't leaving her side until she was awake. He wasn't leaving her side unless *she* told him to.

CHAPTER TWO

DEVON'S MUSCLES had stiffened hours ago, his legs were cramped, and his back sore from the uncomfortable chair. Luther had left as the sun broke over the horizon, taking Chris and Melissa with him to check on Marcy. They hadn't been gone long, but he knew they would be returning soon. Cassie's grandmother sat across from him, her hand on Cassie's arm. She kept most of her attention focused on Cassie, but she would glance at him every once in a while. Sometimes her eyes were the color of the sky, at other times they were a deep, distant brown. He didn't know what brought on the change, but it was fascinating to watch.

Cassie's grandmother hadn't spoken since she'd arrived; Devon knew she had something to say to him though. He was nervous the deceptively delicate looking woman would tell him to stay away from her granddaughter, and that was something he couldn't do. Finally, she turned to him; her eyes a clear blue once more. "Thank you," she murmured.

Devon's hands clenched on the arms of the chair. "For what?"

She swallowed heavily. "For saving her, she's all I have." Tears shimmered in her eyes before she quickly turned back to Cassie. "Thank you."

Devon's back cracked as he leaned forward. "Cassie's parents were killed during the attack?"

She lifted a dainty strawberry blond eyebrow as she studied him. "Is that what your kind calls it? The attack?"

Devon nodded as he studied her. She didn't seem to hate him, but there was a hesitance about her she hadn't displayed in his presence before. "What do you call it?"

"The Slaughter." Her voice was cold and distant. Pain emphasized the lines around her mouth. "*We* call it The Slaughter."

He could understand why they would call it that. Before most of the Elders went into hiding, they had decided to gather as many vampire's as possible in order to destroy the Hunter line, and secure their own safety. Fortunately for him, fate had seen fit to spare Cassie's life, and bring her into his. "I see," he murmured.

"Do you?"

He stared at her before rising and moving to stand beside the bed. Behind her closed lids, Cassie's eyes moved as unconsciousness held her deep within its grip. A soft healthy color was beginning to return to her face and chest. He wanted her awake and speaking; he had to know if she would hate him now that she knew what he was.

"You also saved her life then." His gaze returned to her grandmother as he tried to distract himself from his thoughts.

Her head was quirked as she studied him. "Yes, I kept her safe, hidden, and protected."

"Thank you."

A small smile curled the corner of her full mouth. "You really care about my granddaughter, don't you?" She sounded completely mystified, and he knew exactly how she felt. How could he have not known what Cassie was? What they *all* were?

Love was truly blind, or at least the people in it were, he realized.

The image of her standing at the side of the clearing with her hand clenched around a stake was burned permanently into his mind. She hadn't been astonished to see him there, not as much as he'd been seeing *her* standing there. She seemed to have figured out what he was, but he hadn't been able to put all of the pieces of the puzzle together until then.

The woman he loved, and cherished, was also his sworn enemy. The woman who had brought him back to life had also been created to end it. He still couldn't quite understand it all, and the twisted irony of it was not lost upon him.

Devon met her inquisitive gaze. "Yes," he admitted honestly. "More than I ever thought possible."

Her delicate forehead furrowed as she turned back to Cassie. "I don't understand any of this."

"We are not *all* monsters."

Her gaze shot back to his. "No, I suppose not. I'm just going to have to figure out how to process that astonishing bit of information."

His hand rubbed Cassie's arm as he relished in the feel of her satiny skin. Turning away, he paced back and forth as he tried to lose some of the restless energy clinging to him. Still acutely attuned to the beat of her heart, he felt when it picked up, when she stirred. He froze instantly; his mouth went dry as he waited for his fate to be handed to him.

Her grandmother rose and leaned eagerly over her granddaughter. "Cassie, Cassie can you hear me?"

He could see her lids lift, but he was unable to see the brilliant color of her eyes. "Grandma?"

The sound of her voice was the sweetest thing he'd ever heard. "Yes, dear, I'm here. It's ok; you're going to be just fine."

Cassie's hand grasped hold of her grandmother as the woman bent over to give her a hug before pulling away. "Devon? Where's Devon?"

Her grandmother glanced anxiously at him before taking a small step back. "Here, I'm right here."

He was surprised to find he could barely get the words past the constriction in his chest and throat. He took a guarded step toward her, eager to see her again, eager to *feel* her again, but terrified of what she would say. Stopping at her side, his body froze as her eyes clashed with his. The startling azure of them was vivid, and the pure amethyst flecks speckled throughout shone in the harsh illumination of the room.

"Devon," she breathed as tears filled her eyes and spilled down her delicate cheeks.

"Shh, don't cry love." Bending over her, he tenderly wiped the tears from her skin. "Don't cry."

"I thought you were that… that *thing* and I planned to kill you."

He had already suspected as much. He felt he should be angered, or feel betrayed by it, he wasn't. Their kind knew nothing about the vampires who didn't feed on humans; they knew nothing about the ones who had shunned human blood. All she'd known was a monster was hunting her community, killing people, and somehow she'd managed to figure out what he was. She had no way of knowing he wasn't a murderer anymore.

More tears spilled free; they came so fast he couldn't keep up with wiping them away. "Cassie…"

"I wanted to kill you, and you saved my life." She seized hold of his hand with surprising strength. "I should have known you weren't a monster, I should have *trusted* you. You would never do anything to hurt me. Please forgive me."

He felt as if he'd been punched as he stared at her. He'd been concerned she wouldn't forgive him, and instead she was pleading for *his* forgiveness. Gathering her in his arms, he cradled her as he relished the feel of her. "There is nothing to forgive Cassie. I was worried you wouldn't forgive me."

Her body trembled in his arms. "For what?" she mumbled.

"For what I am."

Her tears wet his skin as she buried her face in his neck. "You are an amazing man Devon."

His gut twisted as his grip on her tightened. That was the worst part about all of this, he wasn't a man, and at one time he'd been a brutal monster. He didn't know what he'd done to deserve her, but he would spend the rest of his life doing everything he could to earn her love. His hand slid into her hair and eased through the tangles that marred its golden beauty.

Never in his life had he felt anything as magnificent as she was, and he knew nothing would ever compare to her. He rocked her as her tears gradually subsided. Her eyes were reddened from her tears as she pulled back from him. He wiped the tears from her cheeks, hating the sight of them. She deserved only happiness and warmth, but unfortunately fate had cast them into roles where darkness was their main reality.

She stared at him with awe filled eyes as she searched his face. The tips of her lengthy lashes shimmered with water. He was unable to resist the tempting lure of her as he bent down and pressed a kiss to her rosebud mouth.

His skin heated, his body tightened as the feel of her burned into him. Hunger for her coursed through him, but he kept it under control. Pulling away reluctantly, he stroked her face once more before turning to meet the newcomers in the room.

Luther, Chris, and Melissa stood just inside the doorway. Chris's jaw hung ajar, Luther's face was an impassive mask, and Melissa's cheeks had become the color of Santa's suit. Rising from the bed, he kept hold of Cassie's hand as he stood beside her. He'd nearly lost her and he wasn't about to let her go anytime soon.

Cassie wiped the remaining tears from her face as she shyly smiled at them. "Hi guys."

Melissa was the first to recover her usual aplomb. "It's so good to see you awake!"

She shot Devon a confused look as she moved to Cassie's grandmother's side. She bent to hug Cassie, careful of the wires and tubes running from her. "It's good to be awake."

Chris's sapphire eyes were dark and brooding as he joined Melissa. Awkwardly, he bent to hug Cassie, but his gaze never left Devon's. Devon hated the idea of another man touching her, even if it was Chris, but he remained immobile as they embraced.

"What happened?" Chris asked.

Cassie quickly glanced at Devon, her hand clenching his as she recounted the awful events of the night. Devon became more and more incensed as he sensed her rising distress. Though he'd only tasted a few drops of her blood, they'd been enough to forge a stronger connection between them. He could sense her emotions more clearly, and though he couldn't read her thoughts, he could almost feel them pounding against the edges of his mind.

When she was done they all turned to stare questioningly at him. Luther finally broke the silence. "I think we have a lot to discuss."

"After Cassie is feeling well enough to go home, we can talk," he assured him.

"I feel fine now," Cassie interjected forcefully.

She'd only been awake for a little bit, but her color had already returned. He was surprised to realize the severe blood loss had been traumatic, but she appeared as if nothing had happened. Her intense sleep seemed to have completely repaired the injuries she'd sustained. It was amazing.

"You have to rest," her grandmother insisted.

"I'm fine Grandma, really. I heal fast."

"Apparently," Devon muttered as his thumb slid over her skin.

"Cassie…" Luther uttered her name in disbelief.

"I'm fine Luther, really. I feel much better; I just want to get out of here, now. I don't like hospitals."

"You've never been in one," her grandmother said.

"And now it's time to go."

Tossing aside her blankets, she swung her legs out of the bed. Devon was startled by the graceful movement and the speed with which she'd done it. She stood before him for a moment before her legs began to wobble. He grabbed hold of her and swung her into his arms as if she weighed no more than a feather. He was once again reminded of how fragile she was as she stared up at him. The beast crawled through him, rippling just beneath the surface as the compulsion to make her immortal reared back to life.

Seeming to sense his tension, Cassie rested her hand on his cheek in order to soothe the monster within him once more. He held her closer, refusing to let go of her. "I want to go home," she told him.

Whatever she asked for, no matter how absurd or difficult, he would give it to her. "I'll get the doctor."

Devon reluctantly placed her back down on the bed. "Devon…"

Luther's voice broke off at the silencing look Devon shot him. Cassie was *his* now. They just needed to realize that. It was one thing he did know for certain, one day he would possess her completely. One day she would belong to him, for eternity.

CHAPTER THREE

CASSIE CLUNG to Devon's hand, unwilling to release him. His hand was strong, calloused, and slightly cool against hers. She couldn't stop herself from reveling in the splendor of his striking face. His strong jaw clenched; the nostrils of his sculpted nose flared as he faced the people surrounding him.

Sensing her attention, his vivid emerald eyes warmed as they met her fascinated gaze. His full lips curved into a small smile. His black hair hung around the edges of his chiseled face and curled boyishly at the corner of his right eye.

He was anything but boyish though with his svelte body and immortal status. No, Devon was most certainly not a boy; he wasn't even a man. He was the one thing she'd hated since she'd learned her parents, and Chris's father, hadn't been killed in a car accident together, but had been murdered during The Slaughter. If it wasn't for Chris's mother Mary, Cassie and Chris would have been slaughtered in the strike also.

Devon seemed to sense the dark turn her thoughts had taken.

His smile faded as he took a step closer to her. The feel of his body suddenly heated her chilled skin, her heart thudded, her toes curled as she fought the desperate urge to pull him into her embrace. Unfortunately there was still too much to deal with before she could allow herself to be lost in the comfort he offered.

Cassie's attention was brought back to Luther as he shifted his stance. His head was quirked as his gray eyes studied Devon over the top of his John Lennon style glasses. His graying brown hair was uncharacteristically disheveled as he anxiously ran his fingers through it. "How old are you?"

Cassie wasn't sure she cared to know the answer to that question. She'd dated an older boy for about a week, but he'd only been a year and a half older than her. Being the girl with the boyfriend who could possibly be a couple hundred years older was something entirely different, and more than a little frightening.

Devon's fingers entwined with hers. "I've been a vampire for seven hundred and fifty-two years. In total, I'm seven hundred and seventy-one."

Cassie's breath exploded from her. Her eyes spun toward him as her hand clenched on his. "Crap," Chris breathed.

Cassie felt *that* was the understatement of the year. He was nearly a *millennium* older than her! Seven hundred and fifty-four years to be exact! It was far more of an age difference than she ever would have imagined, no wonder he seemed so much older than all of the students around him. She didn't want to think about the number of women he'd known over the years. She knew how the girls at school flocked to him, practically throwing themselves at his feet.

She found herself barely able to breathe through the knot of jealousy and disbelief stuck in her throat. His emerald eyes were filled with unease and a desperate need for her to understand as they pierced her own. It was that look that finally allowed air to filter back into her brutalized lungs.

No matter how frightened, lost, and envious she was, she couldn't turn against him. She had to live in the present; she *had* to stay grounded here. She would go crazy if she didn't. No matter how many women he'd known in his past, she knew *she* was his everything now. Biting nervously on her bottom lip, Cassie managed a small nod for him, and his shoulders relaxed visibly.

"You must be very powerful," Melissa said softly.

Devon nodded. "Yes."

"What can you do?" Melissa prodded when Devon didn't say anymore.

Melissa's exotically slanted, onyx eyes, were fixed upon Devon. Her hair, free from its customary French braid, fell around her shoulders in thick black waves that ended just beneath her shoulder blades. Her slender body was seemingly at ease as she leaned against the fireplace, but tension hummed just beneath her outwardly calm surface.

Devon shrugged absently. "I am stronger and faster than a human."

"So is every other vampire. So are *we*," Chris retorted.

Devon lifted an eyebrow at Chris. "But I'm stronger than most, far more. My senses are keener than theirs and I'm faster. Most wouldn't survive a fight with me."

Hostility hummed through Chris's large, football players build. Despite his size, Chris moved with a grace and agility that was both surprising and impressive. It was one of the reasons he was the star on the football team. His sandy blond hair was a mess from tugging on it as he restlessly paced back and forth, only pausing once in a while to pierce Devon with an accusatory glare.

"Except for the one you ran into last night," Chris grumbled.

"I can defeat Julian," Devon snarled.

Chris took an angry step forward. "Then why didn't you?"

Devon's emerald eyes darkened to a deep shade of jade as he glanced down at Cassie. It was because of her that Devon had abandoned the fight. Because of *her* he hadn't hunted Julian down and destroyed the monster plaguing their area. If she hadn't been so distracted, and horrified to realize her suspicions about Devon being a vampire were true, Julian never would have had the opportunity to nearly kill her.

Cassie shuddered at the reminder of her near death experience. She'd come close to losing everything, and everyone, she loved. Closing her eyes, she tried to suppress the disgust and fear the memory aroused. "What else are you capable of?" Chris inquired, apparently deciding to let the fight go.

Devon frowned as his attention was once again pulled away from her. "I have the ability for mind control, and…"

"Excuse me," Cassie interrupted stridently. "Mind control?"

"Yes. Though I can't read them, I am able to sort through people's minds and pick out a certain one amongst the crowd. Or I can pick out a few minds, a crowd's too, if it's necessary. When I latch onto it, I can bend it to my will, inserting memories or altering time." Cassie gaped at him as nausea curdled through her belly. He could control her mind? "I would never do that to you Cassie, any of you, I swear."

"That's how you were able to get into the school," Luther guessed. "I'm assuming you don't have transcripts."

Devon's eyes twinkled with amusement. "No, I don't."

Cassie couldn't help but chuckle as she shook her head in disbelief. This was her life, as strange and odd and fantastic as it was. It was far more overwhelming than she'd thought it would be when she was thirteen, but she wouldn't trade it for anything. Just a few weeks ago there had been many things she would have changed, but then Devon had walked into her world and turned it upside down. She wouldn't even change the Hunter heritage she'd resented for the past four years. To alter one thing might mean she never would have met Devon.

"I think they would be a little expired anyway," Melissa said with a laugh.

"That's why you're always so bored," Cassie murmured. Devon flashed a beautiful, heart stopping grin, it melted the last of her disquiet over his startling ability to control people's minds. "What were you saying before I interrupted you? What else can you do?"

His grin faded as his eyes became distant once more. "I have an inherent ability to lure people to me. It's especially strong with women."

Cassie's eyebrows drew together. The more he spoke of his abilities, the less she liked them. His looks were more than enough to draw any woman, and she was sure some men, never mind adding this to it. "Like a Venus flytrap," muttered Luther.

"Yes, very much so."

"Does anyone escape?" Chris asked harshly.

"I haven't tasted human blood in a hundred and thirty-seven years," Devon retorted. Then his eyes fell to the scratches still marring her neck. Cassie felt her face redden as horror curdled through her. He'd gone so long without tasting blood, until her foolishness had forced him to use the healing agent in his saliva to close her cuts. "Until tonight," he mumbled.

Hunger heated his eyes and turned them a darker shade of green as he met her startled gaze. Need poured from him in waves that left her breathless and frozen. She could feel the turbulent battle he waged with himself as he fought to control his desire for blood, *her* blood. She should be petrified by his obvious longing to drain her, she was amazed to discover she was also oddly tantalized by it. Excitement tore through her at the thought, her toes curled as yearning hotly blazed through her body. He was the only thing she saw; he became the only thing in the *room* as every cell in her being focused on him.

Luther cleared his throat and coughed loudly then pulled off his glasses and began cleaning them with his shirt. Chris and Melissa were studying the far wall, obviously trying to ignore the scene before them. Face burning, Cassie couldn't bring herself to look at her grandmother, she was sure she would burst into flames if she did.

"What made you stop drinking human blood?" Luther inquired after a few more awkward seconds.

Devon shrugged. "Things change."

Cassie frowned as her eyes hesitantly flitted back to him, but it appeared he wasn't going to elaborate any further. "And before this change, were you a killer?" Chris demanded.

"Yes." The simple word, spoken with such a clear and dry tone, hung heavily in the air. Cassie's heart thumped loudly, she bit on her bottom lip, as she tried not to judge him too harshly. "I cannot change the past but I have spent over a hundred years trying to atone for my sins."

"And have you?"

"No." Devon's jaw was clenched, a muscle jumped in his cheek as he stared at Chris. Cassie rubbed her thumb over his cool skin, as she tried to assure him of her unwavering love.

"The sun," Melissa said, obviously looking to change the tense subject. "How are you able to go out in the sun?"

A small smile curved Devon's lips. "That took *years*. As my powers grew, I began to gradually expose myself to the sun's deadly rays. Eventually I could stand more and more of them as I built up a sort of immunity to it."

"How long did that take?" Luther inquired.

"I've been working on it for about three hundred years now. I still burn easily if I'm exposed for a prolonged amount of time, and it still depletes my powers a little faster than I would like, but at least I'm able to be in it for longer periods of time without bursting into flames."

"Why would you take such a risk in the first place?" Cassie demanded as she realized he could have been killed.

His smile slipped a little as he glanced down at her. "In the beginning, simply to see if I could. I knew of one other vampire who had succeeded in being able to walk about in daylight, and I wasn't about to be second best to anyone. After a while I began to remember what it felt like to be in the sun, to feel the heat of it." He shrugged as his gaze returned to the far wall. "I missed it."

"And it allowed for more hunting time," Chris snorted.

Devon's face was impassive as he turned toward him, but his body had gone rigid. Cassie hated the conflict between them, but there was nothing she could do about it right now. Eventually they would come to realize they had to get along, because she wasn't going to part with either one of them.

She only hoped it didn't get to the point where they couldn't be near each other. Chris was her rock, her best friend, without him she would have been lost years ago. But Devon was her heart and soul. Swallowing heavily, she shoved away her trepidation and unease. It had only been a few hours, she was sure with time Chris would come to see that Devon wasn't a monster.

"Yes," Devon answered.

Cassie fought a shudder as she tried to block out the awful image of Devon killing innocent, unsuspecting people. That wasn't the Devon standing next to her now; she had to remember that. She didn't know what had made him stop killing, but she did know the man beside her now was kind, compassionate, and loving. He was *not* a killer anymore.

Still, she couldn't shake the uneasiness she felt. "Can Julian go out in the sun?" she asked.

"I don't know, but I doubt it," he answered thoughtfully. "Julian has always relished the darkness, the deprivation, and pain of our existence. He would not appreciate the warmth of the sun's rays."

"But it would expand his hunting time," Chris pointed out.

Devon simply nodded. Cassie pulled the blanket off of her lap. Devon took a step forward in an attempt to stop her if she tried to rise. Cassie frowned at him as she shook her head. She had no intention of going anywhere, not yet anyway, the blanket was just hot and confining. Besides, she didn't need him hovering over her like a mother hen. Cassie waved him off as she swung her legs to the floor. She knew it wasn't the weight of the blanket making her uncomfortable, but rather all the awful events and truths that had come out. Unfortunately, there was no easy way to throw them off.

"Does Julian have the same powers as you?" Cassie inquired, fearful of the potential for Julian to control minds.

Devon shook his head but his eyes were troubled and dark. "He doesn't have mind control, but he does have Psychometry."

"Psycho what?" Cassie asked, not at all liking the sound of it.

"Psychometry, it's the ability to learn about a person by touching them, or by touching an object they've touched. He gets impressions from these things, he can tell what has happened in the past, and he can learn about you."

"That's not so bad, at least it's not mind control," Chris said with a pointed look at Devon.

Devon shook his head as he ignored Chris's baiting. "No, it's not mind control, but Julian uses it to get inside a person's head, to torture them, to taunt them. He can learn about you, your abilities, and your families. It's fun for him to drive a person crazy with his knowledge of them, before killing them. It's not mind control, but the way Julian uses it, it's worse."

Cassie's mouth dropped, Chris inhaled sharply, and Luther cleaned his glasses off again. Melissa leaned heavily against the fireplace mantle, but her grandmother remained unmoving. "Just great," Melissa moaned as she rubbed the bridge of her nose.

"Psycho, just psycho, that's all I have to know about *that* ability," Chris mumbled.

The heartbeat in Cassie's chest began to increase; the palms of her hands became sweaty. "He touched me," she managed to croak out.

"He won't ever touch you again," Devon vowed. "And he will never get close enough to use his knowledge against you."

"But he does have knowledge of me?"

She could tell he'd like to sugarcoat it, that he didn't want to be brutally honest with her, but in the end, he was. "He didn't touch you for long so he probably only had a brief glimpse into you."

Cassie blinked; it was the only reaction she could make. He knew about her. That *monster* knew about *her*! What did he know? What had he seen? Cassie's fingers curled into the blanket, she was suddenly ice cold, but she knew the blanket would do little to warm her. Devon knelt beside her and nudged her chin up.

"He won't get near you again," he vowed.

Though she managed a nod, she didn't feel relieved. She'd seen that *thing*, she'd felt it's evil. There was no stopping it, not until it was dead.

Devon stroked her face before turning back to the others. "And what powers do you possess?" he inquired.

Chris and Melissa exchanged a panicked look, and then a quiet voice bravely declared, "I speak to the dead."

It was the first time her grandmother had spoken since Cassie had been released from the hospital. Apparently where Chris and Melissa were still hesitant, she'd decided to give her trust whole-heartedly. Cassie's heart warmed, she knew how difficult this must be for her grandmother. She'd lost so much to vampires over the past twenty years, and yet she was willing to trust Devon with one of her most intimate secrets.

Her grandma's sky blue eyes were clear and warm as they briefly met Cassie's gaze. She sat casually in the recliner in the corner of the room, her small legs drawn up beneath her. Her strawberry hair had been pulled into a loose ponytail that fell to her shoulders in flowing waves. Though she was in her late fifties, she still looked as if she were in her thirties. Cassie hoped she looked that good at her grandmother's age but at this point, she just hoped to survive to see her thirties, then she would worry about how she might look in her fifties.

"A whisperer," Devon said.

Her grandmother's mouth quirked in a slight grin as she nodded. "Apparently you know a lot about our kind."

"Seven hundred years is a lot of time to learn things."

Her grandmother chuckled. "I suppose so. It puts us at a disadvantage though."

Devon was silent as he pondered her words. "But you must know The Hunter line and vampires share the same abilities. That is why many vampires know a lot about your abilities, and likewise, why you know a lot about *our* abilities."

"Some of us do." Luther shot a pointed look at Chris and Cassie, who quickly looked away. Cassie was not in the mood for another one of his lectures on their lack of knowledge, and unwillingness to learn, about their ancestry and heritage.

Devon gave her a questioning look, but she didn't feel like discussing it right now. "The Slaughter," Cassie said quietly. The vampire's may not have known which Hunter's possessed which abilities, but they knew the kinds of abilities they would come up against, and they were prepared for them. However, The Hunter's hadn't been prepared for the sudden, violent onslaught.

"I had no part in that, I swear. I was far removed from any of the inner circles, far out of the loop when it occurred. I wouldn't have taken part if I had known." Cassie found she believed him. It was a strange realization considering everything that had transpired in the past twenty-four hours, but though he'd never told her what he really was, he'd never done anything to harm her.

"They will keep coming for you," Devon continued. "Not only do they aspire to have The Hunter line extinguished, but also because your blood is strong, and very powerful. There is no greater rush than a Hunter's blood. There is nothing more empowering, and the effect of it lasts for years. It can be irresistible."

Cassie's hand fluttered up to her neck. He had resisted it. He had tasted her blood, and he had turned away from it. Was there something wrong with it? Cassie's brow furrowed as the disturbing thought occurred to her. She had no special "gifts" like her family, Chris, and Melissa. Did that somehow make her blood less appealing?

She didn't know why the thought bothered her so much, she should be happy she wasn't a magnet for vampires. But for some unfathomable reason, she was *not* happy. She was ashamed to admit that, for once, she would like to be special too. She'd been denied the "gifts" given to those in the Hunter line; she didn't want to be denied this too. No matter how unreasonable her thoughts were, she couldn't shake them.

"Who brought Mr. Good News to the party?" Chris muttered as he folded his arms over his chest and scowled at the floor.

Devon glanced back down at her, his forehead furrowed and his eyes dark and stormy. "This is good; we have an insider's view. He can help us," Luther said.

A muscle twitched in Devon's jaw, and his fingers tightened briefly around hers. "Yes, but I think the best thing for all of you is to leave…"

"No!" Cassie cut in.

Devon continued speaking as if she'd never said a word. "I can defeat Julian, but he's brutal, and merciless. He'll keep on coming, and I can't be everywhere at once. If you leave, then I will protect the town, I will keep everyone safe…"

"I'm not leaving you here!"

"And I will meet up with you when I am done here."

Cassie opened her mouth to protest again, and then snapped it shut as she glared up at him. Luther and her grandmother were practically salivating over his suggestion. It had been a fight to get the two of them to agree to let Cassie, Chris, and Melissa stay in town in the first place. Now Devon had given them the excuse they'd been looking for to rip the three of them out of there as quickly as they could.

"We are *not* leaving," Cassie grated through clenched teeth.

"Cassie, you must listen to reason. Devon can protect this town better than the three of you, and we must keep you alive."

She turned her glare on Luther. "We are here to protect people…"

"Which Devon can do more effectively."

The throw pillow that had been sitting in her lap fell to the floor as Cassie launched to her feet. Devon lurched toward her, for the first time not moving as effortlessly as a panther as she caught him off guard. She shook off his hand on her elbow, but he reached for her again.

"I'm fine!" she retorted before spinning on Luther. "What good is being a Hunter if we have to run all the time?"

Luther glanced briefly at Devon, his gray eyes weary as they met Cassie's once more. "Not all of the time Cassie, only when it's prudent."

"Prudent?" she snorted. "Is that what all of our ancestors did, turn tail and run whenever things got hard?"

"Well no, of course not, but there aren't enough Hunter's left to risk your lives. We must keep you safe, the line *must* continue on."

"Wait, wait, wait!" Melissa threw up her hand as she took a step forward. "So what you're saying is we must be kept alive in order to continue the line? It has nothing to do with us? We're just necessary for *breeding*? What freaking century is this?"

Luther colored somewhat, his glasses slid down his nose as he shook his head. "No, of course not, but you must understand how important it is that the line continues. How important it is you are kept alive to kill other vampires. You can't kill them all, but you can get a lot of them. There are few as powerful as Devon and Julian."

He glanced at Devon who nodded in agreement. "And what if you can't stop him?" she demanded.

Devon quirked an eyebrow; a flicker of amusement crossed his amazing features. "I can."

She didn't appreciate his cocky, arrogant demeanor. "How do you know that for sure?"

Devon's eyes wandered over the room, before he turned back to her with a steely resolve in his eyes. "I made Julian what he is, I *can* defeat him."

A pin dropping would have resounded through the room following his admission. Cassie was the first to recover. "What do you mean *made* Julian what he is?"

His eyes were hooded and distant; he had already shut himself off in preparation for her turning against him. "Julian and I were once good friends, I helped to mold him into the vampire he is today. He's nearly six hundred years old, we spent almost three hundred of those years traveling together, and wreaking havoc wherever we went. I am the one who taught him the joy of the hunt, the torture, the mental anguish." He paused for a moment, a muscle twitched in his cheek. "The pleasure found in drawing out the kill."

Cassie's legs went to rubber; limply she sat back down on the couch. Clasping her hands before her, she bent her head, uncertain how to deal with the turbulent emotions tumbling through her. What kind of a monster had Devon been? What had he done to people? She shuddered, struggling not to fall apart as her hands clenched.

"I see," Luther, the first to recover after the shocking revelation, whispered the words.

Cassie lifted her head as she tried to breathe through the constriction in her chest. "Why?" Cassie mumbled.

His eyes were shards of green ice as he met her gaze. "Because I could. What I am now is not what I was then. I cannot take it back. I cannot change my past, no matter how much I would like to." Her mind tripped over his words as she tried to assimilate everything he was telling her. Taking a deep breath she tried to retain control of her emotions.

"All right, fine, you were once great friends: you think you can defeat him…"

"I *know* I can."

Chris shot Devon an exasperated look over being cut off. "But we're still not leaving."

"Chris…"

"No, Luther, we made the decision to stay, and we're sticking by it. Devon himself said he couldn't be everywhere at once. He will need our help. If even *one* person dies because we left, then we would be responsible for that death. That is something I can't live with, and I'm sure Cassie and Melissa can't either, and I hope that *you* can't."

Luther gaped at him for a moment. "No, of course not!"

"You shouldn't stay here." Devon's hands fisted as he stared forcefully at Cassie. "He'll come for you the most."

Her eyebrows shot up as her mouth parted in surprise. "Why?"

Devon ran a hand through his already disheveled black hair. "He's smelled your blood; he's already been denied what he wanted. Plus, he knows you're *mine*. He will try to destroy that."

Though she thought she should be offended by the "you are mine statement," she was oddly thrilled by it. If any other boy had ever said that to her, she would have laughed in their face and walked away. But with Devon, she *was* his, completely, utterly, and for as long as she could have him. Their bond couldn't be severed and ran deeper than the Mariana Trench. She'd never thought something like this could exist, but it did, and it was so very true and real.

"Why?" She felt like a parrot, but it seemed to be the only word she could get out.

"Because Julian aims to destroy anything good and right in the world, and he hates that I've turned against my nature. He would like for me to return to the way I once was."

Cassie shuddered. "Like him?" Melissa asked.

Devon hesitated briefly. "Worse."

A thick hush descended upon the room. Though the answer was blunt, Cassie sensed the regret, distress, and pain behind the word. "Why did you change?" she inquired.

"That's a long story."

Cassie wasn't so sure if it was a long story, or if he simply didn't want to talk about it. Either way, she wasn't going to push him. She already had enough information to digest without having more heaped onto her. "That's all fine and good, but we're *not* leaving," Cassie said firmly. A muscle twitched in Devon's jaw. "You won't change my mind, or theirs, so don't argue with us."

The muscle twitched more, she could now hear his teeth grinding. "We can't change what we are, or what has been." Her eyes narrowed pointedly as she reiterated his words. She had to accept him for what he was, and he had to do the same with her. "You just have to accept it, as we have."

Muscle twitching forcefully, he slowly turned away from her. His shoulders were thrust back, his hands fisted at his sides so tightly his knuckles had turned white. She had aggravated him, she knew that, but she felt no remorse for it. They wouldn't run from this, or any other problems that arose. They had to stay; it was their duty, hell it was in their *blood.* It was who they were, who they were born to be.

Luther shook his head, and rested his arm on the mantle. "Tell him what the two of you can do."

CHAPTER FOUR

"If you insist upon staying then Devon should know of your abilities in order to utilize them in the best ways possible." Luther's voice was tinged with exasperation as they continued to remain silent.

Devon knew very well the annoyance the man was feeling. It was taking every ounce of self-control he had not to grab hold of Cassie and forcefully remove her from this house, and this town. If she wouldn't hate him, and possibly never forgive him for it, he would do it. When he saw Julian again, he was going to rip him limb from limb for what he had done to her earlier.

At the moment he didn't know if he wanted to force her to leave, or taste her, more. No, he didn't simply want to taste her; he wanted to change her, possess her. A shudder ran up his spine, his eyes closed briefly as a rush of bloodlust rippled through him.

Being around her was a constant battle with his darker, more twisted side. But it also brought out the best in him, drew out a light he'd never expected to find, completing him in a way he'd never thought possible. Eventually his feelings would cause problems between them, and he would have to make a decision she may end up hating him for, but now was a time for strategizing, and learning as much as he could about the people around him. If they had abilities that would aid him in his hunt for Julian, he was going to use them in every way he could.

He would do whatever it took to keep her safe.

Melissa licked her lips nervously, Chris still looked doubtful. "I have premonitions," Melissa supplied. "Some are inconsequential, foolish, and vague. Others, well, others are awful, detailed, and almost consuming. They don't always come true though, like tonight." Though he had exceptional vision, he could barely tell the difference between the black of Melissa's pupil and the near black of her iris as she pinned Cassie with a pointed look. "Devon's intervention tonight stopped my premonition from coming true, but I didn't see him in it. I only saw Cassie, wounded and bleeding… dead."

The color drained from Cassie's face. "You saw my death?" she choked out.

Melissa nodded as her gaze slid to the wall behind Cassie. "Yes, it was awful. Awful." Melissa shuddered as she wrapped her slender arms around herself and took a deep breath. Chris draped an arm around Melissa's shoulders and pulled her against his side. "I hope to never see anything like that again, but unfortunately, I don't have a choice.

"I have no control over my premonitions, when they come, or what they are." Though dismay still filled Melissa's gaze, there was a steel rod of strength running through her. "I had a premonition a couple years ago of your arrival Devon. I knew you would come for Cassie, and you would change things. Make her whole again, so to speak."

Cassie's face flooded with color as she turned away from the eyes that swung toward her. "I've seen nothing else of you though. I had no idea *what* you were, or *when* you would come, I didn't know what you would look like, but I've been waiting." Melissa sighed as she bowed her dark head. "Somehow, maybe because of what you are, you keep us blocked out. I don't know why that one premonition of you slipped through, but I have a feeling no more will come."

Devon frowned as he puzzled over Melissa's statement. He knew why she didn't receive visions about him, but he didn't understand why she'd gotten that *one*. Melissa's gaze was questioning, her dark eyes eager as she stared at him expectantly.

Premonitions were a handy gift to have for a lot of reasons, they wouldn't help him. She wouldn't have any visions about Julian either, maybe some of his actions, but not about Julian himself. "And you?" he ignored the crestfallen look on Melissa's face as he turned to Chris. He liked the girl, he didn't aim to keep her in the dark, but he wanted to hear everything they had to say before he laid all of his cards on the table.

Chris was still rigid, but at least he didn't look as if he were going to attack anymore. "I can read people. I know what they are when I meet them. Good, bad, indifferent to life. I know what they are feeling," he said defiantly.

Devon chose to ignore his tone. "And what am I inside?" he asked quietly.

Chris shook his head. "I don't know," he admitted. "I never really picked anything up from you. There was always a sort of blank surrounding you, except for when it came to Cassie."

Devon frowned as his gaze darted back to Cassie. She sat

stiffly upon the couch, her hand clenched on the throw pillow she'd picked from the floor. "What did you sense then?" Devon asked.

Chris shifted and glanced at Luther. Then, with a small shrug, he seemed to decide it wasn't all that important anyway. "I could sense how much you cared for her, how much she meant to you."

Devon's frown deepened. Bowing his head, he began to rub the bridge of his nose as he tried to puzzle through what they were telling him. They shouldn't have been able to get anything off of him, but for some reason, when Cassie was involved, they were somehow able to pick things up.

"What's wrong?" she inquired.

He shook his head and dropped his hand to take hold of hers once more. "And what can you do?" he asked.

Her frown deepened, a strange flicker passed through her eyes. "I have no abilities."

Surprise coursed through him. She possessed the most powerful blood he'd ever tasted. From just a few precious drops he was stronger, faster, his senses were more honed, and he felt like he could conquer the world. It made no sense that she didn't possess *some* ability.

A wounded look crossed her features; he could feel her starting to withdraw from him. "Are you sure?" he inquired.

She gave him a dark look. "Yes, I'm sure."

"Cassie is an outstanding fighter," Luther interjected quickly. "Maybe the best to ever come out of the Hunter line."

She quirked an eyebrow as she studied her Guardian. "Being able to kill well is not a gift or ability."

Luther's gaze was sad and sympathetic, but his jaw was set in determination. "It is. It's just a different one than what Chris and Melissa have."

"Killing, being fast and strong with enhanced senses is a

natural ability of all Hunter's, not just me."

Luther sighed. "True."

She turned back to Devon, a strange hopelessness in her usually vivid eyes. "I've seen what Chris and Melissa go through. I'm glad I don't have to deal with the burdens they do."

Devon nodded but his mind spun as he tried to place all the pieces of the puzzle together. She had no abilities but she was powerful, he could feel that, he had *tasted* it. But no matter the power he could sense pouring out of her now, he hadn't been able to detect it until her blood had been spilled. He hadn't been able to see the truth about her, for if he had, he never would have gotten the chance to know her. To love her. The thought was staggering, he'd never loved before, and yet the realization was not a surprise.

He'd loved her since he'd first seen her, he suspected he'd loved her *before* he'd even met her. If Melissa had received a premonition of him, then it was quite possible he'd been destined to find her, and although he'd never believed in that kind of thing before, it felt right in this situation.

"Why can't we read you?" Melissa blurted.

Devon couldn't help but smile as he shook his head at her. "My power and abilities, keeps you blocked."

Melissa's brows furrowed. "What do you mean?"

"My powers are much stronger than any of the vampires you've come across. I have learned to keep people blocked out, especially Hunters. It's an ability that has helped to keep me alive all this time."

"But I had a premonition of *you*!" Melissa insisted.

Devon's gaze focused on Cassie. "I don't understand exactly how it all works, but I have a feeling your premonition probably had more to do with Cassie than me."

"With me?" Cassie inquired.

"When it comes to you, my guard is down more; my humanity is stronger and more intense." Cassie's eyes softened, she relaxed as she gazed up at him.

"But that vision was two years ago," Melissa said.

Cassie's mouth dropped as she spun toward Melissa. "Two years?" she squeaked. "You kept this from me for two *years*?"

Melissa drummed her fingers on the mantle. "You never like to hear about them anyway." Cassie was still frowning, but she nodded her agreement as she settled back. "Why would I receive that one two years ago, when you didn't know Cassie then?"

Devon shrugged as he met Cassie's startled gaze. "I don't have all the answers. Maybe it was fate and I was supposed to meet her, maybe something happened two years ago that allowed a vision to slip through. I simply don't know."

"What could have happened?"

He grinned at Cassie as he brushed a strand of her golden hair off her face. Her eyes warmed as they filled with love. Love for him. His hand stilled on her cheek, he was lost to the beauty and sensation of her. It wasn't only her outer beauty entrancing him, but also the pure wonder of her soul. She was the strongest, most giving, and loving person he'd ever encountered, and he'd encountered far more people than he would have liked in his extensive life.

She leaned into his touch, her silken cheek nestled against his cupped palm. Dark lashes curled against her cheeks as she closed her eyes. Devon had to force himself to recall the other people in the room before he took her upstairs, curled up with her, and held her close as he kept her safe.

"Like I said, I don't have all the answers. There are many mysteries in life that are never explained."

Cassie's eyes fluttered open, her lashes brushed against the palm of his hand. A shiver of desire raced down his spine, and left his restraint shaken. He shuddered as he struggled to retain control of himself. "It's still very strange," she murmured.

"Yes," he managed to grate out.

"That's also about the time Cassie really started to withdraw," Chris pondered.

"Yes." Melissa folded her arms over her chest as she leaned against the mantle.

"Hey," Cassie interrupted. "I'm right here."

Melissa frowned as she focused on her. "I think I had a vision of Devon because I was frightened we would lose you. I think I was granted that vision to ease my concerns about you, and your future, and it did help."

"Could have told me," Chris mumbled.

"I didn't *know* what he was," Melissa reminded him.

"Yeah, I guess."

Cassie rolled her eyes as she shook her head at the two of them. "So what do we do about Julian?" she asked. She tried to hide it, but Devon could still hear the undercurrent of fear in her voice. His free hand clenched at the reminder of the brutality she'd experienced last night. A brutality inflicted upon her by a monster he had helped to create, and would soon destroy.

"*We* don't do anything. If you insist upon staying then there is nothing I can do about that, but you are to stay away from him." Anger flashed through her violet blue eyes, she opened her mouth to protest, but he swiftly cut her off. "You can't defeat him Cassie, he will kill you, and I can't allow that to happen. I *cannot* lose you."

Biting her lower lip, she managed a small nod as she turned away from him. "The three of you are to stay by me from now on."

All of their eyes shot to him again. "What?" Chris barked.

Devon met his hostile gaze, impressed by the courage the kid possessed. "Julian will come after you. If he catches you alone, or without me, you won't have a shot of surviving."

Chris's hands fisted, a muscle twitched in his cheek as he clenched his jaw. "He's right," Cassie's grandmother said. "You must stay safe; Devon can help protect you from him."

"The three of us…"

"Are no match." The older woman unraveled her legs and gracefully rose to her feet. "Until this is taken care of, you will be safe, and you *will* stick by Devon. There will be no arguments on the matter."

He wasn't surprised when they remained silent, sullen, but silent. Cassie's grandmother was small, but she bore an air of authority that brooked no room for argument. *He* wouldn't even argue with her, and because of that, he was glad she was on his side. "Now, I think it's time for Cassie to rest."

"I'm fine, Grandma."

She planted her hands on her hips. "You *are* going to rest."

Devon fought back a smile. "I'll help you upstairs."

Cassie frowned at him as she shook her head. "I'm perfectly capable of walking upstairs on my own."

"Let him help you Cassandra," her grandmother interjected.

Cassie's teeth locked, but she didn't argue further. Releasing her cushion, she went to rise, but he moved forward and easily swept her up in his arms. She gasped as her fingers curled around his neck. Her look of irritation vanished as a small smile played across her full mouth. Playing with the hair at the nape of his neck, she curled against him. Her lithe body fit perfectly against his, her supple curves melded to him in all the right places. Her heady scent filled his nostrils as her head rested against his shoulder.

He cradled her as he left the room. He was suddenly desperate to escape for a bit. He needed to hunt, to fill himself with blood, and to regain complete control of himself. Though he was loath to do it, he had to separate from her until he was sure she would be safe around him.

He maneuvered her in his arms to open the door to her room. He knew her room well now, but it still surprised him that it wasn't decorated with posters, and pictures, like most teenagers rooms. The only picture in the room was of her parents, she'd never told him that's who the picture was of, but she looked a lot like the blond woman in it. He suspected the chaos of her life outside of this room made her keep everything within it neatly ordered and meticulous.

He smoothly placed her on the bed, hating to part with her, but he had to. If he stayed much longer he would become a threat to her. "I have to go for a little bit."

Apprehension flashed through her eyes, he hated the vulnerability and alarm suffusing her, but her encounter with Julian had rattled her. From what he'd seen of her, she wasn't afraid of anything. Then, she buried the fear, jutted her chin out and nodded briskly.

His mouth curved in a smile as the brave woman he knew reappeared. "I'll leave the window open for you."

"It wouldn't stop me anyway."

She grinned at him; her hands framed his face as she pressed a chaste kiss on his lips. Heat flooded through him, his skin rippled as he pressed closer to her. He felt himself spiraling out of control; he was losing himself to her. Regaining control of himself, he pulled away before he couldn't. "I'll see you soon," he whispered.

She caressed his face for a moment more before she released

him. Frustration boiled through him as he turned away, he hungered for so much more than blood. His gaze fell upon Chris and Melissa standing in the doorway, he'd been so lost hc hadn't heard them approach. Melissa smiled at him, while Chris continued to scowl.

CHAPTER FIVE

CASSIE GATHERED her books from her locker and just barely managed to resist slamming it shut. Ever since she'd become the social leper of the school, she'd received more whispered comments and nasty asides than she'd ever thought to hear in her life. She tried not to let them affect her, but it had been a tiresome day, and her defenses were wearing thin.

Straightening her shoulders, she held her chin high as she turned back to the whispers and stares. They had all heard about the attack in the woods, but for the most part, they weren't relieved she'd survived. They were especially annoyed she was here, while Marcy was still in the hospital, and probably wouldn't be getting out until tomorrow.

"Cassie."

She braced herself, her hands tightened upon her books as she turned toward the sound of the mellow voice. The girl standing behind her was staring up at her with hazel eyes, heavily outlined with eyeliner and mascara. The dark makeup brought out the gold flecks in her eyes. Her short hair had been dyed a blood red color that stood out at spiky angles around her pretty, heart shaped face.

The girl looked vaguely familiar, but Cassie was too drained, to place her. "Danielle," the girl said, taking obvious pity on her. "We met in the bathroom a couple weeks ago."

Her overwrought mind finally recognized the girl. Dani had been kind enough to give Cassie some towels when she'd freaked out over Devon's arrival at school. It was hard to believe she'd ever fought against the bond connecting them.

"Oh, hi Dani, I'm sorry I just… well I've just been out of it lately."

Dani's smile was sympathetic as she glanced around the hall. Students went out of their way to avoid walking near Cassie, and none of them did a good job at muffling the snide comments they dropped as they moved past. Cassie fought the impulse to start punching them all, or just walk out, but she would *not* give them the satisfaction of seeing her crack.

"I understand. I heard about what happened in the forest, I'm glad to see you're ok."

Cassie's eyes widened, no one, other than the teachers had bothered to ask her if she was ok, and she was fairly certain most of the female student body wished she'd died so they could have a crack at Devon. She would like to think their hatred of her was because of the strong appeal Devon had told them about yesterday, but Cassie knew it had always been there, bubbling just beneath the surface.

"Thank you Dani." Dani smiled and touched Cassie's hand. "You probably shouldn't be seen with me though."

Dani glanced around the hall and gave a small wave of her fingers to Julie Jenks who turned away quickly. "I've never cared what these people thought of me, and believe me Cassie, being on the outside is better. You don't have to play by their rules all the time."

Cassie couldn't help but smile at the eccentric girl. "I suppose you're right."

"I'm always right," Dani declared forcefully.

"Is everything ok here?" Devon's emerald eyes were severe as he appeared at her side. Dani colored as she ducked her head shyly. Although Dani was one of the few who didn't hate her, apparently she was also a Devon groupie. Devon's eyes burned into Cassie's questioningly, his body tensing in preparation to defend her. Something he'd been doing far too much of lately.

"Everything's fine," she assured him. "Devon this is Dani, she was just making sure I was all right."

His shoulders relaxed as he nodded briefly at Dani. "Nice to meet you."

Dani's face was scarlet as she thrust her hand out. He shot Cassie an amused look before taking hold of her hand. "You too," Dani muttered.

Dani pulled her hand away as the heat in her face spread down her neck. "I um… I should be going," Dani stammered. "I'm glad you're ok, Cassie."

"Thank you, Dani."

She turned and quickly disappeared into the throng of students. "Where did she come from?" Devon inquired.

"I met her a few weeks ago, when you first arrived."

Devon slipped his arm around her waist and pulled her against his side. Warmth erupted in tingling waves that enveloped her from head to toe. She pressed closer as she rested her hand on his chest and dropped her head to his shoulder. The strength and comfort he offered helped strengthen her and buoy her confidence once more.

He dropped a kiss on top of her head. "Let's get you some lunch."

She frowned up at him, aggravated at the interruption, she didn't feel like moving. His green eyes twinkled as he grinned at her. She loved it when he smiled like that, it gave him an air of boyishness that was charming and heart melting. "I can hear your stomach rumbling."

Blushing slightly, Cassie ducked her head as she silently cursed his enhanced hearing. Squeezing her once more, he turned her and moved with the flow of students toward the cafeteria. Though she still received dirty looks, the whispered asides drastically decreased. Mainly because none of the girls wanted Devon to think they were catty and cruel, and none of the boys wanted to risk his wrath.

The smile slipped from his mouth as he stared at the students. Apparently they weren't as discreet as they'd thought, at least not around him. His jaw clenched as his hand locked upon her waist. "It's ok," she told him. "I'm becoming used to it."

"You shouldn't have to."

Cassie shrugged and placed a quick kiss on his cheek. There may be nothing he could do about it, but she thrilled at his desire to protect her. "I'll meet you at the table."

"I'm coming with you."

Quirking an eyebrow, she shook her head at him. "You don't eat."

A muscle in his cheek jumped. "I don't care."

"You can't follow me everywhere Devon, I can do this myself." She had to face a good chunk of her day alone as it was, and if she didn't start developing a thicker skin now, then it was going to be a very long, very *hard* year. "I'll be fine."

He reluctantly released his hold on her. Cassie gave him a

small, reassuring smile before heading in to swim with the sharks. The buzz instantly grew around her; the murmurs became louder and nastier as she wound her way through the crowd. She did her best to tune them out, but they only got worse the farther from Devon she got.

Her rumbling stomach clenched as her appetite vanished. Instead of all the talk dying down with time, it seemed to be growing in force, becoming angrier. Regretting her decision to leave Devon behind, she almost turned away from the lunch line, but she couldn't let them know they were getting to her.

She kept her chin held high as people snickered and whispered behind their hands. Though she didn't know why they bothered to stay behind their hands, their whispers were as loud as gunshots to her. "Look who it is."

She didn't bother to look up as Mark Young appeared by her side. Having sensed something off about Mark, Chris had cautioned her to stay away from the muscular boy years ago, but Cassie would have stayed away without Chris's warning. She'd never felt anything for Mark, but he'd been relentless in his pursuit of her.

"Ah, but you're not so special anymore are you?" Cassie continued to ignore him as she moved at a snail's pace through the line. "How the mighty have fallen. Guess that's what you get for being a slut."

She'd been trying not to give him the satisfaction of reacting in any way, but she couldn't stop herself from shooting him a dirty look. He chuckled, enjoying that he'd finally gotten a reaction out of her. Cassie shivered; her skin crawled as his arm brushed against hers. "Truth hurts, doesn't it?"

She kept her chin held high, but inside she was a seething mass of raw nerves and revulsion. She wished she hadn't sent Devon away and that she'd never stepped foot in this line. There were many things she wished for, but none of them were going to do her any good right now. She was here, Devon wasn't, and Mark seemed determined to make her miserable.

"Doesn't it, whore?" Cassie's jaw clenched. If she hit him, she would probably injure him, and she knew her conscience couldn't handle that, no matter how much he deserved it. "I'm talking to you."

Her eyes quickly flickered toward him. His eyes were feral, frantic. She was surprised and horrified by the lack of control radiating from him. She took a small step back, her attempt at bravery forgotten in the face of his unstable persona. She didn't know what was wrong with him lately, but this was the second time she'd seen him half crazed as he came after her. The first time had led to the school hating her; this time she thought it might lead to actual violence.

Cassie glanced around the cafeteria, searching for an escape, but they had slipped into the inner area of the lunch line. A wall now blocked her back and students were crammed around her. Out of habit, and looking for something more to protect herself, Cassie grabbed a tray. She held it against her chest in a poor attempt to shield herself from his bizarre behavior.

She silently begged the crowd ahead of them to move faster. "You always thought you were too good for all of us, for me. Now you're nothing."

She shot a glare at him as exasperation boiled up to replace the disgust inside of her. "I *am* too good for you," she retorted, unable to stop herself.

His eyes bugged out of his head, his hands fisted at his sides, and briefly she thought he might hit her. "Bitch!" he spat.

Cassie had enough. Tossing her tray onto the metal railing, she turned and began to shove her way through the crowd. She ignored the disgruntled looks she received. Pushing free of the crowd, she inhaled a shaky breath as she tried to regain control of herself.

A hand seized hold of her arm and ripped her around. A startled cry escaped her as Mark's grip became painful. "Don't you walk away from me!"

"Let go Mark." She tugged on her arm, but he wouldn't release her.

Cassie's hand fisted, she didn't care what they said about her afterward, she was going to knock him on his ass. Another hand shot forward and seized hold of Mark's arm in a bone crushing grip before Cassie could let her fist fly. Devon's lip was curled and his eyes gleamed dangerously as he stepped forward. "Let her go before I break your arm," he snarled.

Mark's mouth dropped as Devon relentlessly clenched down harder. Mark's fingers released her, not by choice, but because he couldn't hold onto her anymore. He tried to pull his arm free, but Devon refused to let go. Devon clenched his jaw, a muscle twitched in his cheek as he glared violently at Mark.

"I told you before to stay away from her."

The words were spoken quietly, but they caused the hair on Cassie's arms and neck to rise. She could sense the unraveling restraint Devon fought so hard to keep in check. Cassie glanced at Mark's arm; it would only take a little more pressure for it to shatter.

"Devon," Cassie breathed.

Chris blocked the curious stares of the students passing by as he stepped beside them. "What's going on guys?" he asked cheerfully for the benefit of those surrounding them, but his eyes were dark and turbulent as he studied Devon. He glanced at Cassie before focusing his attention on Mark.

Cassie stroked Devon's arm as she tried to pierce the thick cloud of fury filling him. His eyes burned hotly as they flickered to her. She was momentarily frightened of him and what he might do. She'd never seen him like this, frenzied and so very close to killing. Cassie's breath caught in her chest, but she didn't move away from him. She wouldn't abandon him now, this was *her* Devon. She just had to reach him, to stop him from doing something he would regret.

"Devon please, just let him go. It's ok."

His eyes flickered briefly, light came momentarily back into them before the darkness descended over him once more. He turned back to Mark, who was still gaping down at the hand clenching his arm. Cassie shot Chris a pleading glance, but he remained stony as he glared at Mark.

There was no one to help her now, no one to stop Devon if he snapped completely. Devon took a step closer to Mark and pulled his arm against his chest. Abandoning all caution, she threw herself forward, instinctively knowing that Devon wouldn't hurt her. Shoving her way in between them, she stood on tiptoe to grasp hold of Devon's cheeks and bring his mouth down to hers. She stood awkwardly, her lips pressed against his compressed, firm mouth as she waited breathlessly to see what he would do. His body remained unmoving for a moment more, and then *everything* changed.

Cassie had only meant to divert his attention from Mark, to keep Devon from harming him. She hadn't expected all of the frenzy he'd been feeling toward Mark would be diverted to *her*. His rigidity melted away, he released Mark as his arms clamped around her. He lifted her off the ground and pressed her flush against him.

She'd never felt him this wild and savage before. His fingers threaded through the bottom of the loose twist in her hair to cup her head. His mouth was unrelenting against hers, desperate, ardent. She was certain he would never hurt her, but she also realized he was barely in control of himself. His mouth opened against hers as his tongue plummeted in.

A small moan escaped Cassie. She forgot all her doubts and concerns as she melted against him. Heat pooled through her entire being and warmed her everywhere. Her heart hammered in her chest, her hands clenched at his neck; she couldn't seem to get close enough to him. The entire world, and the awful events of the day, disappeared as she became completely focused on him.

He worked the knot out of her hair, letting it free to flow down her back. His tongue caressed her mouth; he tasted her in prolonged deliberate strokes as he savored her. The muscles in his arms were rigid, yet she could feel a small tremor working through him as his kiss became almost bruising in its intensity. She didn't utter a complaint, didn't make a sound. She knew he needed this, he needed *her*.

She just hadn't realized how much.

A shiver raced through her as his teeth sharpened and lengthened. She could feel them against her bottom lip. She was scared, and more than a little in over her head, but she couldn't stop the thrill racing through her.

Curiosity, and an overwhelming impulse she couldn't deny, took hold of her. Gingerly, she flicked her tongue over the tips of his elongated teeth. Devon shuddered as his kiss became harsher. She was lost to him, lost to everything he was, and the breathtaking sensations he made her feel. Never in her life had she experienced anything as breathtaking as this, and she craved more.

She craved *all* of him.

Cassie took a stumbling step back as Devon suddenly released her. It took her a moment before she could get her wobbly legs firmly beneath her again. Breathless she stared up at him, shaken, and unfulfilled. His emerald eyes were dark and tortured as he gazed at her. For the first time it hit her just how difficult it was for him to be around her.

Tears sprang to her eyes; her hand flew to her swollen lips as a choked sound escaped her. The last thing in the world she meant to do was upset him in anyway, but that was exactly what she was doing to him.

"Devon." Her voice was choked with horror and sorrow.

His darkened gaze turned to Chris as small tremors ran through his fisted hands. "Mark?"

Chris cleared his throat; his face was flushed as he glanced at Cassie before focusing on Devon. "Ran off the first chance he got."

Devon nodded briskly. "Get her away from these people. I have to go, but I'm leaving her in your hands."

Cassie blinked away her tears as his gaze turned back to her. She longed to comfort him, but she instinctively knew she shouldn't. He was close to completely unraveling and her touch might just push him over the edge.

With a shaking hand, he briefly touched her cheek before turning on his heel and disappearing into the gaping crowd. Cassie blinked rapidly as she recalled she was standing in the middle of the crowded, oddly silent cafeteria. Questioning, condemning stares were focused upon her. Chris stepped forward and slid his arm through hers.

"Come on Cassie," he said gently.

She stared helplessly up at him, for years Chris had been her rock, the one person she could turn to when she required solace, and right now he was just as lost as she was. He led her through the crowd as it began to come alive again. The comments were no longer whispered as accusations were hurled at her. She barely heard any of them through the haze surrounding her.

They were at the cafeteria doors when Melissa came strolling around the corner. Her eyebrows rose when she saw them, and her mouth parted. Her gaze shot behind them as the buzz in the cafeteria increased. "What happened?" she demanded.

"A lot," Chris muttered. "We're leaving."

Melissa didn't question them further as she fell into step beside them. Cassie made it all the way to Chris's car, and was settled into the backseat, before she started to cry.

CHAPTER SIX

CASSIE PACED her room restlessly as her gaze flitted continuously to the darkened night. Devon should be here shortly, if he came at all. The thought froze her briefly in mid-stride, before she continued on. He *had* to come. She couldn't allow herself to think that he wouldn't. If she did, she would start crying again, and it had only been a couple of hours since she'd completely regained control of herself.

It had taken another hour to convince Chris and Melissa she was fine, and to go home. They had been reluctant to leave, but she didn't want them here when Devon arrived. She had to speak with him alone. Turning on her heel, she paced restlessly back to the other side of the room, feeling as wound up as a yo-yo.

She glanced at the clock on her nightstand, dismayed to realize it was almost ten. *Where* was he? What would she do if he didn't come tonight? Her chest constricted at the thought; it became difficult for her to breathe.

It had happened so swiftly, her love for him had been rapid and all consuming. She should be frightened by it, but she wasn't. To be this dependent on someone else was something she'd *never* wanted to have happen. Loving someone this much left her vulnerable to all of the cruelty she knew resided in the world. But it was too late, she was helplessly in love with him, lost to him, and she could *not* lose him.

All of her pent up, nervous energy, drained from her. She limply slid to the floor and pulled her legs up against her chest and hugged them as she dropped her chin on her knees.

DEVON RELEASED the last fox he'd caught. It staggered as it tried to regain its balance from the loss of blood it had sustained. Though he tried to keep the animals alive when he fed from them, the first two foxes, three rabbits, and one coyote he'd captured hadn't survived. He barely remembered draining them dry, but he clearly recalled their limp bodies left broken on the forest floor afterward.

It was far better it was animals, and not Cassie he was draining dry, because he'd been that close today. A shudder ran through him as he recalled exactly how close he'd been to ravishing her in every way, and not caring who watched. He couldn't be unstable around her again.

But when she'd run her tongue across his teeth, showing no fear of him as her excitement blazed forth, he'd nearly unraveled completely. He shuddered as the memory roused his desire once more. She was far too innocent to know what she was doing to him, but she was going to be his undoing.

Their relationship had come to a crossroads much faster than he'd expected. Rising, he wiped the dirt from his jeans and watched as the fox disappeared. He had fed to the point of near bursting in the hopes it would keep him from desiring her blood as fiercely. He didn't think it would work.

His head fell back as he stared up at the thick canopy of trees. Dropping his head back down, he used all of his senses to search the dark night. He felt nothing out there except for a deer, and a pack of coyotes.

Julian was uncharacteristically lying low, usually once he made his presence known; he liked to keep it known. He was planning something, and Devon didn't like it. He had to find him, and soon. As long as Julian was out there, Cassie was in jeopardy.

Turning away, he blended into the woods as he raced toward Cassie's house. He moved rapidly through the thick forest as he easily dodged any obstacles in his way. Arriving at her house, he stopped at the edge of the forest to study the peaceful Cape style house before him. The weathered grey shingles, and pale blue shutters, were illuminated by the glow of the full moon.

Cassie's room was dark, but the TV was flashing in the window pane. He could feel her up there, lost, upset, and confused. He hated himself even more for putting her through this, for leaving her to stew while he gorged himself on blood.

Climbing quickly up the tree, he paused at the edge of her window to take her in. She sat upon the bed with her slender legs drawn up to her chest, and her golden hair cascading around her shoulders in thick waves. The delicate beauty of her features was illuminated by the flickering TV. His chest constricted as he studied her, he was amazed and charmed by the effect she had over him.

She turned toward him; her shoulders slumped as her rosebud mouth parted. Relief filled her as she leapt gracefully to her feet. "Devon."

Her whisper washed over him, as did her vast relief. She cautiously stepped toward him as if afraid she would scare him away. Hoping to ease some of her apprehension, he gracefully slid through the window. Tears bloomed in her eyes, but she rapidly blinked them back as she watched him move toward her.

"Are you ok?" He could only manage a brisk nod; he found it difficult to think in her presence. "I'm sorry. I didn't know what else to do; I thought you were going to kill him."

Devon clearly recalled the scene in the cafeteria, the haze that had suffused him, the need to destroy the person upsetting her. He also recalled her kiss, her taste, her sweetness. She was the *only* one who could have gotten through to him. He didn't like the way she'd put herself at risk though, stepping between a vampire and its prey was worse than stepping between a charging bull and its target. But she was right; he may very well have killed Mark if she hadn't intervened.

She'd been lucky he hadn't turned on her. But then again, in a way he had. The uncontrollable rage had turned into uncontrollable passion instead. Devon shuddered to think about what he could have done to her and not realized it until he'd been well sated by her luscious blood.

"I was." She blinked in surprise at his flat words. "You stopped me from injuring him, but you can't put yourself in danger like that again."

"Danger?" she croaked.

He nodded briskly. "Never step between a vampire and their prey."

Her mouth pursed as she studied him. "No matter what you might think, I know you would *never* hurt me Devon, and I have stepped in between a vampire and its prey many times before."

She had more faith in him than he did, but then again, she

didn't know the thoughts running through his mind. The things he longed to do to her, *with* her. If she knew any of it, she wouldn't have so much faith in him; she would probably run screaming.

She took a step closer, but he held up his hand to ward her off. "Cassie, we have to talk."

CHAPTER SEVEN

CASSIE'S HEART beat a staccato in her chest, and it took everything she had to keep breathing. She shifted as she braced herself for the worst. She could smell, and feel, the vast amounts of blood he'd consumed, the power coursed through him now. He'd drunk so much she actually picked up on the metallic scent of it for the first time.

He'd done it so he could prepare himself to come and see *her*. Anxiety clutched at her, and her knees began to tremble. She had to sit before she fell down. She perched uneasily on the edge of her bed and clasped her hands in her lap. "What is it?" she managed to force herself to ask.

He was half hidden in the shadows enshrouding his toned body. The night was a little chilly, but he wore only a t-shirt that clung to his muscles and emphasized his washboard abs. For the first time she realized how much he truly belonged to the night, and the darkness.

Cassie was mesmerized and thrilled by him as his emerald eyes perused her with keen interest. Swallowing heavily she forced her mind away from her wandering thoughts. The crickets had retreated, the loss of their melodious chirrups left the night oddly empty.

Tears burned the backs of her eyes again, but she refused to shed them, not yet anyway. She still didn't know where this was going. His eyes were rapt upon her as he stopped just feet away. Though the distance between them was small, it suddenly felt like a vast chasm. There would be no breeching it with a simple word or touch.

"I want you Cassie." Her mouth went dry, her heart hammered so loudly she was certain he could hear it. Excitement spread rapidly through her body and burned through her veins. "But I can't control myself around you."

She swallowed again, fearful she would choke on the lump lodged in her throat. "Yes, you can," she whispered.

He leaned back on his heels as his gaze darted briefly toward the ceiling. Shaking his head, his black hair fell forward across his sculpted face as he looked at her again. "Yes, somewhat," he admitted. "But not enough, and everyday gets tougher for me. Looking at you, smelling you, having tasted your blood, all of it is a temptation that is getting harder and harder to resist. Every day, every *second*, I crave more."

She could barely breathe, let alone find any words for him. She wasn't ready for that step yet. She knew that was crazy, she wanted to spend the rest of her life with him, but she wasn't ready for what he was looking for from her, not yet anyway. There was still so much she didn't know about him, like just exactly how many women there had been over the past seven hundred years.

On second thought, she wasn't so sure she wanted to know *that* at all.

"I'm not ready yet." She felt awkward and so very young and stupid as she issued the words. Heat crept through her cheeks as he stared at her; she hated the almost pitying look in his eyes. She was unable to meet his stare any longer as she focused on the window behind him.

"I know, Cassie," he assured her. "I won't push you into doing anything you aren't ready for, but it's more than just sex." Despite her intentions not to look, her gaze returned to him and her forehead furrowed. "I want your blood also. I want to taste you and feel you and have you fill me."

Despite the fear his words aroused, exhilaration also slid through her gut. What he was describing sent her into a tailspin of confused need. She shook her head as she tried to regain control of her spiraling feelings. She knew she should be troubled by what he was saying, she should be completely against it considering what she was, but yearn for it she did, *desperately*.

"I would also like to change you."

Revulsion slammed through her and knocked away all of her longing. Nausea twisted in her stomach, she felt hollow and cold as the blood seemed to freeze in her veins. Her mouth dropped, she tried to find words, but none would come out. Change her?

Living in the dark, being a monster, being one of the *things* that had killed her parents wasn't something she could do, *ever*.

Bile rose in her throat. She tried to stand up, but her legs wouldn't support her. His gaze was forceful on her, but he couldn't hide the brief flicker of distress that flashed through his eyes. "Cassie…"

She held up her hand, not sure she could hear anymore. She needed time to digest what he was saying to her now, never mind hearing anymore. "I can't," she managed to choke out. "I can't."

He closed his eyes and folded his hands behind his back as he rocked on his heels. He opened his eyes; the stark pain in them nearly broke her heart. He took a step closer to her and knelt down so they were on the same eye level. "I either change you, or I leave when this is over," he said.

She slid off the bed and fell before him on the carpet. She grasped hold of him, her fingers dug into his shoulders as her throat clogged. "You can't," she whispered. "You can't."

He brushed away the tears spilling down her face. Tears she hadn't known she was shedding. "If I stay, I may change you against your will Cassie. You shake me to the very core of my being. I don't want to hurt you, it's the last thing in the world I want to do, but I might."

"No," she breathed. "You would *never* hurt me."

His fingers slid through her hair. "Today in the cafeteria…"

"I won't do anything like that again!"

"So we don't touch, we don't kiss, we keep our distance? What kind of a relationship is that Cassie? You deserve so much better, you deserve someone who can love you completely without having to worry they might break and turn you into a monster."

"I can't lose you, I can't," she sobbed. "I didn't come alive until I met you. I can't lose you."

"Shh love, please Cassie, please don't cry. I'm sorry; I don't mean to hurt you."

"Then don't leave me!"

She could see the battle waging within him, the absolute torture she was putting him through, but she couldn't stop herself. She couldn't lose him, she would never survive it. He nodded briefly, but his were still dark, distant. "Not now," he promised. "Not with Julian around."

"But after?" she asked anxiously.

"After, you are going to have to make a choice. You should be with someone who can give you the life you deserve. I'm not that man, Cassie; I'm not even a man."

She tried to shake her head, but he had a firm hold on the back of her head. She would do anything for him, well almost anything; she simply could not give him *that.*

Her gaze ran over his glorious face, savoring every detail from his chiseled cheekbones to his full mouth. He was everything she'd ever dreamed of and more. No one else would ever make her feel like he did; she couldn't imagine kissing another man, let alone having them touch her. The thought repulsed her almost as much as the idea of becoming a vampire. "You *are* that person. I could never be with anyone else," she said fervently. "Never."

Anguish flashed across his face. "Cassie…"

"You can control yourself," she whispered. "I know it."

Resignation settled over his features as his thumb began to rub her neck. "I don't know for how long Cass. My need for you grows every day. If I lose complete control, I could kill someone, or I could force the change on you, and it might come to that if I continue on this way."

She bit her bottom lip as she tried not to start sobbing again. "You'll have to make a choice, Cassie."

She closed her eyes, unable to meet his hopeful gaze as she nodded. Even if it meant losing him, she didn't think she could do what he was asking her to do. Her heart constricted; it felt as if a hundred needles were piercing her skin and driving the pain into the very marrow of her bones.

She shuddered as her heart labored to push blood through her flayed veins. Slowly opening her eyes, she tried her best to hide the grief tearing through her as she met his gaze. She didn't want to lose him, but this was an impossible choice she wasn't capable of making now, if ever.

She couldn't assure him he would be the one she chose. She couldn't assure him she would give up sunlight and life, for a cold existence of death and darkness. Not all vampires may be the monsters she'd once believed them to be, but she couldn't become the *thing* that had murdered her parents. She couldn't become the thing she'd been born to destroy.

All she could do was hope he was wrong, and he would be able to keep control of himself. It was selfish of her to put him through such torture; it was so much to ask of him. Yet, it was also a lot to ask of her. She refused to let the knowledge their relationship was doomed seep into her brain. If she did, she would completely break down, and she couldn't do that, not in front of him.

For now she was still able to hold him and love him, and she was going to cherish every moment they had together. They were far more limited than she had realized.

Beneath her hand she could feel the fine bristles of his stubble. "I love you Devon."

Hope bloomed in his eyes as they glowed with warmth and love. Pulling her forward he dropped a lingering kiss on her forehead. "I love you too. I'll love you forever."

Tears slid down Cassie's face as she leaned into him and savored the strength, warmth, and eternal love enshrouding her.

CHAPTER EIGHT

CASSIE STUDIED the crowd crammed into the dining room at B's and S's. A few diehards remained around the picnic tables outside, but for the most part the crisp mid October air had chased everyone else inside. The heat from all the bodies, and the noise, were almost more than she could tolerate, but unfortunately they had to be here. Vampires were drawn to the crowds and the fresh blood of the youth within the walls.

The loud ringing of the pinball machine behind her caused her to wince involuntarily. A headache had been nagging at her all day. It was the kind of headache no amount of aspirin could cure; loud noise and stress were best avoided. Unfortunately, she couldn't avoid either of those things right now.

Devon leaned closer to her as his hand massaged the back of her neck. She closed her eyes as he attempted to ease the knots there. A loud shout rang out as the pinball machine went crazy. Sliding lower in her seat, she feverishly wished she was anywhere but here.

"I'll take you home," Chris offered.

Cassie cracked an eye as she focused on his bleary figure. She would love nothing more than to go home, but she couldn't leave the three of them on their own tonight. If anything happened... "No, that's ok. I'll be fine."

He frowned at her, but didn't push it further as he rested her head against his chest. He blocked out some of the noise, making it easier to breathe as she opened her eyes once more. Her gaze drifted across the students giving their table ample berth. Just a little bit ago their table would have been flocked with people vying for their attention. Now there was no one, and she found she didn't miss them. Sighing heavily, she took a sip of water in the hope the cool liquid would help ease the pain in her body. It didn't.

Fresh air would, she was certain of it. "I'm going to step outside for a minute."

"I'll come with you," Devon told her.

She shook her head the best she could. "No, I'll be fine, I'm not going anywhere."

"Cassie..."

"Devon, I just want some fresh air."

His eyes were dark and turbulent as he studied her. His glance toward Chris and Melissa set Cassie's hackles on edge. She was just getting some fresh air for crying out loud, she wasn't a two year old, and she didn't require a babysitter. "I don't need their permission either," she said stridently.

His guilty gaze came back to hers. "All right, but don't go anywhere."

She frowned at him, but didn't argue further. Besides, she wasn't fooled into thinking at least one of them wouldn't be keeping an eye on her, making sure she didn't get herself killed. Devon slid out of the booth to let her escape from her cramped corner, and the endlessly annoying ring of the pinball machine. "I'll be back," she muttered.

In the old days she would have had to push her way through the crowd and stop every few feet to talk with someone. There had been times it had taken her a half an hour just to make it to the door. Now the crowd parted for her as if she were a highly contagious leper.

Cassie kept her face impassive, and her chin held high. It was only high school, she continuously told herself. She only had a little over seven months left, and she still had her best friends, and Devon. That thought helped to ease some of the unhappiness, but it didn't make it go away. She would never get used to people she'd considered friends, turning against her so quickly, and so easily. It was like a knife to the heart, and especially to the back.

Shoving through the double glass doors, Cassie greedily inhaled gulps of the refreshing, crisp air. The doors blocked most of the noise as they slid closed and left her in the near blissful silence of the outdoor eating area. The two tables of people still outside glanced at her, surprise and amusement crossed their features before they turned back to each other.

Cassie turned to ignore them, but her attention was snagged by one of the girls with blood red hair tinted at the ends with neon green. Her mind churned as she tried to place the girl. Then, it locked into place. She'd been one of Dani's smoking friends the day Cassie had first met Dani in the bathroom.

But where was Dani?

Cassie scanned the crowd again, but she didn't see the tiny girl amongst them. Turning back to the restaurant, she searched the packed interior. If Dani was farther than ten feet in the door, Cassie wasn't going to see her. Maybe she had decided not to come out tonight? Or perhaps she was in the restaurant. She tried to assure herself both of these things were possible, but Cassie couldn't shake the feeling neither explanation was right.

With shrewd eyes, Cassie scanned the dark night. The roads winding through the center of town were empty of all but a few souls mingling outside of the bars, smoking or talking loudly. They would be prime targets for Julian, though she suspected he planned to do more damage than what they would offer. Julian aspired to attack Cassie, Chris, Melissa, and Devon the most. Going after high school students would be the best way to do that.

A shiver ran down Cassie's spine, the hair on the nape of her neck stood on end as her thoughts returned once more to Dani. Turning in the other direction she scanned the darkened sidewalk leading to the outskirts of town, the cemetery, and the woods.

Her vision blurred a little from the pounding in her head, then suddenly snapped into focus. At the far end of the sidewalk she could just barely make out the form of someone taking a right into the woods. Cassie's heart leapt into her throat, her chest constricted as panic tore through her.

Spinning back to the restaurant, she wasn't surprised to see Melissa lurking by the door, trying to look preoccupied with the gumball machine. It was a machine Melissa hit up every time they left B's and S's, but they weren't ready to leave. Cassie bet their food hadn't even arrived yet. However, she couldn't find the energy to be annoyed. She was far too relieved to see Melissa for that.

She gained more attention than she'd planned when she banged on the glass to get Melissa's attention. Cassie pointed toward the sidewalk, but didn't wait to tell Melissa more. Turning, she sprinted past the group gathered by the picnic tables. "Hey, stay away from her you freak!" one of the boys yelled after her.

Cassie fought back a bitter laugh, they weren't concerned enough about Dani to stop her from walking home on her own, but they were worried Cassie might bother her. She made it to the sidewalk and skidded around the corner as her sneakers briefly lost traction on the dew dampened surface.

Regaining her balance, Cassie kept her eyes locked on the woods as she tried to pinpoint the exact spot where Dani had entered. A small path made its way into the forest and a few freshly broken branches snagged her attention. Bolting into the forest, Cassie shoved branches out of her way and easily avoided obstacles as she sprinted down the path.

A chill of apprehension caused goose bumps to break out on her flesh. She'd placed herself in jeopardy, but she had to get to Dani before Julian arrived.

And he would arrive, she was certain of that.

DEVON SAT IN THE BOOTH, his body rigid due to the fact he couldn't see Cassie. Melissa had volunteered to keep an eye on her, citing that her favorite gumballs were by the front door. Chris had added Cassie would be upset if she felt she was being babysat. Devon had tried not to care about that, her safety did come first after all, but he found himself unwilling to distress her in anyway.

So in the end he'd relented, but he wasn't happy about it. They'd sent Melissa up with two dollars and seventy-five cents worth of quarters, plenty to keep her occupied for a little while. Slipping her first quarter in, Devon watched as the red ball made its way through a series of ramps, dips, traps, and holes in the intricate machine.

If it had been at any other point in time, he wouldn't have minded watching the thing. Right now all he yearned for was Cassie back at his side where he knew she was safe. He shifted uncomfortably, his gaze returned to the window at his side, but he couldn't see her from this angle. All he could see was a group of teenagers gathered around two tables. They were dressed in dark clothes; their hair was dyed different colors, and they had an array of piercings covering their heads.

The group glanced back toward the doorway, confirming Cassie was still there as they bent close to each other and spoke with each other before glancing at her again. Devon ran a hand through his hair as he fought the impulse to stand up and storm out after her.

"She'll be fine," Chris said.

Devon wasn't at all relieved by his reassurances. He knew Cassie, she didn't think before she acted. It had almost gotten her killed a couple of days ago, and he wasn't willing to take that chance again. Chris's chuckle brought Devon's ire and agitation back to him. "What?" he asked irritably.

Chris lifted a dark blond brow, his sapphire eyes twinkled with amusement. "It's a relief to have someone else share in my frustration. I've been watching over her for the past seventeen years and it hasn't been fun."

Devon scowled at him as Chris grinned annoyingly back. "She is stubborn," he mumbled.

"Ha!" Chris barked loudly. "That's the understatement of the century!"

Devon found himself grinning back at the boy, amused by his easy going nature and cheer. He liked Chris, but since his vampirism had been revealed, there had been nothing but tension between them. Now it seemed as if Chris had decided to throw caution to the wind, either that, or he was going to rely on Cassie's instincts and trust Devon.

"Hey guys." Devon's and Chris's smiles faded, they exchanged a pointed look as Marcy appeared at their side. Smiling cheerfully, she tossed back her long, coffee colored hair. "How are you tonight?"

Stony silence followed her question, and then Chris heaved a sigh. "We're good Marcy, you?"

Marcy shrugged a dainty shoulder, lust radiated from her as she leaned closer to him. "I'm feeling better, but it was still the scariest thing *ever*." She shuddered as she wrapped her arms around herself. "Someone should kill that animal."

Before they had left the hospital, Devon had altered Marcy's memory of the attack, leaving her with a foggy recollection of a wild coyote rather than Julian. "Yes, they should," Devon agreed as his attention focused on Melissa again. He really didn't want to encourage more conversation with Marcy, but she was right, someone should destroy that animal.

Marcy indiscreetly sat next to Devon. He shot a dark look at her as she wiggled in an attempt to push him over. He refused to budge. Her leaf green eyes narrowed, but it was obvious she wasn't moving.

Resting her hands on her knees, she perched precariously on the edge of the seat as a few other girls began to make their way toward the booth. Apparently they considered the absence of Cassie and Melissa an open invitation. Chris's jaw locked, his eyes darkened, as he briefly met Devon's gaze once more.

Devon shook his head, unsure what to do. He didn't like the idea of dumping Marcy on her ass, but when Cassie came back she was going to be upset by what was going on. The other girls hovered around them, grinning and whispering to each other as they giggled. Chris lifted an eyebrow, and shook his head at Devon in disbelief. "Amazing," he muttered.

"Venus flytrap," Devon reminded him.

"What is?" Marcy asked as she indiscreetly pressed her breasts against his arm.

Disgust boiled through Devon as he jerked his arm away. "Don't," he growled in warning. Marcy's eyes widened in surprise and she moved back a little, but she didn't remove herself completely. Instead, she turned her attention to Chris, who was eyeing her like she was some kind of repulsive insect he would like to stomp.

A blur of motion caught Devon's attention and his mouth dropped. He watched in horror as Cassie dashed past the group of students by the table, moving with an agility and speed that left him frozen in disbelief as she raced down the road. The cold stone of his heart seemed to lurch and twist as he followed her movement.

"Son of a bitch!" He slammed his hand on the table with such force it shuddered and threatened to break. "Move!"

Marcy still didn't move out of his way. Unable to wait, and tired of the tiny girl, Devon shoved his way out of the booth. She stumbled and nearly fell to the ground before managing to keep herself upright. People stared at him in surprise, but he paid them no attention as he shoved his way through the thick crowd.

Melissa was waving at them, jumping high to be seen over the top of the crowd. "Hurry!" she cried before turning and rushing out the door.

She didn't have to tell him that. Grasping hold of the banister, he swung himself over the side of the stairs in order to avoid the group gathered upon them. Landing gracefully, he shoved past the few remaining people in his way and bolted out the door. Cassie was disappearing into the woods already, barreling her way through the trees and ground cover.

It took all he had to keep his powers under control as he burst free of the restaurant. Though he was powerful, he couldn't alter all the memories of the human's within, and they couldn't afford to let the humans see him. Racing past the startled group by the picnic tables, he chased after Melissa. Chris was right on his heels as their feet stomped against the sidewalk.

As soon as he got free of prying eyes, he would catch her, and he very well might kill her himself when he did.

CHAPTER NINE

CASSIE IGNORED the briar that caught hold of her hair and ripped it out. Tearing past a large elm, relief filled her as Dani's dark head came into view. "Dani! Dani!"

The girl turned and took a step back as she caught sight of Cassie racing toward her like a crazed banshee. In the radiance of the full moon the red in her hair was the color of blood. Leaping over a rotten log, she panted as she halted before her.

"Cassie? What are you doing?" Dani demanded.

The beam of Dani's flashlight splashed across Cassie's face, momentarily blinding her. Blinking rapidly, Cassie knew she must look ridiculous, but didn't care. She inhaled deeply as she tried to get air back into her tortured lungs. "I saw you walking and thought I'd walk with you," she lied poorly.

Dani lifted a dark eyebrow questioningly. "You ran all the way here to *walk* with me?"

Cassie took another breath. "After the animal attacks last week, I didn't think you should be alone."

Dani tilted her head to the side, a small smile quirked her full lips. "That's nice of you, but I walk this way every night, and I can take care of myself."

Cassie didn't doubt she could, at least with normal things, but Dani had no idea what lurked in these woods now. Glancing nervously around, Cassie searched for any sign of something hiding within the shadows. She used every ounce of her power to explore the dark night as she tried to pick up waves of Julian's evil. Though she came up empty, she wasn't fooled into thinking he wasn't around. He was powerful enough to keep her blocked out if he chose.

"Still thought it would be better if you had some company."

Dani shrugged a dainty shoulder and turned away. "Well, come on, the path is better up here. I'm surprised to see you without Devon."

Cassie hoped he wasn't far behind. He would be infuriated with her, but she was willing to face his wrath. "I'm sure he'll be here," she mumbled.

Dani shot her a questioning look as they stepped onto a well worn, much easier to traverse path. Cassie studied each direction of the trail, but as far as she could see it was clear. "Cassie, are you ok?"

"Fine."

Dani kept the beam focused a few feet before her, but Cassie relied more on the light of the moon as she watched the pathway. Turning to look behind her, she was dismayed to see that Devon, Chris, and Melissa were still nowhere to be seen. She had no doubt they'd come after her, but had they somehow lost her in the woods?

A chill swept down her spine as shadows danced and swayed

over the path as the skeletal branches swayed and creaked in the night. Cassie's heart hammered as a crushing sense of impending doom settled over her. It was too quiet; no animals scurried through the woods, nothing moved within the underbrush.

Swallowing heavily, Cassie tried to push down her rising dread. She had to keep her wits about her if they were going to survive this. She took a step closer to Dani. Dani shot her a questioning, confused look as she shook her head. "You seem awfully jumpy tonight, are you sure you're ok?"

"Yes."

The loud echo of a cracking branch resounded through the forest. Cassie jumped as it tore more branches free on its plummet to the ground. Instinctively she grabbed hold of Dani's arm and pulled her closer. "There's someone out there," Dani said in a wavering voice.

Cassie fought the impulse to turn and flee while dragging Dani through the woods with her. She would have too, if she thought there was any chance of them being able to get away. "Just stay by me," she whispered.

A flurry of motion on her right caused Cassie to spin. A blur raced at them, it was so fast it nearly blended in with the trees. Dani cried out in surprise as Cassie shoved her to the side. Dani fell to the ground and rolled away on the path. Cassie had only a moment to react as she swung out and slammed the palm of her hand upward.

Julian's head shot back, blood burst over her as his elongated teeth pierced his lower lip and his nose shattered. The crazed vampire grunted from the impact, but his attack didn't slow. His arms encircled her waist, and he jerked her to the side as they fell to the ground in a tumbled heap of arms and legs.

A startled cry escaped her as they rolled over the path. Reacting on pure instinct, Cassie pulled her legs up against her chest and wedged them against Julian's well muscled frame. Adrenaline washed through her as she pushed up with all her might.

Julian snarled in rage as she managed to flip him off of her. Rolling away, Cassie bounded gracefully to her feet and scurried back toward where Dani stood at the edge of the path. "Run!" Cassie screamed at her.

Dani's terrified gaze swung toward her as another blur raced out of the woods. Cassie caught a brief glance of blood red eyes and lengthy fangs as Devon rushed past her. Rumbling growls echoed through the woods as he collided with Julian who had been coming back after her. Devon seized hold of him and slammed him into the ground. As they rolled, they clawed and tore at each other; murderous snarls echoed throughout the forest.

Cassie shuddered as the smell of blood filled the air. She knew she should take Dani and run, but she couldn't leave. Devon rolled and bounded back to his feet as Julian knocked him aside. "Devon!" she cried as she spotted the blood oozing from the jagged slices in his magnificent face.

His gaze swung toward her, the blood color of his eyes caused her to inhale harshly. His face was twisted as his teeth extended over his bottom lip. He looked like a monster, but he was still the person she loved, and she couldn't leave him here. "Go!" he barked at her. She took an involuntary step back. "Go!"

Cassie jumped in surprise, tears pooled in her eyes as hopelessness filled her. His gaze swung away from her as Julian went at him again. They fell together, snarling and growling as they tore at each other with the ferocity of savage animals. Cassie's ears rang with the noise as it hammered into her head. A large locust tree shuddered and shook as Devon slammed Julian against it with enough force to cause a jagged tear to race up the trunk.

Melissa and Chris burst onto the path and skidded to a halt as they took in the battle before them. "Move!" Cassie screamed at them.

They broke out of the daze holding them riveted and bolted across the path. Devon slammed Julian into the tree again. The crack gave way with a loud snap that echoed throughout the forest. Devon and Julian were forced from each other as the tree fell with a resounding boom that shook the earth.

Devon bounced across the ground, landing close to Cassie. She moved toward him, but he was back on his feet before she could reach him. Numb with terror and dread, Cassie watched helplessly as they relentlessly fought one another.

The earth beneath her feet began to rumble as a peculiar pulsing energy suddenly flooded it. Cassie's mouth dropped as the earth heaved with an odd new rhythm. A beat began to rise up from the dirt; it throbbed up her legs and made its way down her arms.

Cassie looked up as the earth released a current of electricity that rocked her back a step. Devon and Julian shot backward and bounced across the ground like ping pong balls. They both remained limp, knocked unconscious by the bolt that had smashed into them.

Cassie gasped, her heart hammered as she raced to Devon's side. Falling beside him, she tore at him as she grasped at his life-less body. Instinctively, she rested her hand on his chest, searching for a heartbeat but finding none. It took her a panicked minute to recall he wouldn't have a heartbeat anyway. She had to remind herself that even if he wasn't breathing, there was still a life energy pulsating from him. Cassie looked around the eerily still pathway, unable to understand what had just happened, or where the strange energy had come from.

"What was that?" Chris's voice came out choked and raw. If it hadn't been so frightening and shocking, Cassie would have laughed at the sight of his shaggy blond hair standing on end. It looked as if someone had just rubbed a balloon over all of him as his raised arms revealed the same thing. "What the *hell* was that?"

Melissa stood beside him, her hair wasn't quite as bad because of the braid, but a few strands of it were standing up. Dani bashfully met their gazes from under lowered lashes. "I'm sorry, I didn't mean to," she apologized.

Cassie gaped at her, unable to believe the tiny girl had done this. "You did this?" Cassie inquired as her hands clutched at Devon's motionless body.

Tears shimmered in Dani's eyes. "I'm sorry," she whispered again.

"Is he going to be ok?"

Dani's gaze fell briefly on Devon. Confusion flitted over her face, but she didn't look at all surprised over what had just happened. Knowledge settled over Cassie as she leaned closer to Devon, her hand stroked over his battered face as she prepared to defend him to the death, against one of her *own* kind.

"He should be fine," Dani finally said.

"Should be?" Cassie demanded. "*Should* be!"

"Cassie," Chris said as he gave up on calming his hair down.

Cassie took a deep breath as her attention returned to Devon. Though he remained immobile, the jagged cuts in his cheek had already begun to heal. She could practically see the muscle reattaching itself as the blood dried on his skin. The scent of his blood hinted of spices and power. Even in his bloodied and unconscious state he was still magnificent, and he was *hers*. A protective urge surged through her as she bent closer to him. He had to wake up, she needed him to come back to her, and it had to happen soon.

"What did you do?" she asked.

"It's… it's an electric pulse," Dani answered shakily. Then her gaze sharpened on Cassie. "Why are you defending him? They're our enemies."

Melissa and Chris looked nervously at Cassie before turning their attention back to Dani. "You don't know it all," Cassie retorted. "And neither do we."

"I think we should get out of here, and then we can discuss this," Melissa interjected as her eyes darted to Julian's prone figure fifty feet down the path.

He'd been further away from the blast then Devon, did that mean he would wake faster? Cassie's hand twitched to the stake at her side, her mind and heart hammered with the possibility of destroying him now, of ending the misery of so many people. Could she get down there in time? "How long does it last?" she inquired.

"Cassie!" Melissa hissed.

Dani licked her lips as she glanced nervously at Julian. "I… I don't know. On normal people," she glanced warily at them again. "It can last an hour or two, depending on the strength of the blast. On them," her gaze ran over Devon and Julian. "I have no idea, it varies."

Cassie's gaze settled on Julian again. This could be their opportunity to make it all end. They could stop the murders and the suffering, end the fear they'd lived with since Julian arrived. She just didn't know if she would have time to get to him and kill him before he awoke.

"Can you jolt him again?" she inquired.

Dani's red highlights flashed in the moonlight as she shook her head. "No. I have little control over my ability; it usually comes out when I'm frightened. I've never been able to use it twice in the same day."

"Like a battery," Chris whispered. When Dani seemed a little insulted, he quickly explained himself. "You need time to recharge."

Dani still didn't look appeased as she shrugged. "I guess," she mumbled.

Cassie glanced back at Julian; she was desperate to end it once and for all. Devon showed no sign of awakening any time soon. Would it be the same with Julian? "We can do it," she whispered.

"No Cassie!" Melissa said brusquely. "We have to get to safety. We must get *Devon* to safety."

Reluctantly tearing her gaze away from Julian's body, Cassie shifted as she slid her arm under Devon's shoulders. Melissa was right, she couldn't take the chance of Julian awakening first and coming after him in this vulnerable state. "Give me a hand Chris!" she ordered briskly as her heart hammered with her desperate need to get Devon out of here.

He hurried forward, his wary gaze still on Julian as he bent to help Cassie. It took a few moments but they finally got Devon on his feet. Draping his arms over their shoulders, they drug him toward Dani and Melissa.

"We have to hurry," Melissa implored. Though her dark eyes didn't reveal a recent vision, Cassie knew Melissa's instincts were highly honed because of her premonitions.

They shuffled as quickly down the path as they could while dragging Devon between them. Dani's flashlight bounced across the trail, and flashed off the eyes of a fox as it rushed into the woods. Cassie noted the return of the wildlife, surely that meant Julian was still safely unconscious. Didn't it?

Cassie relentlessly scanned the forest as she searched for any hint of his return in the shadowed interior. "Just a little further," Dani whispered.

Devon twitched suddenly and his hand grasped her shoulder. Cassie stiffened as adrenaline shot through her. "Faster," Chris urged. "Go faster."

A deer bolted through the forest, the loud crash of its passing reverberated around them. "Oh," Cassie breathed, forcing herself to ignore the growing ache in her shoulders, back, and legs as she tried to move faster. The eerie stillness returned once more as a pall hung over the shadows. "Melissa!" Melissa turned and rushed to her side. "Take him."

Melissa's dark eyes scanned her, but she didn't refuse as she slid easily into Cassie's place. Cassie was reluctant to release Devon, but she had to be ready to fight. She was the strongest of them; though she wasn't fooled into thinking she was strong enough to defeat Julian.

"Keep going."

"We're not leaving you here!" Chris said forcefully.

"Go!" Cassie yelled. The hair on the back of her neck stood on end, and goose bumps broke out on her arms. She bounced on the tips of her toes as she braced herself for the attack. "Get him to safety. Please Chris, he's the only hope we have of destroying Julian."

Chris swore vehemently. "I'll take him," Dani offered.

Cassie didn't look back as more rustling ensued. Chris's sapphire eyes were dark as he appeared at her side. "Go," she commanded.

"No," he said simply.

Cassie didn't argue further, there was no need. It wouldn't do any good. They began to back down the path together as they kept an eye out for any sign of movement. She glanced over her shoulder, relieved to see that Dani and Melissa had disappeared around a bend with Devon. "Run," she whispered.

Their feet moved rapidly over the ground as they turned and raced down the path. The hairs on her neck stood up, she could almost feel Julian breathing down her neck. His fury pushed her faster than she'd ever run before. She grabbed hold of Chris's arm as he started to lag behind. A burst of strength, she'd never known she could possess, swept through her as she dragged him along with her. She refused to lose him to the monster chasing them.

She pushed Chris in front of her and pushed him faster with her hands. They rounded another corner, and Dani and Melissa came back into view. Devon was still being dragged between them. "Go!" Cassie screamed.

Something brushed against the back of her neck; an involuntary cry tore from her as ice filled her veins. Turning another corner, the woods suddenly gave way to a large, dark field. The glow of the moon bounced off the tall grass covering the field.

Julian was playing with her as his touch brushed over her once more. She could almost hear his laughter; almost feel the enjoyment he took in playing with her like a cat with a mouse. She wouldn't run from him anymore, she wouldn't give him the satisfaction of tormenting her.

Cassie spun and planted her feet as she braced herself for the attack. There was nothing behind her but open air and dark night. She knew he was there; she could feel his eyes upon her, and his merriment. The faint breeze tickled her hair as it blew it across her face. It was the only thing that moved in the still night.

"Cassie!" Chris bellowed.

The woods exploded with movement. Leaves and branches shredded from the trees, and billowed outward as a blur raced toward her. She became hollow and empty inside, her veins filled with ice as blue eyes of death rushed at her with a merry twinkle in their cold depths. A startled cry escaped her as arms suddenly wrapped around her from behind and pulled her into a strong embrace. "Down," a voice commanded in her ear.

She ducked down as Devon bent over her, using his body to shield her from the blow that followed. A grunt of pain escaped him as he was knocked forward. He pushed her to her knees but his body remained folded over hers. Cassie shuddered as she waited for the attack to come again.

Devon rose, pulling her up to stand beside him. She clung to his firm body, savoring the feel of him awake and alive as she struggled to catch her breath. "Where is he?" she demanded.

Devon's jaw was clenched as he stood protectively against her. "Gone."

Cassie searched the area, but Julian did appear to be gone. Shuddering again, she buried her face in Devon's chest as she tried to forget all the awful events of the night. His arms wrapped around her as he buried his hand in her hair.

"It's ok now," he whispered reassuringly.

Cassie nodded, but she couldn't stop the shudders racking her. So close, they had all come *so close* to dying tonight, and if there was one thing she wasn't ready to do, it was die. Now that Devon was in her life, she had every intention of staying around for as long as possible. He turned his face into her hair as his hold on her went from one of protection, to one of desire. Despite her terror and confusion, Cassie's body reacted instantly to his.

His hand tensed on her hair as his body trembled. She knew she should pull away, she was only rattling his control, but she couldn't move. She'd nearly lost him tonight, nearly lost her own life, and she couldn't let him go.

His mouth turned into her neck, his shaking increased as his lips brushed over her skin. Clinging to him, her body became limp as he pressed butterfly kisses against her flesh. Cassie couldn't stop the breath that escaped her as her hands dug into his arms and her knees went limp. His strong arm around her waist kept her on her feet as he supported her weight.

The chest high grass rustled as footsteps rapidly approached. Devon pulled away from her, his hands clenched on her. His eyes flashed between their beautiful emerald color and a volatile red as he met her gaze. Cassie rested her hand upon his cheek as she wiped away his dried blood. The gashes in his cheek were completely healed; the small scratches were disappearing before her eyes.

He dropped his forehead to hers. "Cassie," he breathed. "*My* Cassie."

"Yes," she agreed. She was his, she would always be his.

"Are you trying to get yourself killed?" Cassie shook her head. "I can't lose you it would destroy me."

Her hand tightened on his cheek as tears burned the backs of her eyes and throat. "I'm sorry," she whispered.

Cassie lost herself to the beauty of his emerald eyes. They burned with a fiery intensity that left her speechless and frozen. In those eyes she could feel, and see, the endless depth of his love for her. She suddenly understood his overbearing compulsion to keep her protected, because he would *not* survive her death. Swallowing back her tears, her heart hammered with an answering need that left her shaken. She gladly would have given him anything he asked from her, and more.

"Are you ok?" Chris demanded as he burst free of the grass and broke through the web ensnaring them.

"Fine." Cassie caressed Devon's face once more before turning to face the three of them. She could feel Devon's annoyance over being interrupted. He kept his arm firmly around her waist, refusing to release her. "Are you guys ok?"

"Yes," Melissa answered. "Where is he?"

"Gone," Devon answered flatly.

"But why would he just leave like that? He gave up too easily."

They all turned to Devon with questioning gazes. He lifted an eyebrow in amusement. "If he stayed he would have had to take on a vampire more powerful than him, and four Hunters. There wasn't much thought required in abandoning his quest, especially with a Grounder present."

"A what?" Melissa, Cassie, and Chris asked in confusion.

He nodded toward Dani. Heat crept up Dani's face as she studied her sneakers. "A Grounder. I'm right, am I not?" Devon inquired.

Dani nodded as she lifted her head to look at them. "Yes, you're right."

"What is a Grounder?" Chris demanded.

"Would you like to tell them, or shall I?" Dani shook her head as she turned her attention back to her sneakers. "A Grounder is a vampire, or Hunter, who can pull energy from the earth and turn it into an electrical current they release in a burst of power. It's meant to stun the prey, though sometimes it kills."

Cassie inhaled sharply; Chris and Melissa took a hasty step away from Dani as their eyes turned wary and distrustful. "I've never killed anyone," Dani said defensively.

"No, that is rare, and it usually involves someone with a lot of power. But you are new to yours. What are you fifteen, sixteen?"

"Fifteen," Dani whispered.

Devon shifted his hold on Cassie. "You're still young and inexperienced. With time your emotions won't control your ability, you will."

"But she could kill us?" Melissa asked as she studied Dani.

"No, since you're Hunters you're not affected by her ability. You can withstand it. You can't withstand a vampire with the same ability, just as Julian and I can't completely withstand Dani. Next time, Julian will be more prepared for her though. She won't knock either of us out again. If Dani and a vampire Grounder come up against each other, they can mostly withstand the attack of the other. Though they will get banged up a little, possibly slightly singed by the shock."

"Singed?" Cassie asked.

Devon held up his arms to reveal the healing burns marring his skin. Cassie seized hold of him and twisted his arms in her grasp. The burns ran all the way up to his shoulder, where they disappeared beneath his shirt. The hair on his arms was seared and for the first time she noticed the smell of burned flesh on him.

She turned back to Dani and pinned the girl with a heated glare. "I didn't know," Dani whispered. "I didn't mean to, I was frightened."

"It's ok," Devon assured her as he ran his hands up Cassie's arms. Though his touch calmed her, her protective instincts were still running high. "Do you guys know nothing of your heritage? Of your people?"

Cassie shot him a look, as Chris scowled at him. Melissa's forehead was furrowed as she studied the forest. She knew far more than Cassie and Chris about their heritage, but apparently this little bit of info had somehow been left out. Luther's biggest pet peeve with Chris and Cassie was they didn't *want* to know their history. Cassie had always been resentful of it and Chris was bored by it.

Melissa had grown up with Luther though; he'd been teaching

her their history since she was a child. Melissa also believed the study of their history, *any* history, helped to pull her free of a world comprised mostly of tomorrows for her.

"Chris and I don't know much," Cassie admitted reluctantly.

Devon frowned at her. "Dani?" he inquired.

She shrugged, but she shifted uneasily. "Yes, I know some of it," Dani said. "My brother has taught me."

"Your brother?" Cassie inquired as she took a small step toward her. "Where is he?"

"At home."

She glanced at Devon and then back at Dani. "I think we should go meet him, and we have to speak with Luther."

"Good idea," Devon agreed.

"Who is Luther?" Dani inquired.

"Our Guardian," Melissa answered.

"You have a Guardian?" she asked eagerly.

"Yes." Cassie's ire over Devon's fading injuries diminished in the face of Dani's hope. "He's a good man."

"Maybe this time we'll listen to him." Chris looked slightly chagrined as he kicked his shoe in the dirt.

"Would be helpful," Devon muttered.

His hand remained in hers as he stepped around her to survey the dark night. A startled cry escaped her and her hand flew to her mouth. His back was marred by jagged gashes crisscrossing it. Blood stained his shirt and caused it to cling to the torn edges of his skin. Nausea boiled up her throat as her stomach somersaulted violently.

Hatred boiled through her as she realized Julian had done this to him. Devon had taken the blow meant for her; a blow that would have flayed her open, and possibly killed her. She hadn't thought it was possible to love him more, she knew now she'd been wrong. It filled her completely and nearly burst from her as it flowed up in powerful waves that pulsed through her veins and warmed her to the tips of her toes.

"Your back," she whispered.

He glanced at her. "It's fine." She reached toward him in order to comfort him and ease the pain she knew he had to be in. Seizing hold of her hand, he subtly shook his head. "It's ok, it will heal soon."

Tears slid down her cheeks. She hated the pain and the hunger blazing from his eyes. He'd been wounded badly, lost a lot of blood, and although his face was completely healed and his back was well on its way, it was obvious the battle had drained him. The burns still marring his skin hadn't helped his energy level either.

Sensing her distress, he pulled her a step closer and encircled her waist as he kissed her forehead. "I'll be fine," he assured her again. "I barely felt a thing."

She knew he lied, but she didn't push him further. Resting her head on his chest, she simply relished the comfort of his body and the love enveloping her like a warm cocoon.

Dani watched them in amazement as her eyes flickered back and forth. "I know, it's confusing," Chris said as he dropped an arm casually around her shoulders. "But he really is one of the good guys, strange as that sounds. So, we've found another Hunter, there are four of us now."

"Five," Melissa corrected. "Dani's brother. We'll definitely give Julian a run for his money. It's amazing you live here also, and we never knew what you were."

Dani looked shyly away. "We just moved here at the beginning of the year."

"Works great for us!" Chris said jovially. "Especially with that little zapping gift you have. He may be one of the good guys, but that was pretty impressive." He shot a grin over his shoulder at Devon who glowered back at him. Cassie shook her head and rolled her eyes at Chris.

"It's not all it's cracked up to be," Dani mumbled. "Especially when you can't control it."

Cassie sensed more behind the words, and her heart went out to the younger girl.

CHAPTER TEN

DANI'S BROTHER, Joey, was wearing the already bare carpet even thinner as he spun on his heel and paced back across the room. His whipcord lean body was as taut as a bowstring and his dark auburn hair was in disarray from running his fingers through it. He was older, at twenty-four he was probably one of the oldest Hunter's still alive.

Melissa and Chris watched him suspiciously, thrown off by the resentment and tension radiating from him. Joey's gaze focused on the open doorway, where Devon was leaning casually against the frame with his legs crossed at the ankles. Though he appeared relaxed, tension hummed through Devon and undermined his casual posture. Joey frowned at him, his scathing gaze raked over all of them before he returned to pacing.

Joey refused to invite Devon in and none of them could really talk with the apartment door open. "Why don't we go to my house," Cassie suggested.

Joey shot her a look before shaking his head. "I'm not going anywhere that *thing* can go inside of!"

Cassie's skin prickled against the assault on Devon. "Devon is on our side," Luther said, not for the first time, as he shot Cassie a warning look.

"None of *them* are on our side. I don't think any of *you* are on our side!"

"It's true Joey," Dani murmured.

His lip curled in a sneer as he stared at his sister. "Have you forgotten what they did to our family? To mom and dad and Rachael."

"Rachael?" Luther inquired.

"She was our sister. They," he thrust a finger viciously at Devon, who lifted an eyebrow, but otherwise showed no reaction to the hatred directed at him. "Murdered her."

Nausea rolled through Cassie as revulsion washed over her. It so easily could have been her or Chris, and it would have been if Chris's dad hadn't been gifted with premonitions also. She glanced at Devon, but his face was a stoic mask. She craved his comfort, but she sensed he'd shut down from the accusations, and the brutal reminder of what he'd once been.

He may not have been part of The Slaughter, but at one point in his prolonged life he'd been a killer. She didn't know how many he'd killed, she wasn't sure if *he* knew. She didn't like to think about the past, she only wanted to focus on the present where he was good and loving, and hers.

"I barely got Dani out of there alive," Joey said. Dani was staring at her sneakers again with her hands folded behind her back. "And I was only eleven. Do you know what it's like to try and keep your sister alive when you're only eleven years old and living on the streets?" he demanded.

No one spoke. Cassie couldn't find words to offer him. Though she and Melissa had lost their parents, and Chris his father, they'd all been lucky enough to have someone there to take care of them after. Luther had fled with Melissa, Cassie's grandmother and Chris's mother had taken them to safety. Although Chris's mother had retreated into a world of alcohol and drugs, Cassie's grandmother had been there to nurture and love him as they grew.

To live on the streets, struggling to survive while trying to raise a baby was something she couldn't begin to fathom. Her heart went out to him, and she began to understand why his hatred was so entrenched. "That must have been awful," she said.

Joey's gaze slid to her, his eyes blazed with hatred. Devon's casual stance was forgotten as he stepped away from the doorway. "Awful doesn't begin to describe it!" Joey barked. "You know nothing of what I went through."

"We all had a difficult time of it." Chris was trying to defuse the situation though he looked almost as agitated as Devon.

Joey snorted as he tugged at his hair and ran his hand through it once more. "It must have been really awful for you with your homes, and your families."

"Joey," Dani said, looking embarrassed and discomfited by her brother's attitude. "They lost their families too."

"Not all of them!" Joey's gaze disdainfully raked Chris before turning on Cassie. A low growl emitted from Devon, his hands fisted at his sides as he glared at Joey. "I told you, animals," he sneered at Devon.

"Cassie come here," Devon ordered forcefully.

She bristled at his commanding tone, but she sensed he was near his breaking point. Though he couldn't enter the apartment, she was frightened he would tear the building down if she didn't get further away from Joey. Glancing anxiously back and forth between him and Joey, she was uncertain what she should do. She didn't like the idea of alienating Joey any further, they might need him, but she didn't want Devon's control tested anymore than it already was.

She glanced helplessly at Luther, seeking some sort of guidance from the man who'd been very much like a father to her over the past four years. He gave a subtle nod toward Devon, though his eyes didn't leave Joey as he continued to pace restlessly. For the first time she noticed Chris had been moving protectively closer to Melissa and Luther.

It was Chris's reaction that bothered her most. He didn't trust Joey.

"Cassie," Devon said again.

Joey glared at her as she moved away from the back of the old couch and edged her way toward the door. The moment she was partly past the frame, Devon seized hold of her hand and pulled her outside. She gave him a disgruntled look he chose to ignore as he pushed her behind him.

"Devon," she said angrily, not at all pleased with being relegated to the back.

He didn't look at her, nor did he move. Cassie nudged him as she stepped around his back. He slammed his hand into the doorframe as his eyes briefly flared ruby red. "No!"

Cassie blinked in surprise, she'd seen his eyes red before, but it had never been directed at her. Though she knew he would never harm her, he could hurt someone else if he lost control. Swallowing heavily, Cassie rested a hand on his arm as she sought to ease some of his tension. "I'm not going back in," she kept her voice low so Joey couldn't hear her.

He relaxed and his hand fell away from the frame, but he didn't allow her to go any further past him. Joey was glaring at her as if she were a distasteful thing that was better off dead. Despite her intention to stand her ground, Cassie found herself taking a small step back from the loathing blasting against her.

The corded muscles of Devon's arms stood out distinctly as his hands fisted. His back was ramrod straight, and the jagged tears in his shirt revealed that his vicious cuts had completely healed. Cassie found herself fascinated by his amazing healing abilities. She was a little unnerved by the acute reminder he was anything but human.

"I think you should all leave," Joey said briskly.

"Joey!" Dani cried as she leapt off the couch. "They're like us! We've found others. That's what we've been searching and hoping for. You can't send them away."

"They are *not* like us Dani, they're traitors."

Dani pleadingly glanced around the room before her eyes landed on her big brother. "No, they aren't! No, Cassie came after me to help me. She was frightened for me and she was trying to save me! If they hadn't come, I would have died. The real monster is still out there!"

He shook his head, his jaw set, and his eyes pitiless. "I will have nothing to do with people who have aligned themselves with our enemy."

Dani seized hold of his arm. "He saved her Joey!" she cried as she jabbed a finger at Devon. "He put himself in between her and that thing out there. He put his own life at risk to save her!"

Joey threw her hand off. "I don't care," he snarled. "They both should have died."

"Don't you ever say anything like that again!" Devon bellowed. He took an aggressive step forward, only to be blocked by an invisible wall of air.

Cassie grabbed hold of his arm and squeezed as she tried to

calm him. Glancing back at her, he relaxed visibly, but it wouldn't take much for him to lose it. "I told you, nothing but animals," Joey spat.

"No, you're wrong Joey, you're wrong." Tears streamed down Dani's face as she hopelessly stared at her brother.

Cassie's heart ached for Dani, the girl was desperate to find acceptance, a family, *anything*. Cassie longed to go to her and comfort her, but she knew it would be the worst thing she could do. Devon would go crazy if she wasn't near him, and Joey wouldn't react kindly to her presence in his home again.

"That's enough Dani!" he snapped. "All of you get out of my house."

"Let's go," Luther said as he nudged Melissa toward the door. "I'm sorry we've troubled you. You're safe here, if you change your mind about joining us."

Joey's look of abhorrence was enough to let Cassie know that was never going to happen. "My sister and I will have *nothing* to do with you. *Ever!*" Tears continued to stream down Dani's face as she stared helplessly at them. "We will be leaving this town."

"No!" Dani cried. Cassie's heart lurched, she took a step forward but Devon shot her a look that froze her in her place. "I don't want to leave!"

"Too bad," Joey retorted.

Devon pushed Cassie back a step when Chris, Melissa, and Luther stepped through the doorway. "We will be sad to see you go, but if you feel it's best…" Luther started.

"It is." Joey stalked across the room as they stepped out of the apartment. Cassie jumped in surprise as the door forcefully slammed shut. The echo of it reverberated throughout the dingy hall of the apartment building.

"Well, he was pleasant, we should invite him over for tea and crumpets sometime," Chris quipped as he rolled his eyes and shoved his hands into his pockets.

"Not funny," Luther reprimanded. "We could have used their aid, especially Dani's. A Grounder." He shook his head in amazement as he ran his fingers through his disordered hair. "Maybe he will come around."

"No," Chris said firmly. "He won't be coming around. He radiated hatred and revulsion for us; there were waves of it coming out of him." He shuddered as he huddled deeper into his coat. "He is set in his opinion, and he will stick to it."

Cassie was disheartened by Chris's assessment but she wasn't surprised by it. She took hold of Devon's hand and massaged the knuckles of his fingers as she tried to calm the anger still radiating from him. "Let's get you home," he said. "Luther can explain about your powers there."

Chris and Cassie groaned, not at all looking forward to a lecture from Luther. "Maybe we should just wait till tomorrow; it's been a long day…"

"It's about time you learned at least a little about your heritage." Luther shot Chris a stern look that dared him to continue protesting. "It will help in your fight against Julian. It will also aid in your understanding of where your abilities come from."

"I have none," Cassie reminded him but she didn't hold out much hope that would get her out of this.

"You do have abilities a human doesn't possess," Devon reminded her. "You should know where those come from."

Her nose wrinkled as she realized she'd lost the battle.

CHAPTER ELEVEN

CASSIE'S GRANDMOTHER met them at the door; a strawberry eyebrow was raised questioningly as she studied them. Holding the door open, she ushered them inside and made a sweeping gesture toward the living room. Crackers, cheese, bottles of water, and glasses of soda had already been set out on trays for them. The enticing smell of shepherd's pie drifted from the kitchen, and reminded Cassie they hadn't had a chance to eat yet.

"Food," Chris groaned. He plopped himself on the couch as he grabbed a handful of crackers and cheese.

"You guys look like you've been through hell," her grandmother said.

For the first time Cassie noted how dirty, bedraggled, bloodied, and exhausted they all looked. "Hell came to us," Chris's words were garbled by the crackers he was chomping on.

Her grandma shook her head as she moved into the living room. She shooed Chris's feet off of the coffee table. He gave her a bashful grin, but it didn't hinder his chewing process. "Good thing

Adam told me you were coming," she announced as she slid into her favorite recliner. "Dinner should be ready soon."

"Have I ever told you how much I love you?" Chris asked with a grin.

Her grandmother rolled her eyes, but she couldn't stop the cheerful smile spreading across her youthful face. "Suck up," Melissa muttered as she slapped Chris's hand away so she could snag a handful of crackers. He sulked for a minute before dipping his hand back into the cracker bowl again.

"Who's Adam?" Devon inquired.

Cassie's smile was sympathetic. "He's one of the ghosts she talks to; the other two are Caleb and Julia. She mentions them often."

"So, who is going to tell me what happened?" her grandmother asked.

Cassie squeezed Devon's hand and released it. Moving around the couch, she stopped to drop a kiss on her grandmother's head before grabbing some of the few crackers left. "I will," she said as she slid onto the loveseat and Luther took up his customary position by the fireplace.

In between munching on crackers, Cassie filled her grandmother in on the details of the night. When Cassie finished, her grandmother sat back in her chair, and her eyes darkened to a deep brown as she began to converse with her ghost friends. It was a few moments before her eyes returned to their normal sky blue and focused on Cassie.

"I can't believe you ran into the woods on your own," she scolded.

Cassie shifted uncomfortably, but she didn't bother to look for help elsewhere in the room. "I was worried she was going to be killed."

Her grandmother quirked an eyebrow. "I understand that, but you were reckless and *you* could have been killed."

"Not to mention Dani was better able to defend herself than any of us," Chris mumbled.

Cassie shot him a look, not at all pleased with his interference. "Very true," her grandmother agreed. "But none of you could have known that. I've only ever met one Grounder before and it was a little disconcerting."

Cassie, Chris, and Melissa nodded their agreement. Devon remained immobile, though his gaze did flit down to his now healed arms. "It's a lot of power for a young girl, especially if she doesn't have control over it." Luther shook his head as he pulled his glasses off and rubbed the bridge of his nose. "I could have helped her if her brother would have let me."

"Stubborn, foolish boy," her grandmother whispered as her eyes darkened once more. "There will be no changing his mind though."

"No, there won't," Devon and Chris agreed simultaneously. They shot each other an amused look before Chris's attention was once more diverted by food.

Her grandmother turned to Devon as she began to speak. "If you continue to hang out with our kind, I'm sure you'll find some of them will feel the same way. Though, there are so few left I doubt you'll meet many more. It's a miracle they moved into the same town as us. Imagine the odds."

"They move frequently, it was probably only a matter of time before they stumbled upon Cape Cod," Luther murmured. "But yes, the odds are astronomical. I do wonder what the brother is capable of, considering the power his sister possesses."

Cassie tried not to contemplate what the infuriated, hate filled man could do. Though she suspected if it was anything as destructive as Dani's ability, he would have used it today. Her glance slid to Devon, he was exceptionally powerful, but Dani's power had left him vulnerable and wounded. What if it happened again, but this time they weren't there to keep him safe from someone seeking to kill him?

"What happened today won't happen again," he told her. Cassie frowned at him as he grinned at her. "I don't have to be able to read minds to know what you're thinking; you wear your thoughts on your face. Dani's power knocked me and Julian out because neither of us expected it. If I run into her or her brother again, I will be better prepared. She won't knock me out next time, she may give me a good blow, but she won't knock me out."

Cassie sighed in relief. "I don't think Dani meant to injure you."

"No, she didn't," Chris said emphatically. "She felt pretty bad about it. Her brother though, he would have hurt you, all of us actually."

Devon sat beside Cassie and took hold of her hand. "They'll leave," Luther said. "Probably already packing their things now. What a waste," he mumbled.

"I feel bad for her," Cassie said. "She wanted so badly to stay and be a part of something."

"Maybe we'll run into her someday in the future, but for now she isn't part of this group, and we must come to that sad realization." Her grandmother rose to her feet and smoothed her pants as she looked them over. "This is a pretty powerful group here though."

"Yes, it is," Luther agreed. "And I suppose it's time we finally have that conversation."

Cassie and Chris exchanged sullen frowns. "Just let me get dinner out of the oven first," her grandmother announced.

"I'll help you," Cassie offered.

Her grandmother waved her back. "Sit, you need a break. I've got it."

Cassie leaned back in the loveseat and rested her head on Devon's shoulder. No one spoke as they listened to the clink of silverware, and cabinets opened and closed as her grandmother bustled about. She was carrying two big plates of steaming, delicious looking food when she reappeared in the room. Chris and Melissa eagerly accepted their plates; Chris nearly salivated at the mound of meat and potatoes on his. Melissa had a big slice of vegetable lasagna on her plate.

"You drop any on my carpet and you're going into the dining room," her grandmother scolded Chris.

Chris nodded, but he didn't respond as he dropped the plate to the table and began to wolf it down. "Could you at least eat like a human being?" Melissa inquired.

"I'm hungry," he retorted.

Melissa rolled her eyes but refrained from eating until everyone else had been served. Chris finally caught sight of this and eased his onward rush to choke himself to death. Her grandmother reappeared with two more plates and handed them out to Luther and Cassie. "Thank you," Cassie murmured.

She dug into her dinner, savoring it as the eager rumbling in her stomach quieted a little more with every bite. Devon was studying her with shrewd eyes. "You haven't eaten today." The low tone of his voice didn't carry beyond her.

Cassie shook her head. "No, I had a headache."

She was surprised to realize the headache was gone, apparently having disappeared when fear for her life had taken over. "That's no reason not to take care of yourself."

She couldn't meet his gaze again. She suddenly realized it took more than just him staying well fed, and strict self-control, to be around her. She also had to take care of herself, and try to stay out of trouble. If she wasn't going to take care of herself, then he would do it for her. He would keep her out of harm's way by making sure she couldn't be wounded anymore, ever.

Grasping hold of his arm, Cassie met his unsettled gaze. "I promise it won't happen again."

Though he visibly relaxed, a muscle in his cheek jumped. It took every bit of control he had to be around her, every ounce of self restraint he had to be with her every day. A knot formed in her throat as tears burned her eyes; her appetite vanished. She loved him so much, but it wasn't enough. For the first time she fully realized the finality of their love. Deep down she'd still been holding out hope they would somehow get through all of this without losing too much, and with her still being human.

She realized now that wasn't going to be possible. She either joined him, or they ended this. Right now, she didn't know which was worse.

Devon turned back to her, his eyebrows drew together questioningly as his gaze shot to her barely touched food. Cassie swallowed heavily and dropped her head before he could see the hopelessness engulfing her. Though she wasn't hungry anymore, she forced herself to eat. She couldn't give him everything he required, but she would give him as much as possible.

No one spoke as they ate. Chris helped himself to seconds before anyone else was done. Cassie managed to choke down almost three quarters of her plate before putting it aside. "I think everyone is ready Luther," her grandmother said as she pulled her small legs beneath her once more.

Luther nodded as he pushed his glasses up on his nose. He rested one arm on the mantle as he stared at the far side of the room. "About fifteen hundred years ago, vampires were beginning to run rampant in the world. They weren't overly concerned about people knowing of their existence, why should they be when there was no one to stop them? At this time, a group of humans gathered together, determined to hunt down the monsters and destroy as many of them as they could in order to stop the killing and regain some control of the earth."

"They were the first Hunters?" Cassie inquired.

"Sort of," he hedged.

Cassie lifted an eyebrow at his "sort of," not at all liking the way he responded to her question. "What do you mean, sort of?" Chris inquired as he temporarily forgot the plate of food still on his lap.

Luther and her grandmother exchanged a look and Devon rested his hand on her knee. Melissa's shoulders were slouched as her gaze was focused on the floor. Cassie's frown deepened, it was becoming more than apparent she wasn't going to like what Luther had to say. Luther slid his glasses off and cleaned them on his shirt before slipping them back on. Her hand tightened around Devon's as a growing knot of apprehension began to twist in her body.

"As a group, the humans were able to do some damage against the vampires, but not much. When they came up against a more powerful vampire, they were useless. They were getting slaughtered and the vampires were becoming stronger. As the years passed the vampire's numbers grew, and the human fighters dwindled as most became afraid to continue the battle.

"That was when they decided to recruit the help of an emerging group of scientists."

The knot in Cassie's stomach turned into a noose that spread up her throat and threatened to choke her. Chris still looked confused, but a chill of apprehension swept down her spine. "And what did these scientists do?" Chris inquired as he placed his plate on the table.

Cassie fought the impulse to cover her ears and block out whatever else Luther had to say. It may have been a childish urge, but it was one she desperately sought to fulfill. "They began to experiment on the vampires they managed to capture during their hunts."

Chris looked confused as he glanced around the room. It wasn't that he couldn't grasp what Luther was saying, he didn't want to, and Cassie didn't blame him. "What kind of experiments?" Chris demanded harshly.

Luther heaved a loud breath. "They were determined to know how vampires worked, how they functioned and where their powers came from."

"And did they succeed?" Cassie asked in a choked voice.

"Somewhat, but not completely. They learned the source of a vampire's power comes from their blood. To become a vampire an exchange of blood is required, and death must occur."

Cassie turned toward Devon, these were things she knew, but for the first time she truly realized he'd died. Someone had *killed* him. Or he may have willingly allowed himself to be changed, may have embraced death for the promise of eternal life. Her forehead furrowed as she once again recalled how very little she knew of him. However, right now she was learning more than she'd ever wanted to know, and her curiosity about Devon was going to have to wait.

"During the exchange of blood, the demon within the vampire is passed on to the victim. This demon blood is thought to be the source of the vampire's power; it was also the reason why everyone believed all vampires must be monsters and murderers."

His gaze turned briefly to Devon as his gray eyes flickered. "Obviously we were wrong."

Devon looked briefly at Cassie as he nodded. His face was tense, and Cassie knew he was thinking about his effort to keep himself restrained around her. "It is difficult, but it can be controlled. Most simply don't control it; they enjoy the hunt, the thrill, the power. They revel in the evil, or at least their demon side does, and they have no inclination to suppress it. Others may not know it can be done, but there are still others who *do* control it."

Luther nodded as he rubbed the bridge of his nose. "Yes, I understand that now. We should have understood it earlier, but arrogance and ignorance go a long way in keeping the truth hidden."

Chris rose so suddenly he knocked the coffee table with his knee. It skittered back, but he made no move to fix it as he paced away restlessly. Running a hand through his hair, he turned toward Luther and pinned him with his gaze. His broad shoulders were set as if he awaited a blow. Which Cassie was certain they were going to receive.

"Where did our abilities come from?" Chris inquired.

"When they discovered the source of the vampire's powers they started to try and isolate it. They could never successfully isolate the gene, but they began to experiment with trying to harvest that power into humans."

The hair on the back of Cassie's neck stood on end. Her fingers began to tighten around Devon's, but for the first time his touch wasn't enough to soothe her. Shifting uncomfortably, she found she was unable to sit still anymore. Sliding her hand free of Devon's she launched to her feet. She fought against fleeing the room and this conversation, but she knew she couldn't.

"And how did these experiments go?" she asked.

"At first, not well," Luther admitted. "There were many failures and many were caught in between. They were caught in a world where they were neither…"

"Neither?" Cassie croaked.

"A monstrosity," Devon answered when Luther seemed unable to. "A thing that is neither human nor vampire, a creature with no thought or reason. All it does is destroy. All it craves is blood and death."

Bile flowed up Cassie's throat; it burned into her esophagus as her stomach threatened to heave up its contents. She could picture these monsters, these *things* caught in between. Neither human nor vampire but a fiend worse than anything any horror writer could have dreamed up.

"What happened to these things?" she asked.

"They were destroyed," Luther answered flatly. “They couldn't be allowed to roam the earth. The destruction would be incalculable."

"Were these experiment victims willing?"

"Some, but not all."

Swallowing heavily, Cassie paced to the doorway before turning back again. This time she didn't return to Devon's side. Instead she felt the desperate compulsion to be closer to Chris and Melissa. "And how did it all turn out?" Chris inquired when she stopped next to him.

"Eventually they succeeded in planting enough of the vampire blood into a human without changing them completely, or leaving them in the void. They turned these humans into something that still appeared completely human but was stronger, faster, and possessed gifts and talents of their own."

The truth wasn't as shocking after all. She had expected this. She didn't like it, but at least she'd been braced for this blow. "They became The Hunters," she stated flatly.

"Yes."

"And the genetic alterations were passed onto their children?"

"Yes. Even if a Hunter and a normal human are together, the Hunter genetics are stronger than the human's DNA. Those children will inherit the Hunter line, develop abilities, and carry on the gene. Though for the most part, Hunters tend to stay with each other, or with The Guardians. It's rare when they go outside of those lines."

Chris shifted uneasily beside her. His father had gone outside of those lines, and his mother had been the one to pay for it. "The experimenters, the perpetrators of this abomination, became The Guardians," Chris stated bluntly.

Luther inhaled loudly as he nodded. "Yes, originally The Guardians were meant to make sure nothing happened to these humans, and they didn't change to become more like vampires."

"They were meant to destroy them if they did," Chris said dully.

"Yes, but fortunately nothing occurred. As each generation emerged with no mutations The Guardians became relegated to the role of training the Hunters to fight, and hunt vampire's. They also became keepers of the history and they stayed close to The Hunters in order to record each generation's efforts."

"Wasn't that nice of them," Cassie muttered, unable to keep the bitterness from her voice.

"It needed to be done," Luther said gently.

"Needed to be done!" Cassie nearly screeched. "They tortured human beings! They turned us all into monsters! They shortened our life spans!" She jabbed a finger at Chris, Melissa, and herself. "They sentenced us to a nightmare life while they sat back on their haunches and recorded *our* history. Needed to be done my *ass*!

They were cowards who were too weak to try the experiment on themselves."

"Cassie," her grandmother chided.

"They tore our families away from us!" her voice broke on a sob as her shoulders sagged in defeat.

The anger fled from her as despair rushed up to take its place. Devon was watching her with a sad and knowing look. They'd also torn him away from her, she realized with a start. If she'd been human, if she'd been *normal*, she probably would have embraced a life of immortality with him.

If she'd been human she never would have known such hurt from vampires, she never would have known the cruelty they'd bestowed upon her loved ones. She would still have her parents, a normal life, and a boyfriend who loved her and wanted to spend eternity with her. She imagined it would all be romantic and appealing to a human, but to her it was a world of darkness, blood and death. A world she'd been genetically altered to fight.

Or to embrace, she realized with a start. After all, her beginnings had come from his kind. She was far more like him then she'd ever realized. She dealt out death and destruction also, and unlike Melissa and Chris, it was the only gift she'd received. She, more than the others, was the most like his kind.

Devon's expression changed as he rose to his feet and glided toward her with the elegant grace of a tiger. She didn't move as he came toward her, didn't stiffen when his arms encircled her. She leaned into his embrace as she took comfort in his strength.

"You are not a monster." His voice was a breath in her ear as she searched his face questioningly. She wasn't surprised he knew what she'd been thinking, he knew her well enough for that, but she had to know he truly believed what he was saying. "You never could be."

Tears burned her eyes and she rapidly blinked them back. Nodding, she rested her head against his chest as she relished the comfort and peace he brought to her. The constriction in her chest eased as she inhaled his familiar, enticing scent.

"I know this is a lot to take in, a lot to understand," Luther said after a few moments. "But something had to be done to stop the vampires. Imagine the world if there had never been any Hunters to stop their murderous rampages."

"There are barely any Hunters now, and it's not so bad," Chris pointed out.

"Things are different now. Then, the world was consumed with war and blood and death. The world is modernized now and the Elders are content in the old ways, and what they have always known. The young ones are the menace, but there are fewer of them as the Elders have grown tired of creating, and the Hunters have always been able to take out the younger, weaker ones," Devon explained.

"Then why did the Elders come after the Hunter line to begin with?" Cassie demanded.

"Revenge," he answered honestly. "The war between the Hunters and the Elders has waged on for over a millennia. They saw a chance to win it, and they took that chance. Boredom also, I suppose. The Hunters are probably the only thrill, and the only challenge the Elders have left to them anymore."

Cassie's frown deepened as anger blistered through her. Her parents had been slaughtered because of *boredom*? "How many of these Elders are left?" she inquired as the need for vengeance sparked to life inside her.

Devon shook his head as his eyes darkened. "I wouldn't allow it," he growled. "And you could do little against them."

She ducked her head so he wouldn't see too much of her thoughts. "I understand that," she admitted. "I'm only curious."

His hand rubbed her arm as he shrugged absently. "Fighting amongst the Elders is common, they tend to take each other out for power, and greed, so there are only ten left. The oldest is a little over nine hundred; the youngest is about five hundred and twelve."

"*You* are an Elder?" Cassie gasped.

He nodded briskly. "As is Julian. I am second in line."

"Will they come for you? For your power?"

"Not if they wish to live. I may not be the oldest, but I am the strongest. Just as with the Hunter's, vampires often develop their own gifts, my speed and strength have always been enhanced, and the mind control helps."

"Oh," Cassie breathed in relief.

"Not to mention, the infighting stopped shortly before The Slaughter. That was when the Elders realized they had all but destroyed each other, and the young vampires didn't care for the traditions, or them. The Elder's grouped together after that; hoping to take out the Hunters in an attempt to eliminate the enemy once and for all. Afterward they retreated back to the old country where they hid themselves away."

"And you didn't want to go with them?" she asked nervously.

A harsh bark of laughter escaped him. "They don't want me; I'm a traitor to them. The shunning of human blood is an atrocity they don't understand or particularly tolerate. They may covet my power, and my strength to help protect them, but they would prefer not to have me there."

"Good." He chuckled as he dropped a kiss on her head and pulled her against him.

"So," Luther continued. "Now you know where your abilities come from."

"And that we're not human," Chris muttered bitterly.

"We always knew we weren't completely human," Cassie reminded him.

"Yeah, but we never knew we were less than human, I always assumed we were *more*."

"You *are* more," Devon said. "Don't think of yourself as less than human when you do more for the human race than many people ever will. Though you may not like how you were created, you should take pride in what you are, and what you do."

"I couldn't have said it better myself," her grandmother said. "It took me awhile to come to terms with this also, but you will, and you will see that Devon is right."

Though the words were meant to comfort, Cassie found little in them. How many people had been sacrificed in order to create their race? How many lives had been lost? A shiver raced up her spine. Devon rubbed her arms, but it did little good to put any warmth back in her body. She wasn't sure she would ever be warm again.

"Well, now I know why I never learned this crap," Chris muttered as he ran a hand through his disordered hair.

Cassie completely agreed. "So all of our *gifts* come from them?" she inquired.

"Yes," Luther answered. "The weapons they used against us, we were able to turn against them."

"And me?" Cassie inquired.

Luther's forehead furrowed over the bridge of his glasses. "There have been Hunters in the past with no abilities."

"Not many though."

"No, not many."

"So I'm a bigger genetic mutation," she muttered, unable to keep the bitterness from her voice.

"Your speed, strength, hearing, and vision are amplified Cass, those are also gifts only vampires possess. You didn't receive any of the other abilities, so those ones are enhanced in you. I keep telling you that is a gift."

Cassie stared doubtfully back at him, but she refrained from commenting. "Your hearing and sight?" Devon asked.

"Yeah eagle eyes over there could see a mouse from a mile away," Chris answered with a crooked, half hearted grin. "And hear a pin drop from the same distance."

"Ha ha," Cassie replied. Devon became rigid against her. Looking up at him, it surprised her to find his forehead furrowed and his eyes distant and thoughtful. "Are you planning on talking about me behind my back?"

His attention returned to her, but his eyes were still distant. Shaking his head, he bent to kiss her forehead. "No, of course not." His wan smile and distant gaze weren't convincing though. "Someone is here."

"What?" Cassie asked a second before the doorbell resounded through the house.

She frowned up at him before slipping from his arms, but he didn't move far from her as he followed her into the foyer. She opened the door and blinked in surprise at Dani huddled on the doorstep. Her gold streaked eyes were bloodshot as she smiled tremulously. "Can I come in?"

Cassie nodded as she stepped back. She searched the night but saw no sign of Joey. "Did you walk over here by yourself?" Dani nodded as she stepped inside and huddled deeper into her flimsy windbreaker. Dani eyed Devon inquisitively, but there wasn't any apprehension in her gaze. "Don't you learn?"

Dani smiled feebly as she shook back her hair. "I told you I can take care of myself."

"You also told me you couldn't use your ability again tonight."

"Yeah, but that other vamp doesn't know that."

Devon snorted with laughter, but Cassie was nowhere near as amused. "Come on in." Leading Dani into the living room, she gestured toward the loveseat she'd abandoned. "Grandma, this is Dani. Dani this is my grandmother."

"You can call me Lily," her grandmother replied.

Dani smiled hesitatingly as her hands folded into the sleeves of her coat. "It's nice to meet you."

"You also; it appears you're a truly talented girl."

Heat burned up Dani's face as she ducked her head. "Yeah," she mumbled.

"We were just discussing where those powers come from," Luther said smoothly.

"Vampires."

"You knew?" Chris demanded.

Dani frowned in confusion as she nodded. "Since I was old enough to understand, you didn't?"

Chris scowled as he turned on his heel and began to pace once more. "No, they didn't," Melissa said flatly.

Cassie blinked, surprised to hear such dismay in Melissa's voice. She was reserved, thoughtful and aloof, but there was always an optimistic air about her that was refreshing. Now she seemed hard, distant, lost. Chris walked over to Melissa and swung his arm around her shoulders as he pulled her close in a brotherly embrace.

"It will be ok, we're no different than the people we were an hour ago."

"No, we're not," Cassie said firmly. "We can't change the mistakes of our ancestors…"

"Without those *mistakes*, the world would have been an entirely different place. It would have been filled with fear and death and murder. It would be governed by vampires. Would you have rather have had that?" Luther interjected hotly.

They gazed at each other for a long moment before Cassie turned to Dani, unwilling to admit that Luther was right. She was still too angry and confused for such an admission right now. "What brings you here?" she inquired.

Dani shrugged, her gaze darted nervously around the room before settling on Cassie again. "I don't agree with Joey, I think we should help."

Cassie's heart fluttered with excitement; with Dani's help they would have a much better chance of killing Julian. They would be able to save more lives, and maybe they could find some peace for a little while. She desperately yearned for peace, and some time with Devon to try and sort out the pieces of their lives.

"Does he know you're here?" Luther asked.

Dani nodded, tears shimmered in her eyes but she didn't spill any. "He knows," she answered in a choked voice.

"Dani, what happened?" Cassie inquired.

"He left."

The hush in the room was heavy with shock. Melissa was the first to recover from the news. "He left you here alone?"

Dani's dark head bowed. "Yes, I refused to go and he refused to stay."

Cassie's heart broke as the tears in Dani's eyes finally slid down her cheeks. They plopped onto her lap as she made no attempt to stop them. Pulling away from Devon, she joined Dani on the loveseat and rested her arm around her delicate shoulders. "I'm sorry," she whispered as she tried to soothe the pain radiating from her. "I can't imagine how tough this must be."

Dani continued to cry silently, but her words were clear. "We'll keep in touch, and one day we'll reunite, but for now each of us has to go our separate ways. We both feel very differently about this. It had to be done and we couldn't be together forever."

Cassie could understand that, but she couldn't understand how Dani's brother could have just abandoned her here. She was barely old enough to get a job, let alone support herself. Apparently his hatred went far deeper than Cassie had begun to fathom.

"Well, then," her grandmother said as she rose to her feet. "We should go get your things."

"Excuse me?" Dani asked in surprise.

"Your things. You can't stay on your own, and we have an extra room here you can use."

Cassie couldn't stop herself from smiling as Dani stared at her grandmother in disbelief. "Really?" she croaked, her voice breaking for the first time.

"Of course," her grandmother replied with a dazzling smile.

CHAPTER TWELVE

CASSIE TRIED to stay strong against the new barrage of whispered comments following her down the hall. Her chase of Dani the other night had managed to set off a new wave of gossip and innuendo. She clutched her books tighter to her chest as she reached her locker, spun the dial, and flung it open.

"Who knew she was such a freak," Jess whispered.

Cassie glanced over her shoulder at the group of girls gathered fifteen feet away. They glanced discreetly at her and looked away when they found her staring at them. Kara, Jess, and Marcy were gathered close together, obviously enjoying her downfall.

Exasperation and betrayal burst hotly through her. She'd once considered all of them her friends. She'd held sleepovers with them, gone to their pool parties, partied on the beach with them. They had talked of boys, and shared their hopes and dreams as they discussed their futures with eager anticipation. Though they'd grown apart when Cassie had discovered her heritage, she'd never once stopped thinking of them as friends.

And they had turned against her so easily. Cassie slammed her locker shut but her pride wouldn't allow her to just walk away again. Throwing her shoulders back, Cassie made her way straight over to them without any hesitation. Their eyes were wary as they watched her approach.

"Hello everyone," she said with a forced grin. "How are you this morning?"

They glanced at each other before turning back to her. "Fine," Marcy answered though resentment gleamed in her eyes. "What is it Cassandra?"

Cassie opened her notebook and pulled out the notes she'd made awhile ago on the homecoming dance. It was a poor excuse, but she didn't care, she was tired of hiding from these girls, tired of slinking through the halls like a leper. She handed the notes to Marcy as she met her gaze head on.

"You asked me for these."

Marcy took them from her but barely glanced at them. "Things have changed since then."

Cassie forced herself to smile at the small girl as she tried to keep her temper in check. "I am well aware of that Marcy, but I am still on the homecoming committee."

Marcy's jaw dropped as she glanced at the other girls. "Uh, you know Cass…" Kara started awkwardly.

"You haven't been to any meetings in the past two weeks," Marcy interrupted.

"I've been busy, but I'll make sure to attend the next one. It's today right?"

"You can't be serious!" Marcy exploded as her leaf colored eyes narrowed severely.

"Oh, I'm very serious. You said yourself Marcy that I do have the best ideas, and we would like our senior year to be the best dance it can be."

Marcy looked at her like she'd sprouted another head. "But…"

"It will be fun; we can catch up on all the gossip. I can't wait to find out what's new and exciting in your lives."

They shifted uncomfortably and everyone except for Marcy appeared somewhat ashamed. Marcy looked like the top of her head was going to blow off and her face had turned magenta. If they hadn't been standing in the midst of a crowded hallway, Cassie was certain Marcy would have launched herself at her.

Cassie grinned back at her. It was good to have the tables finally turn, if only a little. She would never regain her social standing in the school, nor did she wish to, but she was damn tired of skulking around.

Maybe if she confronted them head on they would back off. Yeah right, and pigs would fly, she thought with a sigh. But at least she was making a stand; she was sticking up for herself in some way. It was a small jab, but it was a jab that made her feel a little better.

Even before Marcy's gaze shot behind her, and blatant lust shown in her eyes, Cassie knew Devon had arrived. Her body had become so attuned to his, so in sync that she would know him anywhere. His hand landed on her shoulder as he sought to give her comfort.

"What's going on?" he asked his voice low and grating.

"We were just discussing plans for the homecoming dance."

Devon's eyebrows drew together severely as he glanced questioningly around the group. "Really?"

"Yes, there's a meeting today, and since I haven't gone to one in a while I thought it would be a good idea to attend."

He stared at her in disbelief. "Really?"

Cassie smiled at him as she pressed closer to his side. Confusion radiated from him, but he didn't say anything more. "So I will see you later," Cassie said as she kept the false grin plastered to her face.

It was obvious Marcy felt like arguing this point, but with Devon present she wasn't going to say a word. Turning to Devon, Cassie slipped her hand into his and kept her smile plastered on as she pulled him away. "What are you doing?" he asked.

She waited till they turned the corner before her shoulders slumped and she relaxed against him. "I don't know," she admitted. She should have just kept on trying to fly below the school population radar. Now she was anxious she may have just poked the bear. "I really don't know."

He slid his arm around her shoulders and pulled her against him. "Are you really going to this thing?"

Taking a deep breath, she nodded as she nervously chewed on her bottom lip. She'd jumped before looking, but she was committed now, and she planned to stay that way. They turned another corner and Dani, Melissa, and Chris came into view by the cafeteria doors. "I am. It will be ok," she muttered.

Devon quirked an eyebrow, a smile twitched at his lips, but his eyes remained clouded with unease. "I suppose."

DEVON LEANED CASUALLY against the wall as he studied the ticking clock. Cassie had told him to stay away, she intended to do this on her own, but he wasn't willing to go far from her. Through the thick double doors of the gymnasium, he could feel her distress. He didn't know why she'd insisted upon this, but she was determined to go through with it.

Shifting a little, he shot a look at the group of freshmen boys eyeing him warily as they scurried past. He quirked an eyebrow, but paid them little attention otherwise. Chris strolled around the corner, a towel tossed over his shoulder, and his hair still wet from his shower. He was whistling as he walked, but tension hummed through him.

"How was practice?"

His whistling died off as he shrugged and pulled the towel from his shoulder. "I'll be glad when the football season is over."

Devon's attention turned back to the closed doors when Cassie's anxiety clicked up a notch. He fought against going in there and pulling her out. She would be infuriated with him though, and she was having a rough enough time without him adding to it. Chris studied the closed doors behind him as Devon's agitation grew. He was growing to hate the bitchy, cruel girls in this school. And he wasn't too fond of the lust filled, envious boys who were annoyed she hadn't chosen them either.

"Not going well?" Chris rested his hand against the wall as he studied the closed doors.

"No."

"I can't believe she's doing this."

"I can."

Chris snorted softly. "True. Are they almost done in there super ears?"

Devon shot him a disgruntled look that Chris easily ignored. Pushing aside the waves of distress pouring from Cassie, he turned his attention back to the room. He couldn't concentrate on what was being said if he didn't block her emotions out. They were talking about decorations, debating whether or not to go with the crystal disco ball. Devon was hoping they decided against the ball, as Marcy declared it was a necessity.

"I don't know," he answered Chris. "They're discussing disco balls right now."

Chris groaned as he rolled his eyes. "I hate those stupid things, they're blinding."

"Tell me about it."

Chris grinned at him as he used his fingers to bounce himself off the wall. "Yeah they bother Cassie a lot too, give her headaches. She has to wear sunglasses around them most of the time."

Devon frowned and withdrew almost completely from the monotonous conversation within. Chris's words had his attention far more than what color to use for the tablecloths. "She does?"

Chris nodded as he continued to bounce. "Yeah, the light bothers her eyes."

Devon dropped his head and rubbed the bridge of his nose. There was a nagging feeling in the back of his mind he couldn't shake. "How good *is* her eyesight?" he asked.

Chris shrugged negligently. "Don't really know. It's definitely better than perfect, far better than anyone I've ever met before." Chris eyed him for a moment as he tilted his head. "Except maybe for you."

Devon couldn't shake the nagging feeling something was wrong. That something wasn't quite right and there was something about Cassie they were all missing. "I see."

Chris stopped bouncing off the wall. "What's wrong?"

Devon shook his head and stepped away from the wall as the conversation inside turned to dresses. Cassie's boredom beat against him and he took that as his leave to rescue her. "I'll be back."

"Want me to come with you; those girls are like a bunch of leeches with you around." Devon couldn't help but grin at him. The kid had gotten on his nerves for a little while, but he was beginning to grow on him now. "Plus you might need some help with Cassie, she can't be mad at both of us."

"You would like to think."

Chris chuckled as he wrapped the towel around the back of his neck. Grasping both sides of it, he pulled it back and forth across his neck. "Lead the way."

Devon pushed the doors open and stepped into the dimly lit gym. The group of girls was gathered at the far end with a pile of papers scattered amongst them. Cassie was off to the side, leaning against a wall. Her head was bowed and her golden hair cascaded in front of her in thick waves. She lifted her head when the door opened; her eyes were vivid in the darkened room. Relief radiated from her as she took a small step away from the wall.

Laughter drifted in the air as Marcy waved her hands in an arch. Bending down, Cassie grabbed hold of her bag and swung it easily over her shoulder. The conversation stopped as their attention briefly turned to her before their heads spun toward Devon and Chris. There was a collective inhalation of breaths.

Devon paid them no mind as he strolled past, eager to get to Cassie. He craved her touch like a man in the desert craved water. A breath of relief and joy escaped her as his hand slid into hers. He saw no ire in her amused, twinkling gaze. Only love radiated from her as she stood on tiptoe to kiss him on the cheek.

"I thought you could use a rescue."

"I could," she agreed. "It took you long enough to get in here."

He grinned at her as he brushed her hair back from her exquisite face. His fingers stroked her silken cheek as she turned into his touch. He yearned to take her face in his hands and taste her lips. At the same time he longed to sink his teeth into her elegant neck and devour her sweet blood.

He shuddered as his hand tensed upon her. He knew he would never conquer his desire for her, but he'd hoped it wouldn't be as intense all the time. Just once, he would like to hold her, and know what it was like to savor the touch and feel of her without having to fight his own nature.

He reluctantly pulled away from her. She gazed up at him from under her thick lashes; sometimes he wished she didn't understand him as well as she did. He knew she saw into his soul, he wished he could keep his turmoil hidden from her, but it was impossible.

"Let's go." He was eager to get her out of here and take her somewhere she felt safe and sheltered.

"I'll see you guys Thursday," she called to the silent group.

Marcy's mouth dropped, strange sputtering noises escaped her. "You can't be serious!" she squawked, stunned into letting her resentment of Cassie show in front of him.

"Completely."

Devon shot Marcy a dark look as she continued to gape, and those strange noises still escaped her. "But we don't require any more help."

Cassie grinned at her. "After the ideas I heard today, I would say you do."

There was a collective inhalation of breaths. Pride bloomed through Devon as he pulled her closer and kissed the top of her head.

CHAPTER THIRTEEN

Cassie spent the next couple of weeks dragging herself to the homecoming meetings. She remained standing on the outside and any ideas she offered were immediately shot down. She hadn't expected any of them to be accepted, and she hadn't expected to be, but she couldn't stop herself from going and taking the abuse three times a week.

Her reception got colder every time she went, the iciness at school grew, but she continued to forge on. Continued to try and ignore it. Having Devon by her side was the only thing keeping her going consistently. Without him, she wasn't sure she would be able to drag herself out of bed in the morning, let alone drag herself into the school that despised her. It was taking a toll on her, beating her down. She was tired all the time, but she hadn't backed down. She couldn't.

"You look beautiful."

Dani stood in Cassie's doorway, a bowl of popcorn in her arms as she leaned against the doorframe. Cassie managed a wan smile for her. She wasn't feeling beautiful, and although she should have been excited for the dance, she wasn't.

"Thank you."

Dani smiled at her as she came into the room and dropped the bowl onto Cassie's bureau. Dani had been a little unsettled when she'd first moved into the house, but over the past couple of weeks she had become far more at home. Cassie had started to look at her like a little sister, and was grateful for her company during those few hours when Devon was away hunting, and Chris returned home to watch over his mother.

She was also glad for Dani's unwavering friendship, a friendship that had been given easily, and with no conditions. "Just giving you a heads up, Lily already has the camera set up and ready to go."

Cassie laughed as she smoothed the front of her deep violet dress. It was strapless and hugged her upper body before flowing out to her knees. When she'd seen it, she'd known instantly she had to have it. She didn't regret it, even if it was a little more daring than she would normally have liked.

She didn't know how Devon was going to react to the dress. She hoped he liked it, but she didn't want to test the boundaries of his control. Tonight she simply wanted to feel normal again, to be a normal teenage girl for once.

"You don't think it's a little too much, or actually less?" she asked nervously.

Dani chuckled quietly. "I think it's perfect, and you're wearing waaaaay more clothing than most of the other girls will be."

Cassie nodded, but she couldn't shake the uncomfortable feeling that had settled over her. "Yeah, but they're not dating a vampire," she muttered.

Dani laughed as she shook back her dark hair. The blood red

tips had been replaced with white blond ones. "They all just wish they were dating him," Dani told her. Cassie chuckled as she twisted her hair into a loose knot against the nape of her neck. "It will be fine; the dress really isn't that revealing, Cass."

She nodded but she didn't feel as reassured as Dani had intended, but she decided not to stress about it anymore. It was too late; she was already wearing the dress and Devon would be here any minute. The second the thought crossed her mind, the doorbell rang. Cassie's hand fluttered nervously up to the pearls at her neck. They were her grandmother's, her mother had worn them on her wedding day, and one day they would be Cassie's. A wave of sadness washed over her, she loved her grandmother dearly, and would never trade a moment of her life with her, but sometimes she wondered what it would have been like to have her parents in her life.

With a soft sigh, she pushed the melancholy thoughts aside. There was no place for them tonight. Tonight was about her friends, Devon, and this dance. Tonight was for fun, and she was going to have it for a change. Taking strength from the pearls, Cassie grabbed her pea coat from the bed and draped it over her arm. She listened as her grandmother let Devon, Melissa, and Chris in. "I wish you could come," she said as she turned back to Dani.

The younger girl studied her for a moment. "I don't, I'm glad I'm too young. It's not exactly my thing."

"Mine either," Cassie admitted. "Not anymore anyway."

"Are you ok?"

Forcing a smile, Cassie nodded. "I'm fine."

"Come on then, you can't keep them waiting."

Dani grabbed her bowl of popcorn, and was fairly skipping as she led the way down the hall. Cassie realized the popcorn hadn't been made for a movie, but *this* was Dani's show. Shaking her head, she fought back a chuckle as Dani dashed down the stairs. Cassie made her way down and turned the corner into the living room.

Her breath froze in her lungs as she spotted Devon standing by the mantle. His hair had been brushed back from the rugged plains of his face. The finely tailored sports coat he wore clung to his broad shoulders. He looked magnificent, strong, powerful, and so handsome he made her heart leap in her chest. Need tore through her, along with the overwhelming impulse to touch him, to feel him, to never part from him again.

Hunger blossomed in the brilliant depths of his emerald eyes. His mouth parted as his gaze raked leisurely over her and caused heat to burn through her everywhere his eyes touched. An inner quaking took root in her and shook through her muscle and bone. Her mouth was a desert; her heart hammered as her skin began to tingle.

His gaze returned to hers, it burned with a fire the likes of which she'd never seen before. Cassie's tremors left her weak kneed. No, the dress hadn't been a good idea at all. But then, she felt she could be wearing a sack and he would still look at her like she was a treat he'd like to devour.

His movements reminded her of an animal stalking its prey as he moved toward her. She didn't know if she was more frightened to be his prey, or excited to be it. Stopping before her, his gaze perused her once more. Cassie shivered, her breath exploded from her as he took hold of her hand. His touch seared into her skin and burned its way into every molecule of her body as she was branded by him for the rest of her life.

She would always remember how he felt against her, the delicious way he made her feel. She would never forget how perfect his skin was against hers, how right and true it was. Even if she couldn't have him forever, she would have the memories.

He bent low over her hand; his eyes never left hers as he placed a kiss upon the back of it. Cassie's mouth parted, her pulse pounded in her temples as liquid lava pooled through her. His head bent over her hand, his lips pressed so gently against her skin was the sweetest, most debonair thing she'd ever seen.

He kept hold of her hand as he rose again. "You look exquisite," he whispered.

Heat flooded Cassie's face; she looked away from him, unable to take the overwhelming sensations his very presence caused her to feel. Her body was a tumult of emotions and feelings crashing riotously against each other. The stroking of his thumb over her hand did nothing to ease the flames of an already simmering fire.

"Let me get a picture of everyone," her grandmother's voice was slightly strained.

Cassie met her grandmother's amused gaze. Devon moved to her side and his arm encircled her waist. The feel of him caused her skin to hum with electricity. "Everyone smile!"

Dani munched on popcorn and watched in amusement as everyone was moved around and ordered to smile repeatedly. Cassie's face ached by the time her grandmother was done taking pictures, but it was worth it to see the glow on her pretty face, and the happy gleam in her eyes.

"Ok, you guys can go now!" her grandmother announced as she let the camera drop back around her neck.

Devon approached with her coat in hand. "Will you come out in those pictures?" she inquired.

A small chuckle escaped him as he slipped the coat around her shoulders. "Not all the myths are true, love." His lips brushed against her skin and sent a shiver throughout her whole body.

She had to get control of herself around him, or this was going to be a tortuous night. Slipping his hand into hers, he led her toward the door. "Cassie, wait!"

She turned as her grandmother hurried over with a small box in hand. Cassie frowned as her grandmother handed her the box. "I think it's time you had this."

Cassie took the box from her and opened it. A small gasp escaped at the delicate emerald ring. Surrounding the emerald were four petite, perfect diamonds. Cassie's hand shook as she pulled the ring free and carefully handled the small gold band.

"It was my mother's wedding ring and was meant for your mother."

Cassie glanced up at her as tears welled in her eyes. "Grandma, I don't think I should take this."

Her grandmother's hands enfolded hers. "Of course you should. Your mother would want you to have it. She would be so proud of you dear, just as I am."

A single tear slipped down Cassie's cheek, but her grandma wiped it away. "I'm not giving it to you to make you cry," she said happily, although a strange sadness enshrouded her. "You're a woman now; you should have the things that mark you as such."

Cassie could only nod as her grandmother took the ring from her and slipped it onto her right hand. "Perfect fit!"

Rapidly blinking back tears, she threw her arms around her grandmother and hugged her close. Her grandmother's slender frame shook as she patted Cassie's back. "I'll always be proud of you, always love you dear."

Cassie pulled away to stare questioningly into her grandmother's sky colored eyes. It seemed like such an odd thing to say, but then again it was a big night, for most people at least. "I'll always love you," she whispered as she dropped a kiss on her grandmother's cheek.

Her eyes were sad as Cassie pulled away, but she was smiling brilliantly. "Go on now; I've held you up long enough."

She patted Cassie's shoulder as she all but shoved them out the door. Cassie flashed a grin over her shoulder as they made their way to Devon's sleek Challenger. He held the door open for them, Chris and Melissa piled into the back. Taking hold of her hand he helped her slide into the passenger seat. His hand lingered on hers before he shut the door and hurried to the driver's side.

Arriving at the school, they piled out into the crush of students making their way through the doors. Cassie handed her coat over to the parent running the coat check. Without the material around her shoulders, she felt more exposed and vulnerable. Sensing her distress, Devon slipped his arm around her waist and pulled her against his side.

"It will be ok," he assured her.

Swallowing heavily, she managed a nod. She kept her shoulders straight as she allowed him to lead her into the heavily decorated gym. Marcy and company had decided to make the theme of the party Cape Cod in the fall. Though it was neither creative nor original (as it had been done three years ago), it was pretty.

The walls were decorated with a vast array of leaves in every color of the rainbow. Play box sand was spread across the dance floor, there were already groups dancing without their shoes on. Scattered amongst the sand were leaves that had been sorted through and brought in from outside. Hurricane lanterns, with tapered white candles, had been set out on the tables. Sand, seashells, starfish, and sand dollars were spread out around them. Banners hung from the ceiling in the school colors of blue and gold, and the annoying disco ball was in place.

Cassie winced as she shaded her eyes to block out the sparkling light. At the back of the large gymnasium the band was playing. She recognized John Parks and Lyle White playing bass and drums. They'd graduated last year, and their band was one of the few in town that was actually decent. The slow song they were playing switched and one of their own, faster paced songs blasted from the large speakers set up beside the stage.

Cassie winced again as the noise pounded into her ears. She'd forgotten how uncomfortable dances could be for her. Forgotten about the noise and the lights, or at least she'd tried to forget anyway. Digging into the black clutch purse she'd brought, she pulled out her sunglasses. Slipping them on, she was able to ease at least one of the annoyances.

Devon was studying her with concern, but she shook her head as she smiled reassuringly at him. With the pain in her eyes eased, she was able to take in more of the students milling around, and greeting their friends as they talked eagerly. Dresses sparkled in an array of colors from the reflection of the ball.

Cassie couldn't help but smile. These people may not like her anymore, but she'd grown up with them, had once been a big part of their world, and she was happy they'd been given this night. Devon's hand on her elbow was tender as he led her over to one of the tables tucked against the back wall.

Though the gym was packed, Devon parted the crowd easily. Either that or they parted away from *her*. Pulling a chair out, he waited till she was seated before pushing it in. Bending low, he kissed her cheek. Cassie smiled up at him, and slipped her glasses off as the table was far enough away for the ball not to irritate her as much anymore.

"It looks good in here Cass," Chris said as his eyes scanned the decorations.

"I didn't have much to do with it."

He shrugged absently as his attention returned to the crowd. "I was hoping there would be some new girls here," he muttered.

Cassie lifted an eyebrow. "If there were any, they would probably be here with their boyfriends."

"Like they'd be any competition," he replied with a cocky grin.

Cassie laughed as she shook her head at him in disbelief. "There are other girls here."

"Yeah but they're all from our school, and I'm not that fond of them anymore."

His eyes were severe as they met hers, his jaw clenched. Cassie ducked her head, she opened her mouth to apologize, but she knew he wouldn't appreciate it. Melissa appeared at his side and placed three drinks on the table. The sleek black dress she wore emphasized her caramel colored skin and onyx eyes. It hugged her slender body and showed off her curves. Her black hair had been pulled into a twist at the nape of her neck and her long hair flowed from it in curls.

"Too bad the people weren't as nice as the décor," she muttered.

"No kidding." Chris grabbed one of the drinks and sipped it as he continued to survey the crowd. Cassie settled back in her seat and leaned into the arm Devon had draped around the back of her chair. He rubbed her shoulder as he sought to ease the tension inside of her.

They sat for an hour, watching the people milling about, mingling and dancing. Melissa and Chris occasionally strayed away, but for the most part they stayed close. Though they weren't as disliked as Cassie, their close association with her had definitely lessened their popularity. Devon leaned close to her, his nose brushed against her cheek as he caressed the nape of her neck.

She studied him with wide eyes, he studied her as if he were about to devour her. Shivering in delight, she leaned closer to him. "Would you like to dance?" he asked.

Excitement blazed forth as she eagerly nodded. She couldn't imagine anything better than being wrapped in his arms as they danced. Helping her from her chair, he led her out to the dance floor. Reaching the edge of the dance space, Cassie kicked off her heels and allowed her toes to dig into the fresh sand.

Wrapping his arms around her, Devon lifted her briefly off the ground as he pulled her close. Cassie forgot all about the decorations and the catty whispers as she lost herself to the sensational feel of him. Resting her hands against his chest, she traced the rigid muscles beneath the thin cotton shirt he wore. His eyes sparked as his nostrils flared.

Cassie's breath escaped her; she was unable to look away from the burning intensity of his emerald gaze as he moved her. The disco ball didn't bother her as every ounce of her was focused upon him. She could see nothing else, feel nothing else. Deliberately, tantalizingly he bent his head, and his lips brushed over hers. Cassie's hands clenched on his shirt, she stood on tiptoe as she met his butterfly kiss eagerly.

Heat flamed through her, her toes curled as her eyes closed. Bliss spread over her as heat raced through her whole body. His hand wrapped around the back of her neck, the kiss deepened as his tongue flickered against her lips. Opening her mouth, Cassie eagerly accepted his heady invasion. The heat burning through her built to a boiling point as his tongue ravaged her mouth.

She couldn't get enough of him, she wanted *all* of him, and at the moment she didn't care what had to happen in order to have him. Pulling her more firmly against him, she gasped in pleasure as their bodies were pushed firmly against each other as seamlessly as two puzzle pieces. Her fingers dug into his skin as she struggled against ripping his shirt from him, and ridding him of the annoying hindrance of clothes separating them.

He pulled away suddenly; his smoky gaze was dark and bewildered as it met hers. Loss consumed her, she coveted more than his kisses; she *required* more. She needed all of him, forever. Ducking her head, she knew there was only one way that could happen, but for the first time the idea of it didn't petrify or repulse her.

Devon wasn't a monster; she didn't have to be one either. She would have to drink blood, which was repulsive to her, but she was sure she could eventually get over that. Maybe, after a few centuries, she would be able to go out in the sun again. Sighing, she rested her head against his chest.

She realized she would give up anything for him rather than lose him, even her mortality. Was it really such a bad thing to give up?

Suddenly a floodgate opened inside her. Hopes and dreams rapidly bubbled forth and shot out like an erupting geyser. No, they weren't normal dreams as there would be no college, and no children, or at least she didn't think there would be children; she wasn't entirely sure how that worked. But she and Devon would be a family; she would be loved and cherished, for eternity.

They could share so much together, and though she would have to give up some things, she would be gaining so much more. Besides she hadn't had any dreams of college, and a home or a family, for the past four years. She'd given them up when she'd learned about her Hunter heritage. Devon had returned some of her other dreams to her, and given her more than she'd ever dared to hope for.

A lump formed in her throat, tears burned her eyes. His hand cradled her neck as his thumb stroked her skin, in his arms she was enshrouded in a cocoon of love and warmth. Her world became one of peaceful bliss as all of her insecurities and doubts were brushed away by his tender touch.

His lips were tender as they brushed over her hair, touched her cheek, before pressing against her neck. Her hands clenched on the firm muscle of his arms and curled into his skin. She could be with him forever. She knew it in every one of her cells. She had no concerns their love would dissipate, she believed it would grow stronger every day.

She would tell him tonight that when school was over, she would join him. Though she had no need for high school, she felt she *had* to finish it. She'd come this far already, and it would mean a lot to her grandmother. She also had to stay human until Julian was taken care of. She couldn't disappear from town during the day, only to be seen lurking through the shadows at night. That would open up a can of worms she wasn't willing to deal with.

She hoped Devon could wait that long, and it wouldn't be too much stress on him. But maybe once he knew her decision, things would be easier for him. She hoped they would anyway. The last thing she intended was to cause him anymore distress.

She was so entrenched in the feel of him she didn't realize the music had stopped until the loud tapping of the microphone pierced her lovely haze. Lifting her head she blinked blearily at the stage. The band was standing in the background now and Mrs. Dickson had taken the microphone.

"Excuse me everyone, it is time to announce the homecoming king and queen!"

Cassie groaned inwardly as she rolled her eyes. She may be a nominee, but she didn't think they'd read her name. She had no prayer of making queen, and no matter how much she told herself she didn't care, she did. Especially since Devon had a good chance of being king, and Marcy queen. The idea of Marcy getting to share even *one* dance with Devon was enough to make her blood boil.

Reluctantly pulling away from Devon, she kept her arm around his waist as they made their way to the edge of the dance floor. Wiping her feet on one of the mats at the edge of the sand, she slipped her heels back on. Devon led her through the crowd toward their table.

The buzz about the coming announcement had quieted the buzz about her, and for the first time people didn't scatter to get out of her way. Chris was still standing by the table, and off to the left Cassie spotted Melissa's dark head coming through the crowd. Chris grinned at her and folded his arms over his chest as they approached.

"I thought I was going to have to get a fire extinguisher for you two."

Cassie's face flamed red, Devon shot him a warning glance that only caused Chris's smile to grow as he chuckled. "Just what I've been waiting for all night," Melissa muttered sarcastically as she arrived at their side.

"Do you already know who's going to win?" Cassie was unable to stop herself from inquiring.

Melissa grinned as she shook her head. "Nope, only had a vision about the nominees, this one is a complete surprise to me. Well, as much as it could be anyway. I think we all know who's going to win."

Devon frowned at her. "Who?" The three of them just stared at him until he got the point. "Me?"

"Yes, you," Chris replied, laughing as his tone took on that of the childhood cookie jar song.

Devon glanced over the three of them. "Humans," he muttered, causing the three of them to laugh. "What is this thing anyway?"

"A tradition, I suppose," Melissa answered.

"Hmm," he grunted, clearly still not getting it. Cassie didn't try to explain further, she wasn't entirely certain she understood it either, not anymore anyway.

The gymnasium became silent as Kara made her way onto the stage and took the envelopes from Mrs. Dickson. Kara grinned as she stepped up to the microphone. "Hi everyone," she greeted. "As Vice President of the student body I have been chosen to announce the winners." She unfolded a piece of paper and read off the names of the male nominees. Chris and Devon shifted beside her as their names were called.

"And the winner is..." Kara paused for dramatic effect as her eyes scanned the crowd. Melissa rolled her eyes. Turning her attention back to the envelopes, Kara eagerly tore one open. "Devon Knight!" she announced happily.

Cassie closed her eyes as pain bloomed in her chest. She had no reason to be upset, but she couldn't help it. She didn't like the idea of him dancing with some other girl. "Devon, where are you Devon?" Kara cried eagerly into the microphone as a spotlight blazed from the stage.

Cassie blinked as it flashed into her eyes and burned her retinas. She turned away from it as she tried to block it with her hand. Devon stepped in front of her, his sleek body shielded her far better than her hand did. "Cassie?"

She blinked him into focus as she admired the masculine beauty of him highlighted by the glow around his edges. "Go on, get up there before they blind me with that thing." Her tone was far more cheerful than she felt, but the faster he went up there the faster this awful experience could be over.

He grabbed hold of her, a desperate urgency radiating from him as he drew her against him. Cassie didn't have time to react before his mouth descended upon hers and ravaged her with an intensity that left her boneless and limp. When he pulled away from her, Cassie managed to wheeze in a ragged breath.

"You'll always be my queen," he whispered in her ear.

A lump formed in her throat as she nodded. Reluctantly releasing her, Devon turned and made his way through the oddly silent crowd. Cassie rapidly glanced around as she realized their kiss had been the center of attention. All eyes turned away from her as Devon climbed onto the stage. The silence was suddenly broken by loud clapping, shrill shrieks, and whistles from the girls. "Really?" Cassie muttered.

"He's like the freaking Beatles," Chris said as he shook his head in disbelief.

Melissa stepped closer to Cassie and draped her arm around Cassie's shoulders. Kara looked like she was going to explode with excitement as she gestured Devon down to slip the crown onto his head. Cassie bit her lip, trying not to laugh as a look of utter disbelief crossed his face. It was a look that could have been mistaken for humility, but she knew he simply didn't understand this human custom.

A full bodied laugh began to rumble out of Chris. Despite herself, Cassie couldn't help but join him. Melissa rolled her eyes again as she began to chuckle. "He looks so lost," she laughed.

"Yeah he does," Chris agreed enthusiastically. "Big bad vampire taken down by a crown!"

The three of them burst into loud laughter that drew the attention of the few students closest to them. They didn't pay attention though as they embraced each other. At some point through it, Cassie realized they weren't laughing at the situation. They were laughing because they needed to. It had been awhile since she'd heard their laughter, and she'd expressed any of her own. The release was wonderful.

Kara stepped up to the microphone again. Wiping back the tears forming in her eyes, Cassie was able to regain control as she focused on the stage. Devon was watching her with a raised eyebrow as amusement shone in the depths of his emerald eyes. She waved at him, unable to completely rid herself of the silly grin she wore.

"And now nominee's for Homecoming queen!" Kara announced eagerly.

That was enough to make her smile slip away. Melissa's hand tightened on her shoulder as the names were read off. Cassie felt a small jolt of surprise when she was mentioned. She'd expected her name to be as eradicated as she'd been in the eyes of the student body. Well not completely eradicated, as she was still the center of attention. She was just the most hated person in school now.

"And the winner is…" Again the dramatic pause as Kara ripped into the envelope. Her dazzling grin caused Cassie's stomach to roll violently. "Marcy Hodgins!"

Loud applause exploded through the room. Cassie didn't move, didn't even breathe as she watched Marcy eagerly climb onto the stage. Marcy's grin was so big every one of her teeth showed. She waved like a queen to the crowd as she eagerly accepted her crown and flowers. "Thank you everyone!" she announced into the microphone. "Thank you so much!"

"They love me, they *really* love me!" Chris said with a high falsetto as he fluttered his lashes and folded his hands demurely before him.

Despite the sick feeling in her stomach, Cassie couldn't help but laugh again. Chris always seemed to know exactly what to do in order to get a laugh from her. He grinned back at her as his sapphire eyes twinkled merrily. Without Chris, she would have been lost long ago, adrift in a world she didn't understand.

The band began to play again, catching Cassie's attention as the melodious song drifted from the speakers. The lead singer moved forward to reclaim his microphone. "Now it's time for the king and queen to share a dance!" he announced.

Cassie ran her hands up and down her arms as her skin began to crawl. This was the part she'd been dreading. Devon glanced helplessly at her as Marcy seized hold of his hand. Cassie managed a wan, reassuring smile as she gave him a quick wave. Marcy practically pulled him down the steps of the makeshift stage.

"Could she be any more desperate?" Melissa muttered in disgust.

"She's been looking forward to this for months. If I hadn't fallen from grace I think she would have stuffed the ballot box just for this dance," Cassie said.

"I have to agree."

They stepped onto the dance floor and Marcy released Devon's hand as she practically threw herself into his arms. A disapproving frown marred his attractive face as he took a step back. Marcy chose to ignore it; stepping close once again, she wrapped her arms around his waist and rested her head on his chest.

The tingling of Cassie's skin became worse as her heart lumbered in her chest. She couldn't stand to watch this, but she couldn't bring her frozen legs to move. Devon rested his hands on Marcy's shoulder and held her back when she tried to get closer. Which Cassie didn't think was possible.

Groaning, Cassie tore her gaze away when Marcy's hands drifted down to his ass. Devon wanted nothing to do with this dance, or Marcy, but she couldn't stand to watch anymore. "I have to go to the bathroom," she blurted and spun out of Melissa's flimsy hold.

"Cassie." Melissa grabbed hold of her hand and halted her progress. "He doesn't want this."

Cassie nodded as she tugged her hand free of Melissa's. "I know, but I also don't have to watch it."

"I'll come with you."

Cassie shook her head as the crawling of her skin became more intense. She couldn't see what was happening anymore, but she was certain Marcy was still doing her best to grope Devon. "I just need a few minutes. I'll be right back."

Melissa's eyes were sad but Cassie didn't stop. Hurrying through the crowd, she ignored the stares and mutters following her. She also ignored the satisfied smirks on the faces of Marcy's friends, girls who had once been her friends too. The only one who didn't look completely smug was Kara. Cassie met her gaze for a brief moment, a burst of hope shot through her at the regret filling her old friend's gaze.

Then Kara's eyes flitted to the girls surrounding her and she turned away. Anger at Kara, and anger at herself, surged through her. She should have known Kara wouldn't risk the censure of the rest of the school. She wouldn't go against the grain by alienating herself, and becoming the outcast Cassie had become.

Turning away, she hurried through the rest of the crowd as she forced herself not to bolt from the room, and the people inside it. She burst out of the gym and took a deep breath of the cooler, fresher air.

Her hands clutched at her arms as she tried to stop the shaking seeping into her bones. Heels clicking on the linoleum floor, Cassie made her way to the bathroom as she attempted to regain control of her emotions. Pushing the bathroom door open, she poked her head inside.

Kelly Jackson was at the sink washing her hands. She froze as her eyes met Cassie's in the mirror. Cassie gave her a brief nod before continuing onto one of the stalls. Closing the door, she leaned her forehead against the cool metal as she inhaled and exhaled deeply. She listened as Kelly left the bathroom before popping the door back open and stepping outside once more.

Making her way to the sink, she turned the cold water on and splashed her face with it. Her control was returning as the water shocked her out of the dull haze suffusing her. Grabbing some paper towels, she dried her face. The door opened and closed again, but she didn't look up; she couldn't take the shunning and loathing anymore.

Footsteps rang across the floor and stopped behind her. Cassie frowned, a chill swept down her back as her heart leapt into her throat. A shimmering wall seemed to come down upon her as she froze like a deer in the headlights. Her heart lurched and leapt as her muscles and locked them in place. She *knew* who was behind her, knew who had come in, but her body refused to react to such knowledge.

Slowly, ever so achingly slow, she lifted her head to look in the mirror. Julian stood behind her; a cruel smile twisted his beautiful face as his icy blue eyes clashed with hers in the glass. His white blond hair was spiked up in disarray, and showed off the hard angles of his perfect face. Petrified into immobility, her mind somehow managed to process that the just out of bed style looked good on him, but there probably wasn't much that *didn't* look good on him.

For a moment they gazed at each other as they silently assessed the competition. He was enjoying playing with her like a cat with a mouse, practically salivating at the thought of draining her dry. She was simply trying to get her brain to work again as she struggled to grasp the ramifications of this situation.

"For what it's worth, you definitely had my vote."

Cassie's mind lurched into action as his melodic voice pounded into her ears. The terror tearing through her was pushed aside as her survival instinct finally kicked into high gear and years of training poured through her. He would kill her if he got a hold of her, and there was no one around to help her. She was extremely grateful she'd turned Melissa down and her friend wasn't here now. At least they wouldn't *both* be killed tonight. Melissa could go on with her life, even if Cassie couldn't.

No matter what happened, no matter how this all turned out, she wasn't going down without a fight, and Julian wouldn't walk away from this without injury.

"Though you aren't a queen, you can be my princess."

With those purred words, Julian launched at her.

CHAPTER FOURTEEN

DEVON FINALLY MANAGED to extricate himself from Marcy's desperate clutches. There had been a time when he'd thrived on his inherent ability to attract women, a time when he'd reveled in the endless parade of them, not anymore. Now he would like to flip a switch and turn the ability off, but unfortunately it didn't work that way.

Making his way across the floor, he steered clear of the girls attempting to approach him. The only thing he cared about was getting back to Cassie, taking her in his arms, and ridding himself of the lingering feel of Marcy. The girl had no shame whatsoever.

He stepped clear of the crowd and frowned as he spotted Chris and Melissa, minus Cassie. Disquiet filled his gut as he scanned the students gathered near them. "Where's Cassie?" he demanded far more abruptly than he'd intended.

Melissa lifted an eyebrow as she studied him with an amused expression. "The bathroom, she'll be right back."

Uneasiness grew in him as he perused the crowd once more.

Folding his arms, he tapped his foot impatiently. She required her freedom, without it she would rebel and chafe against the restraints placed upon her. Even as he reminded himself of this, his anxiety level hiked up a notch.

Reaching out, he used his powers to search for her presence. He'd become so in tune with her it was easy for him to shift through the people surrounding him to find her. His mind clicked onto hers, his body went numb with cold fear. For a moment he couldn't move as he was buried beneath her emotions.

He had to pull away from her, had to remove himself from the edges of her frantic mind, otherwise he wouldn't be able to move. Breaking free of his paralysis, he shoved people aside in his heedless rush. Ignoring the astonished looks he received, he leapt easily over a table as he raced out of the room. He didn't care that a human wouldn't be able to move as fast as he was, or with as much agility. He didn't care if his reaction put doubts and questions into their minds; all he cared about was getting to her before it was too late.

CASSIE DASHED to the side as Julian came at her in a nearly indistinguishable blurring rush. She just barely managed to avoid his questing grasp as his hand skimmed over the skin of her back. He spun at her again, coming at her with a ferocious hunger that sent her heart racing as her fight or flight instinct kicked into hyper drive.

She turned to the side and grabbed for the first thing her panicked fingers could seize hold of, the soap dispenser. Fear enhanced her strength as she ripped it from the wall in a wrenching jerk. He grabbed hold of her shoulders and shoved her backward as he slammed her into the sink. A cry escaped her as pain flashed up her bruised and battered spine and her head smashed into the mirror. Shattered glass spilled around them in a tinkling wave as it cascaded upon the sink and floor. She was momentarily stunned into immobility from the force of the impact.

The harsh light of the room reflected off of the shattered pieces, they momentarily blinded her with their brilliance. Blinking back the stars briefly filling her field of vision; she strained to bring him into focus. His beautiful face twisted into a snarl as his fangs extended past his lower lip. Her breath rushed from her as he struck at her, moving faster than any rattlesnake.

Reacting on pure instinct Cassie swung up and slammed the soap dispenser into the side of his face. Soap and plastic bits exploded over them as his assault was knocked off balance, and his grip on her was jarred. Cassie tore free of his grasp, and scrambled to get away, but she realized her folly too late. The soap had poured all over the floor making the linoleum treacherously slippery.

Her heels skidded through it, her arms pin wheeled as she fought desperately to keep her balance, but it was too late. With a startled cry, she fell backwards and crashed to the floor with enough force to knock the breath from her. Dazed, Cassie shook her head as she tried to clear it of the waves of pain saturating her. Her tailbone screamed in agony, pieces of glass sliced into her hands as she sprawled inelegantly across the shard coated floor.

Dismay filled her as her heart sank. Maybe if she had stayed on her feet, maybe if she had been able to get to the door, she might have had a chance at escape. She wouldn't be able to do so now. Shoving it all aside, she rolled to the side, not caring her dress became covered in the slippery liquid and torn by the shards of glass. She had to keep moving, it was her only hope, a small one, but it was all she had. As she moved, she kicked off her heels to rid herself of the hindrance they caused.

Julian recovered speedily from the blow she'd given him. She lifted herself to her feet, but remained crouched as she rested her injured hand on the cold linoleum. She froze as she met his heated gaze. Through the pain and annoyance, she saw his amusement, saw how very much he was enjoying toying with her. He was going to drag this out for as long as possible, and he was going to enjoy every second of it. Though she was bleeding, the scent of her blood didn't seem to send him into a frenzy this time as his eyes remained their crystalline blue color.

For a moment she couldn't move, she could only stare at him as despair and anger crashed over her in conflicting waves. She wasn't ready for this; it wasn't her time to die.

"You are a feisty one," he said in a low purr. "No wonder Devon lusts for you so." Cassie shifted slightly, careful not to draw his attack quite yet as she tried to adjust herself into a better position. "I'm going to enjoy taking you away from him."

She froze, trapped by his gaze as realization crashed into her. "That's what this is all about," she breathed. "That's why you're here. *We* didn't draw you in, *he* did."

Julian flashed his perfect white teeth as his fangs cut into his bottom lip. Even with soap dripping off the side of his face, he was hauntingly beautiful and perfect. Kneeling before her, he rested his hands on the floor as his eyes twinkled with merriment.

"Yes love, that's what *this*, is about. Or at least why it started. Now I've decided I will have you. I will keep you, and break you, and parade you around in front of Devon because when I get into you, I won't let you go. You won't know who he is by the time I'm done with you. Your mind will be mine. *You* will be mine."

She shook her head, unable to speak as his words brought forth a rolling revulsion she couldn't escape. "I would *never* forget him. I would *never* allow you to do that to me," she breathed.

His grin broadened. "You're so cute," he taunted. "You actually think you'd have a choice, but you won't. I wouldn't allow it. For eternity you will be at my every beck and call. You will do everything I ask you to do, and I do mean *everything*."

Bile heaved up her throat, images of what he would do to her smashed through her brain. Grabbing hold of her pride, and her strength, Cassie tilted her chin as she met his gaze. "I'd rather die."

A short bark of laughter escaped him as he leaned forward, and his body coiled for attack. "I won't make that mistake princess."

She glared at him as her upper lip curled into a sneer. "*Don't* call me princess."

Leaping easily to her feet, she dashed to the side as she ran a zigzag pattern toward the door. Toward the only hope of salvation she had. She didn't care anymore if he killed her; that would be far better than the alternative he had planned.

He was right on her heels, so close she could feel the heat of his body. Spinning, she just managed to avoid him as he rushed past her. A growl of fury escaped him as he slid to a halt. Scurrying back a few feet, she avoided the puddle of soap and debris as she rushed toward the stalls.

They offered her no protection, she wasn't foolish enough to think they did, but the longer she stayed free of Julian the longer she stayed alive. Her evasion of him might also infuriate him to the point he did kill her by accident, instead of seizing control of her mind and body like he had threatened.

The door slammed off the wall as she lunged into one of the stalls, she didn't bother to attempt to lock it. What would be the point? Leaping onto the toilet, she threw her hands on top of the metal stall divider. She ignored the acute pain the motion caused her torn and damaged hands as she lifted herself up. She catapulted herself into the next stall as Julian slammed into the door. The metal shrieked in protest as it twisted and bent beneath the force of his impact.

Cassie leapt her way over the stalls as she headed back toward the door. A roar followed her as Julian's frustration became palpable in the bathroom. Reaching the last stall, she leapt easily over it and swung her legs over the soap puddle. He was on her, coming at her with the rushing force of a locomotive.

Cassie ran as fast as she could, but it wasn't fast enough, nowhere near fast enough. He was far too powerful for her, far to hell bent on destroying her and Devon. The door was mere feet away when his arms encircled her. His iron tight grasp knocked the breath from her as he squeezed. A rib cracked, a cry escaped her as his hands tore through the fabric of her dress and sliced her skin.

This was it; this was the way it was all going to end.

She wasn't ready; she so very much was *not* ready for this. Her thoughts turned to Devon, desolation consumed her as all of her dreams from earlier shattered. Cassie tried to dig her feet in, but it was useless as Julian's aggressive rush propelled them toward the door.

CHAPTER FIFTEEN

DEVON SKIDDED around the corner of the hall but didn't lose a step as he raced forward. His body thrummed with dread as his skin crawled. He couldn't move any faster, yet it wasn't fast enough. Not *nearly* fast enough. Too much time had passed; she'd been alone with Julian for far too long, and he knew she was with Julian, she *had* to be. Only Julian could have inspired the amount of terror emanating from her.

Devon tried not to think about the many things Julian could have done to her already. Things Devon could never fix. The bathroom was right there, just out of range, but so very close.

The door shattered outward, wood splintered as the door was forced to go in a direction it wasn't designed to. Cassie and Julian tumbled out of the wreckage; they bounced off the wall on the opposite side of the hall before tumbling to the floor. Cassie lurched up in an attempt to free herself of Julian's grasp, but he didn't relinquish her. Swinging around, her fist connected with Julian's cheek and snapped his head to the side.

The scent of her blood and soap hung heavily in the air, but Devon had prepared himself for the scent of her blood. Instead of the smell sending him into a blood frenzy again, it only served to enrage him further. Julian also seemed to have prepared himself for the scent of her blood this time. Instead of becoming feral and crazed with his drive to get at her, he remained in complete control of himself as he grasped for Cassie again.

Cassie was nearly free of him when Julian snagged hold of her ankle and jerked her back. With a startled cry, she fell to the floor. Her chin bounced off the ground with a harsh crack as her hands gave out. She screamed as Julian pulled her toward him. Turning onto her back, she kicked forcefully out. Devon was momentarily astounded by the force of her blow. He knew Julian's strength, knew his powers, and what he was capable of, but his head shot back and the crack of his jaw resonated down the hallway. Though she connected hard, he didn't let go of her.

Devon's bellow echoed throughout the halls of the school. Cassie's head whipped toward him, her relief was nearly palpable as her eyes latched onto his. A small smile curved Julian's mouth as he released Cassie and leapt to his feet. Devon bounded over top of her, and seized hold of Julian's throat as he slammed into him.

For the first time in over a century he fully released the beast he'd been struggling to keep locked away. It tore free of him with a savage intensity that was more of a relief than he cared to acknowledge. He would annihilate Julian, not only for hurting her, but for daring to touch her at all. All reason fled, his humanity vanished as the monster in him took complete control and his lust for the kill sprang forth.

The metal of the lockers twisted and folded as it bent beneath their weights with a tortured screech. Devon was so infuriated he didn't feel the blow that sliced through his side, to expose his ribs and spill his blood. Nor did Julian slow when Devon shattered his arm against the water cooler in the hall.

~

CASSIE CRAB CRAWLED BACKWARD as Julian's grip was torn free. Her heart leapt into her throat as Devon collided with him and bashed him into the lockers. The growls and roars filling the air caused the hair on the back of her neck to stand up. She should flee, but she found herself unable to move as she remained riveted upon the brutal fight.

She'd never seen so much violence and hatred. They tore at each other with the frenzy she associated with sharks when they smelled blood. The copper scent of it filled the air, but neither of them eased in their assault as they were determined to kill each other.

She couldn't move, couldn't breathe. It was like watching a train wreck, but this wreck involved the love of her life, a man she didn't recognize right now. His eyes were crimson and his face was twisted into a brutal snarl. His fangs were longer than Julian's, extended past his lower lip as he slashed at Julian. She didn't know this person, but she did know he would kill for her.

They rolled across the lockers, twisting and warping the metal as they moved. Locks were torn off and shattered upon the ground beneath their feet. Blood dripped down Devon's side and splashed on the ground. The sight of that blood jolted her back into action. Leaping to her feet, Cassie's gaze darted back to the bathroom. Her purse was somewhere in there with a small stake tucked discreetly inside. She didn't want to leave the fight for a second, let alone the amount of time it would take for her to find the thing.

Her attention was snagged back as Devon bellowed loudly and

smashed the palm of his hand into Julian's chest. The loud crack of Julian's ribs reverberated through the air. Cassie's mouth dropped as Julian flew backward a good ten feet before slamming into a classroom door. The glass in the center shattered, the frame bent, and the doorknob was torn off as Julian flopped against it.

She took a step back as she realized she didn't belong here. This was not her fight, not anymore, but no matter how much she tried to get her feet to move, no matter how much she longed to escape, she wouldn't leave him. If something happened to him, she was going to be here, and she was going to give him whatever help she could.

Julian shook his head as he attempted to rise to his feet. A wheezing sound escaped him as he stumbled back. Attempting to rise to his feet again, he staggered forward before dropping once more. Devon stepped in his way; a loud snarl escaped him as Julian's gaze focused briefly on her. Though he wasn't smiling anymore, there was an oddly amused twinkle in Julian's ice blue eyes that unsettled her.

She didn't like the way he studied her. It was too intense, too questioning, and there was a strange, unsettling gleam in his eyes. It was as if he saw too much, as if he understood her in a way she didn't even understand herself. His blond eyebrows rose into his hair as a dawning realization settled in his eyes. She yearned to wrap her arms around herself and shrink from his strangely comprehensive stare, but she found herself unable to move.

"Don't look at her!" Devon spat as he took a defensive step forward. His shoulders were locked, his hands fisted at his sides as his body thrummed with fury.

"I'm going to be looking at her for eternity when I'm done with her."

Devon released a sound that was part growl, part snarl, and

something utterly terrifying. Julian grinned as he gave Devon a come here wave with that caused all of the hair on her arms and neck to stand up. Julian had something up his sleeve. Devon must have sensed the same thing as he didn't heedlessly rush back at him again.

Cassie jumped and a startled cry escaped her when a hand seized hold of her elbow. She spun, ready to fight again until she saw Chris and Melissa standing there, their eyes wide as they scanned her ruined, blood stained dress. Another bellow brought their attention back to Devon and Julian. This time however, Devon's attention was not focused upon Julian, but on *them.*

Mouth parting in alarm, Cassie pulled her arm free of Chris's grasp. Devon's red eyes continued to gleam as his focus centered upon Chris. Trepidation pounded through Cassie as realization hammered throughout her. Devon was so far gone he would attack anyone right now.

Swallowing heavily, she held up her hands as she tried to ward him off. "No Devon," she whispered, praying she could still reach him. "No, he didn't hurt me. Chris would *never* hurt me."

Devon's blood colored eyes were more than a little disarming. She'd never seen him like this, had never known he could be like this, and she was terrified he would kill her friend. She wasn't sure she could stop him when he was so far gone. She didn't know this person, this *creature* before her, but she still loved him. She just had to keep him from killing Chris.

Chris pushed Melissa back with him. "Devon," Cassie whispered as her gaze briefly shot to Julian.

He was still on the ground but his attention was focused upon them. Upon *her* still. If it hadn't been for Chris, he would be dead by now, but he wasn't taking the opportunity to run during his brief reprieve. He had to realize he'd lost this fight, why would he stay?

Devon took another step toward them, his intensity still focused on Chris. Instinctively, Chris grasped hold of her elbow and tried to pull her back. Cassie knew it had been the wrong thing to do, the wrong move to make.

Another bellow escaped Devon as he leapt over the debris generated by the brutal fight and raced at them. A strangled cry escaped Cassie as he launched himself at Chris. Though he'd told her once never to get in between a vampire and its prey, she didn't take the time to think about the consequences of her actions. She just hoped it didn't end badly. Cassie stepped in front of Chris to block Devon's attack with her body. She would willingly die before she allowed him to destroy her best friend. Ducking her head, she held her hands up as she braced herself for the blow she knew was about to ensue.

Devon's arms wrapped around her as lifted her up and pulled her away from Chris's hold. His touch was surprisingly gentle considering his frame of mind, and the murderous intent humming through his body. His hands entangled in her hair as he cradled her head against his chest.

The tension thrumming through him eased as he buried his face in her neck. Cassie stayed perfectly still as she sensed the tenuous hold he had upon his control as his lips skimmed over her flesh. The beast was fighting with the man as it strived to break free once more. Fought to satiate itself on her blood. If she moved a millimeter she was afraid she would set it free.

He shuddered; his hand upon her waist became painful. She could feel the bruises he left, but she didn't protest, didn't flinch away from him. His lips stopped over the pulsing vein going haywire with her heartbeat. Despite the apprehension pounding through her, she couldn't stop the thrill of excitement enshrouding her as his fangs scraped her skin ever so slightly.

Cassie's knees wobbled and threatened to give out. Despite her plan not to move, she couldn't stop her fingers from digging into his back as she fought against offering him her vein. Though she yearned for this far more than she'd realized she knew here was not the place. *This* was not the time.

He would never forgive himself if he took her here, and he would blame it on his lack of control. Nor did she wish for Melissa and Chris to see it, and she especially didn't want Julian to be there. This was something for the two of them to share, something to cherish and remember for the rest of her life, and she didn't want the memory to involve the hall of her high school.

Yet she didn't fight him, didn't push him away. He needed her now, she was also the only one who could calm him down. He shuddered once more and his grip on her eased. She tried not to feel disappointed as his mouth left her neck, but she couldn't help it. He was back; she knew in her soul what held her now was the man. The man, whose love for her was stronger than the demon's thirst for her blood.

"Don't *ever* put yourself in front of me again." His hand constricted in her hair as he kissed her forehead roughly. "I could have killed you."

She hated the self-contempt in his voice. "Never," she whispered.

Devon's head jerked up, a low growl escaped him as Julian launched to his feet and finally managed to stay upright. Julian's icy eyes gleamed with contempt as he surveyed them. "How the mighty have fallen," he murmured as he shook his head.

Though Devon didn't release her, he subtly shifted his body more in front of hers and took a small step toward Julian. Julian grinned as he flicked his fingers through his disheveled white blond hair. "Now, now, Devon stay calm, things are just starting to get interesting."

"What are you talking about?" Devon demanded.

Julian's grin only spread as his eyes flickered behind them. The foreboding creeping through her made it difficult to breathe. A new presence filled the hall, one just as malevolent and cold as Julian, but this one also emitted a jealousy and loathing so thick it was nearly choking.

Cassie braced herself before turning to face this new presence. A woman stepped around the corner of the hall and moved toward them with the eerie grace of the undead. Cassie's mouth parted as she took in the woman's astonishing beauty. The black dress she wore swayed with her hips and provocative walk. The pale beauty of her face contrasted vividly with the color of her dress and ruby red lips. Her features were elegant and refined; her cheekbones high, and her nose slender. Dark auburn hair spilled down her back, swaying against her knees in flowing waves as she moved.

Devon straightened to his full height as the tension in his body notched up to a whole new level. The woman lifted a dark eyebrow as she studied them with amused disdain. She had the most astonishing, frosty eyes, Cassie had ever seen. They were the color of pure molten gold and shone brilliantly. Those eyes pinned Cassie to the spot as the full force of the woman's hatred blasted against her.

"Forgive me," Devon breathed in her ear.

Cassie questioningly glanced up at him, but he wasn't looking at her. Forgive him? Forgive him for what?

His emerald eyes flashed with hostility as he focused on the beautiful woman. "Isla," he greeted with icy disdain.

The woman smiled seductively to reveal her already extended fangs. "Hello lover," she purred.

The breath wheezed forcefully out of Cassie, the beat of her heart stopped for a frantic moment as uncertainty and hurt tore through her in equal measures. If his hands hadn't been clenched upon her, she would have fallen down. *Lover*? Her gaze darted between them as pain cracked through her with the force of lightning bolts.

She'd known there were women in his past, there had to be. But this woman, *this* woman! Cassie trembled as she looked back at the stunning doll before her. This woman was something Cassie had never remotely fathomed. She was exceedingly beautiful and radiated a raw sexuality and poise Cassie could never possess. How could she possibly compete with her? Her confidence shaken, Cassie simply tried to breathe through the constriction in her chest.

Struggling to stay composed, she met Isla's feral gold eyes once more. From the gleam in those eyes Cassie knew she'd already let too much of her emotions slip.

CHAPTER SIXTEEN

DEVON FELT Cassie's body shudder. He wished he could take her somewhere where she would be sheltered from the cruelty of the world. Somewhere she would be sheltered from the mistakes and wrongs of his past.

But there was no escaping this, and it seemed as if his past had come to a head with his future, in of all places, the hallway of a *freaking* high school. Hatred blazed through him as he met Isla's malicious golden gaze. Merriment and vehemence radiated from Isla as her small smile grew and she tilted her head to the side.

"You were right Julian, she is delicious," Isla purred as she licked her lips. "Such a little innocent though, how could she possibly satisfy your twisted passions Devon?"

Self hatred tore through him as Cassie trembled again and her fingers dug into his back. Isla took a step closer; hunger throbbed off of her in rolling waves. Chris and Melissa instinctively moved closer, as their eyes briefly darted toward him. Devon kept his gaze focused upon Isla, but with his mind he monitored Julian's movements, which were still none. He'd been injured, but Devon wasn't fooled into thinking he was incapable of fighting.

Devon didn't know why Julian wasn't rushing into the fray, or why he'd been studying Cassie so raptly. There had been no desire in his gaze, no bloodlust as he had watched her keenly, apparently trying to decipher something about her. What that something could be Devon didn't know, but Julian's scrutiny was unsettling. Just what was Julian's plan, and why was Isla here?

"What are you doing here Isla?" he demanded.

She shrugged an elegant shoulder as she tossed her hair over her shoulder with a flick of her blood red nails. "When Julian called I just had to come and see if what he was saying was true." She glanced briefly at Chris, Melissa and Cassie. "I had to see for myself that The Hunter line had survived, they were here, and they were *thriving*. How could I turn down the offer of so much power from such a tempting treat?"

She licked her lips again. Melissa's shoulder brushed against Cassie's as she moved closer. "I also had to see *her*." The deep purr left Isla's voice as her gaze once more locked upon Cassie with a loathing that infuriated him. He would have attacked her, destroyed her, but he couldn't bring himself to release Cassie when she was so shaken.

The worst thing he could have done was show Isla how much Cassie meant to him, but it was already too late for that. All he could hope for now was to keep Cassie safe, and to convey his fierce love for her with his touch.

"What's the matter Julian can't fight your own battles?" Devon hissed as he glanced briefly at him. Julian's face was twisted in pain, and his skin was far paler than normal as he stepped away from the lockers. He wouldn't die from his injuries, but it would take him a little while to completely recover.

Julian's lip curled into a sneer. "Why would I deny Isla the pleasure of this?" he inquired.

"Coward."

Julian's eyes flashed red, but he made no move to come at them. "I think he might like this girl more than the last one," Isla taunted. Cassie's nails dug into his skin. "What was her name again?"

"Annabelle, beautiful, tempting, Annabelle," Julian replied with amusement.

Devon silently cursed himself as he felt a fresh wave of pain radiate off of Cassie. He'd meant to keep her sheltered from his past, to keep it buried. He'd so badly wanted to only focus on the here and now, and her. To bury the mistakes and atrocities he'd committed. He realized he'd been wrong to do so. If he had told her the truth, she may have been upset by it, but she wouldn't be experiencing the distress she was now. He wanted to reassure her, but there was nothing he could do at this point. Not here anyway, later he would work hard to ease her doubts as he tried to take away her pain.

"Ah yes, Annabelle, she was a pretty little thing." Isla tapped a nail against her lip as she pretended to think.

Devon knew Isla was already well aware of what she planned on saying, but one thing she'd always loved was drama and torturing her victims. Unfortunately, her victim this time was Cassie. He was going to rip Isla's throat out for this, when he got his hands on her, he was going to make sure she could never speak again.

"You gave up human blood for your love of Annabelle, and now you've crawled into bed with the enemy. You will do anything to get into the pants of a pretty little thing won't you Devon?"

Cassie went rigid against him. "You bitch!" Devon spat.

Isla grinned at him as Cassie's hands slipped off his back. Devon fought back his panic. He had to get them out of here before Isla succeeded in tearing Cassie away from him for good. "Did you not tell her about Annabelle?" Isla taunted. "Oh honey, believe me, you aren't the only girl he's lost his head over. Is she Devon?"

"First there was Elizabeth, after that there was me…"

"There was *never* you," Devon snarled. "I *never* loved you."

A cold laugh escaped her. "And you love this one?"

Devon's nostrils flared as abhorrence poured through him. He'd allowed his temper to get the best of him and he'd walked right into Isla's trap by doing so. She would do anything in her power to destroy their love, to destroy *him*. "This is not the place Isla. There are too many humans here."

"I don't see any humans; all I see are three little treats. You know you would like to sample one too. I bet it's killing you not to taste her." She flipped a hand idly at Cassie. "I can smell her power from here, and I know you were never one to deny yourself anything. That's why you were always so exciting to be with. You were a vampire of worth, one who matched my appetite in *every* way." Her gaze fixed pointedly on Cassie as she licked her lips hungrily once more. "*Every* way," she emphasized again.

Cassie trembled again and inhaled a ragged breath. She deserved far more than what his life had to offer her. The best thing he could have done for her was left her alone, but it was too late now.

If he thought it would help, he would leave tomorrow, he would set her free to live the life she deserved. He may be able to separate himself from her, if it was in her best interest, but he knew what she was to him now, and he knew he would *not* survive the loss of her life. He also knew Julian and Isla wouldn't leave until the Hunters in this town were destroyed.

Forgive me, he prayed silently to her. Please forgive me.

"There are three Hunters here, and me. Do you think you can win this battle?"

Isla sashayed her hips as she took a step closer. "Oh honey, I *did* win the battle." A grim smirk spread across her mouth. "And I *will* win the war."

A small snarl escaped. "I'll kill you for this," he vowed.

She lifted a delicate eyebrow as she laughed wickedly. "I doubt it. It is my bed you always return to after all."

Pain didn't wash off of Cassie anymore; instead numbness seemed to have descended over her as she remained limp in his arms. "Not in centuries, and never again Isla, *never* again."

She seemed nonplussed by his response. "When she is dead…"

"If you finish that sentence I swear I will make your death pure torture!" he snapped. "I will make you beg for mercy Isla; I will make you wish you'd *never* survived this long. You want the old me back, you *will* have it if you touch her. If you come near her, I'll destroy you!"

Fury radiated from Isla's eyes as they flashed the color of rubies. It seemed as if his words were finally sinking in. Cassie seemed to come alive again as she clung to him. Until recently she hadn't been used to people hating her, but the dislike her schoolmates had for her was nothing compared to the abhorrence radiating from Isla.

Chris settled into a fighter's stance. Beside him, Melissa dug into her purse and her hand wrapped around something. It wasn't only Cassie he had to see safely out of here, but them also. If they didn't *all* survive this, it would destroy Cassie. Devon's head shot around as Julian moved a couple steps closer. Blood had formed at the corners of his mouth, but he seemed to be doing better already.

He leveled Julian with a ferocious glare. "You take one more step and I'll kill you!" Julian froze, but his eyes shot about as he calculated the odds. "Three Hunters and *me*."

"They're not armed," Isla purred.

"We can still fight, and we're still dangerous." Cassie's spine straightened as her jaw clenched. He was proud of her for standing up for herself, but he was also terrified her defiance would only enrage Isla further.

Isla laughed as she tossed her hair over her shoulder. She became a blur as she charged at them. Devon turned as Isla shoved Melissa before crashing into his back. The force of the blow staggered him forward. Cassie cried out as she was shoved against the locker and his body was slammed forcefully against hers. He tried to absorb most of the impact, but he knew Cassie had been hurt by the blow.

Isla's claws raked down his back as she beat at him. His blood spilled forth, but it wasn't him Isla was truly after. Cassie ducked her head and turned away from the raking claws seeking to destroy her. His vision became a murky red. He would rip Isla limb from limb before he ever let her get her hands on Cassie. He swung back violently; his fist and shoulder connected with Isla and flung her back.

She skidded across the floor before hitting the lockers with a loud thud. Releasing Cassie, he spun around and kept her firmly pinned behind his back. His lips pulled back as a harsh hiss escaped him and his teeth extended. Isla shook her head as she staggered back to her feet. Chris pulled Melissa to her feet, a bruise was already beginning to form on her cheek, but she appeared otherwise unharmed.

Voices filled the hall, laughter trailed ahead of the students making their way toward them. Isla and Julian moved closer together as they silently communicated with their gazes. To expose themselves to a bunch of humans would be reckless and risky. They wouldn't be able to kill them all, and to do so would leave a trail of bodies that would only get the authorities involved.

"Later lover," Isla whispered.

Julian and Isla easily slipped down the hall, disappearing into the shadows before a group of four girls turned the corner with Marcy in the lead. They froze as they spotted the carnage of the hall, and the blood stained floor. Feeling tired, beaten, and worn, Devon took a step toward them.

Marcy's eyes widened as she took in his bloodied shirt and gashes. "Devon! Are you ok?"

Her gaze shot accusingly to Cassie before focusing on him once more. Taking a deep breath, he drew on his strength as he marshaled his powers. He hadn't had enough strength right now to take hold of Isla or Julian, but he could handle four humans. Reaching out, he shoved his mind forward and wrapped into theirs to seize hold of their will. Their eyes became glazed as their mouths became slack.

"You saw nothing here, and *no* one. Go back to the dance, there is nothing going on here." He kept hold of their minds as he twisted their memories. In their minds the doors and lockers were still intact and the hall was empty.

They nodded and turned around before moving away. Feeling drained, it took all he had to keep himself standing upright. The use of his ability on so many people, on top of his blood loss, was exhausting. The three of them stared at him in silent awe of the power he'd never shown them. Cassie grabbed hold of his arm as her violet blue eyes apprehensively searched his face.

"Devon?"

The scent of her blood was overwhelming him in his weakened

condition. Tremors shook him as he fought against his thirst. He couldn't be near her right now. "Chris," he muttered.

Chris shot Cassie an apologetic glance as he took hold of Devon's arm and wrapped it around his shoulders. Devon reluctantly released her as she stepped back. He hated to see the distress in her eyes, and he despised being the cause of it, but he didn't trust himself to be near her now.

"We have to get out of here," Melissa said hurriedly. "Before other people come."

"I need to grab my purse and shoes, my ID is inside," Cassie whispered.

A low rumble slid through his chest as she disappeared from view. Forgetting his injuries, he drug Chris into the bathroom after her. He froze in the doorway as he took in the wreckage littering the floor. The soap dispenser lay in the middle of the room, its liquid was scattered across the floor, sinks, and broken glass. One of the stall doors had been ripped free and tossed aside. It wasn't the wreckage that left him immobile, but the blood staining the linoleum, sink, floor, and tops of the stall doors. *Her* blood.

Cassie emerged from one of the ruined stalls with her stained purse clutched in her trembling hands. Her gaze flitted around the room as her breath came more rapidly. She looked so lost, so child-like and wounded it broke his heart. His fury evaporated as he took in the room once more. All he could do was be thankful she was still alive, that she had somehow managed to survive Julian's attack when no one else would have. At least no human would have, and probably *no* other Hunter.

She may not have the special abilities Melissa and Chris possessed, but Devon suspected there was far more to her than any of them had begun to imagine.

He removed his arm from Chris's shoulder as a fresh well of

strength infused him. She needed him more than he needed blood right now. She hesitated for a moment as he opened his arms to her, but when he made no move to turn away from her, she ran forward. Throwing her arms around his waist, she buried her face in his chest. He held her close as her shoulders began to shake and heart wrenching sobs escaped her.

Burying his face in her hair, he tried to focus on the sweet scent of fruit from her shampoo instead of the luring scent of her powerful blood. Her need for him was a great motivator for this. He was careful of the cuts on her side as he lifted her gently. She wrapped her arms around him as she pressed her tear stained face into his neck.

They used the back doors as they made their way outside while Chris retrieved the coats. Devon adjusted his hold on Cassie and flung open the passenger side door as Melissa hurried inside. He placed her into the passenger seat and knelt beside her. He stroked her hair back from her face as his fingers lingered on her cheek. Turning her hands over, he noted the jagged gashes marring her delicate palms as he pulled a piece of glass free and tossed it aside.

"Are you going to be ok?" he inquired.

She managed a small nod and closed her eyes. Picking her arm up, he surveyed the gashes on her side as he fought back the thirst crashing through him in rising waves. She winced and jerked away from him. "Sorry love," he whispered.

His forehead furrowed as he realized the blood had already stopped flowing and the cuts were already becoming smaller. The rate in which she mended astonished him. He recalled the hospital when she had said she healed fast, but this fast? She was not healing at *his* rate, for he could already feel the muscle reattaching itself to his bone and his skin rejoining once more. No, she didn't heal at his rate, but it was at a rate that far exceeded anything she *should* be capable of. Even as a Hunter.

Doubts gathered in his mind, little pieces of a puzzle suddenly scattered across a table before him. They were pieces he didn't understand, and couldn't quite put together, but they troubled him nonetheless. He couldn't make sense of what he was looking at, and he realized it would take far more than him to make sense of this. He just didn't know who to turn to for help.

"Don't worry about it, I heal fast remember," she told him.

"I can see that," he muttered.

Her finger was tender under his chin as she lifted his face. "You have to feed."

His frown intensified in confusion. Then, ever so subtly, her thumb brushed over his extended fangs. He trembled at her touch. He hadn't realized his fangs had extended, he'd been too caught up in his amazement of her to realize his hunger was so obvious.

Recoiling from her touch, he moved out of her range. Her hand fell away, but there was no offense in her gaze, only deep concern. Chris jogged up to the car with their coats draped over his arm. "Go," Cassie implored. "I'll be fine, I've suffered through worse."

Her tender reassurances, and the growing anguish in his body, made up his mind for him. She would be in good hands, and once she was home, she would be safe. Digging into his pocket, Devon pulled out his keys and tossed them to Chris. Fumbling with the coats, Chris managed to keep hold of them as he caught the keys.

"Drive slow, I'll follow you home."

Chris's mouth dropped as he looked at the keys, and then the car. "You ok?" he stammered.

"Yes, just make sure you take care of her." They both knew he didn’t mean the car. He turned his attention back to Cassie. "I'll see you in a little bit." She managed a nod, but he saw the fear and anxiety in her gaze. Feeling like the worst kind of ass, he quietly shut the door. He didn't trust himself to get close to her again. "I'm sorry about almost attacking you earlier."

Chris managed a listless smile. "I understand where you're coming from, just don't let it happen again."

Chris was trying to sound cheerful but his voice was strained. Devon nodded and closed his eyes as another tremor ripped through him. Shaking, desperately thirsty, he took a step back. He watched as Chris pulled out of the parking lot with the only person who could completely satisfy the arid torture blazing through his veins.

Turning, he fled into the woods, keeping pace with the car as it made its way down the side streets.

CHAPTER SEVENTEEN

"WHAT HAPPENED?" Cassie dropped her coat tiredly on the banister as Dani froze three steps from the foyer. Her mouth dropped as her eyes damn near bulged out of her head.

"Where's my grandma?" Cassie inquired.

Dani blinked in surprise as she stared at Cassie's ruined dress. "Her friend Martha called, they went to Bingo. She thought she would be home before you, but…" Dani's eyes darted to the grandfather clock in the living room. "You're far earlier than expected."

"Party kinda got crashed," Chris mumbled.

"I can see that," Dani said.

"Glad she's not home." The last thing Cassie wanted was for her grandma to see her like this. The retelling was going to be bad enough, but to actually see it would have made matters much worse.

"What the hell happened?"

"You got it, hell happened." Chris shut and locked the door behind him.

Cassie rolled her eyes at Chris and shook her head disapprovingly. There was no reason to frighten Dani more. Chris tried a sheepish, apologetic smile, but it failed miserably as his face didn't cooperate with his objective.

"Where's Melissa?" Dani demanded.

"Dropped her off already," Cassie answered. Dani's shoulders slumped in relief. "I need some ice cream, but first I have to get out of this dress. Chris, why don't you make us some sundaes?"

"Are you ok?" Dani demanded as her focus locked on Cassie's blood stained side.

"I'll be fine," she assured her.

Cassie padded up the stairs, she was acutely aware of every ache and bruise as each step intensified the pain. Though she wasn't looking forward to retelling the horrifying events of the night, she was grateful for the distraction Dani offered. Otherwise, she would be consumed with her concern for Devon, and everything that had been revealed tonight.

How many women were in his past? How many of them had he loved? And *who* was Annabelle?

Cassie's hands trembled as she pulled the zipper of her dress down. She tried not to think about those questions, they would only rattle her already shaken confidence more. Tossing her ruined dress on top of her bed, she took a shower to wash the blood from her body. She tried to scrub herself clean of the memories threatening to choke her. No matter how rigorously she scrubbed though, she couldn't clean away the events of the night.

Tears burned the back of her throat once more, but she refused to cry anymore. She hated the weakness she'd allowed to slip through earlier with Devon. She was a big girl; she'd been in life threatening situations before. She should be able to handle her reaction to them far better than she had today.

Although, she'd never had an experience as bad as the one she'd had tonight. She really had thought her life was over, and she'd never been confronted with a beautiful, psychotic girlfriend from centuries past before either. Cassie shuddered as she scrubbed at her skin with renewed vigor.

Though she tried not to think of Isla, it was all she could think about. How many years had they been together? She didn't want to contemplate the things they'd done together, but she couldn't stop the images flashing through her mind and the jealousy consuming her. She was *nothing* like Isla. That woman had experience; she knew what a man liked, and how to please them. She knew what *Devon* liked. She'd satisfied him with her body, and Cassie was certain, with her blood. She'd satisfied him in ways Cassie hadn't, and maybe never could. Revulsion nearly threatened to drown her in its thick waves.

Her certainty that she would join Devon had been shaken, if not destroyed. His was a world she didn't understand, a world of cruelty, sex, and blood. One she wasn't certain she could belong to and one that may destroy her.

Despite the hot water, Cassie was shivering and numb when she stepped out of the shower. She dressed carefully, feeling hollow and devastated. The night had started out with so much promise, it was all gone now. Like a burnt out log, all of her hope had turned into a pile of ash that was choking her from the inside out. No matter how much she hoped things would be ok, that Devon would explain everything, she wasn't sure it would ever be right again. She wasn't sure they could ever be the same again.

Ever so carefully, she cleaned and bandaged her injuries with the ample medical supplies she kept under the sink. She wasn't at all surprised to find the blood had stopped, and the healing process was well under way. She'd always healed fast, ever since she was a little girl, and she'd never been sick.

She used to wonder about it until Luther walked into her life, now she just chocked it up to her Hunter capabilities. Chris and Melissa didn't heal quite as fast as her, but they'd never had a cold either. Once her wounds were bandaged, she fingered her cracked rib and winced as a sharp pain tore through her. Though she couldn't use disinfectant and bandages on it, it would heal just as quickly as the gashes on her side.

Slipping her favorite baggy sweatshirt on, Cassie wrapped her arms around herself as she made her way to the kitchen. Chris and Dani were already sitting at the counter. Chris pushed a strawberry sundae with no whip cream and extra cherries toward her. Though she'd told him she would like a sundae, she shook her head at it. Her body was already a block of ice, she couldn't stand to add more coldness to it.

Making her way to the window, Cassie stared out at the dark night. She recalled when she had first met Devon, when she had sensed his presence out there, watching over her. That was before he'd started coming to her room. That was when things had been simple and easy, when she'd thought him human and had intended to keep *him* protected. How foolish she'd been. She could no more protect him than she could stop a charging elephant. Her protection was unnecessary, her strength nothing compared to his.

Now as she searched the night, she sensed nothing out there, good or evil. It was simply an empty void that did nothing to ease the void inside her heart. Chris's house was silent; his mother apparently having passed out already, or retreated to bed with whatever man she'd brought home tonight.

Cassie turned and focused on Chris and Dani. "Did you tell her anything yet?"

"No." Chris pushed his bowl aside, but instead of grabbing for hers as he normally would have, he leaned back in his chair. "I thought you should be here."

Cassie leaned against the sink as she began to fill Dani in on the details of the night. When she couldn't continue on, Chris picked it up for her. Dani sat silently; her eyes became as large as saucer's as her half eaten sundae was forgotten. When Chris finished, Cassie turned back to the window and once again searched the empty night.

"So, now there are two?" Dani's voice was hoarse.

"Yes," Chris confirmed.

"Is this Isla also an Elder? What can she do?"

"We don't know," Chris answered. "We didn't ask Devon that."

"Piss me off," Cassie mumbled. She struggled to ignore the twinge pulling at her heart as jealousy reared its ugly head once more.

"How are you feeling?" Chris inquired.

Cassie shrugged absently. "I'll be fine." She turned away from the window, unable to stand the quiet of the night anymore. "I'm going to go to sleep," she lied, knowing there would be no sleep until Devon arrived. Knowing she wouldn't sleep until he answered some of the many questions rapidly swirling through her mind.

"Cassie." Chris's stool slid out from under him as he abruptly rose. She felt like a wooden marionette as she turned back to him. "I'm going to stay on the couch tonight." She opened her mouth to protest, but he held up a silencing hand. "My mom will be fine for one night, she's already home."

Cassie nodded and fled the room before the tears burning her eyes started to fall. Racing up the stairs, she closed the door, and leaned heavily against it as she tried to breathe evenly. Before she'd met Devon she'd never cried, and she'd never been emotional. Ever since he'd walked into her life, she'd been a basket case. Devon had shaken her to the very core of her foundation. He'd shattered her walls, torn into her heart, and ripped into her soul to bring her back to life.

She'd allowed herself to trust again, and she was terrified that trust had been misplaced. Terrified this astonishing reprieve she was experiencing with life, and hopes, and dreams, was all a lie. She was petrified she would become the lost, walking dead person she'd been before his arrival. She didn't think she could survive the loss of everything again.

Taking a deep breath, she pushed away from the door. There was no point in losing it now when she didn't know the whole truth. It wouldn't do either of them any good if she turned into a raving loon. Cassie flipped the TV on in the hope it would drown out her thoughts as she restlessly paced the length of her room.

She watched each minute tick by with excruciating slowness, but still he didn't come. At eleven she slumped onto the bed. Her nervous energy wasn't enough to keep her exhausted body moving anymore. Drawing her legs up to her chest, she rested her chin on her knees as her thoughts became more troublesome.

What if he didn't come to her tonight? What if seeing Isla reminded him of what he was missing? Of what she could never be?

Cassie bit down on her trembling bottom lip. She would *not* cry. He would come, she told herself. Though she tried to reassure herself of this, doubt kept rearing its ugly head. Isla had managed to plant a field of uncertainty in her.

A subtle shifting of the shadows snapped her head around. A cry of delight rose up in her throat; it strangled and died before she could release it. Devon sat outside her window, his emerald eyes eerily vivid in the glow of the half moon. Cassie was unable to move as she was captured by the mesmerizing beauty of him. She wasn't sure she was ready to hear the answers to her questions, and she certainly wasn't ready for their relationship to end tonight.

Gathering the last dregs of her remaining strength, she forced herself up from the bed. The window was unlocked, but she knew he wouldn't come in unless she let him in. Her hands shook as she slid the window up and stepped back to allow him access.

He hesitated for a moment before slipping as silently as a wraith inside. Her breath hitched, her fingers tingled, and it took all she had not to fling herself into his arms. He was the one she took solace in, in order to shut out the rest of the world. Now he was the one she was trying to shut out or at least shut out his past. But she couldn't continue to be an ostrich with her head stuck in the sand when it came to him.

She had been avoiding his past for too long, and tonight it had nearly cost them all their lives. No, no matter how much it upset her, and no matter how much she didn't like hearing it, she *was* finally going to hear it. She was going to be strong again, not the weakling she'd become and she was going to learn everything she could about him.

She opened her mouth and asked the first question that came to mind. "Who is Annabelle?"

CHAPTER EIGHTEEN

DEVON CLOSED his eyes as his hands twitched at his sides. He'd known this was coming, that one day she would speculate about his past. He'd just hoped it would be under better circumstances. Her pain and confusion beat at him with the force of a tsunami. He longed for nothing more than to take hold of her, pull her close, and ease the anguish he'd caused her. But he knew she wouldn't appreciate his touch now. He couldn't make the first move here; she would have to come to him. He just wasn't sure if she *would* come to him when he was done.

Devon opened his eyes. He'd fed well before coming here, but he wasn't sure it had been enough. This was going to be much more draining then the fight earlier. Her misty eyes held his, the violet within them stood out vividly to his heightened vision.

How did he tell her who Annabelle was without driving her further away? Without increasing the doubt and lack of self-confidence she radiated now? He decided to just rip the band-aid off and plunge in.

"Annabelle was a woman I was in love with."

She inhaled loudly and bit into her bottom lip hard enough to draw blood. Devon winced for her, it wasn't her physical pain, for she didn't feel *that*, but he could feel the twisting emotional agony wrenching through her. She didn't flinch though; her eyes didn't flicker. She remained as still as stone, and though she was only four feet away from him, it suddenly seemed like miles.

"Or at least I had thought I was."

His eyes latched onto the drop of blood quivering on her lip as she released it. Although he had glutted himself, he couldn't stop the thrill that shot through him. If she sent him out of here tonight it would destroy him, but if she didn't…

Well, if she didn't, he may well destroy them both. He didn't know which was worse.

Then he met her unwavering gaze again, and he knew. He could keep control of himself for her; he could do *anything* for her. To lose her would be a far worse torment than the ninth circle of hell. Yes, though it was the hardest thing he would ever do, he would stay by her, if she would still have him.

"What happened?" she asked.

"*I* happened." Confusion marred her brow. "Maybe you should sit."

She frowned at him, but she turned toward her bed. When she reached the bed she stopped but didn't sit. Instead, she turned back to him and hugged herself. She seemed to have forgotten to sit as she watched him from shadowed eyes. The subtle shifting of the trees outside cast shadows over her face and hair and hugged her lithe body.

"Go on," she encouraged.

Devon ran a hand through his disheveled hair, he tugged on it as he began to pace. "Annabelle was a simple farm girl when I met her."

"When did you meet her?" Cassie interrupted, her voice carrying a steel edge of resolve.

He stopped pacing to face her. "Over a hundred and fifty years ago."

Her eyes widened as she promptly made the connection to the time when he'd stopped feeding on, and killing, humans. "I see."

He saw the quick retreat she made as her walls slammed into place to keep her sheltered from pain. To keep her sheltered from him before he could shatter everything she was. Desperation seized hold of him as he was faced with the girl he had originally met. He couldn't be the one who drove her behind that wall of hopelessness and despair again as she simply waited to die.

"Annabelle was the oldest of seven children, a good girl who helped her mother take care of her younger siblings. I met her at a barn dance in Iowa. She was young, beautiful, and so very innocent and sweet." Cassie's head bowed as she squeezed her eyes shut. Devon clenched his teeth, his hands fisted at his sides as he realized he'd just described Cassie. Heedlessly he continued on, knowing his next words might drive her further away, but he had to get them out.

"And I wanted to destroy all of that."

Her head shot up as she frowned at him. "I don't understand."

No, there was no way she *could* understand what he'd once been. "I was a different person back then, Cass. I wasn't even a person. I was a monster. I lived to kill, to destroy. I lived for the thrill of the hunt and the game."

"Game?"

"Yes, it was all a game to me, and Annabelle was perfect for it.

She had no idea about the cruelty of the world, no idea of the monsters lurking within the shadows. Annabelle was sweet and she was in love with Liam, a boy just like her. I was driven to ruin that love. I was determined to have her for myself, simply because I couldn't have her. At first I tried to seduce her, tried to lure her away like I could with any other woman. She refused my advances, which only increased my interest in her. I convinced myself I was in love with her and I would never be happy without her. I became obsessed with her and the challenge she represented."

The tips of her lashes were silvery in the moonlight as she stared out the window. Her delicate jaw was set firmly as her nostrils flared. Though she remained unmoving, he could feel the distress she radiated. "So what did you do?" she asked.

"I spent a month trying to lure her away from Liam, but she was having none of it. Her mind and heart were filled with dreams of their future, their children, and *their* happiness. I hated him for it, and I was going to demolish that love no matter what it took." She looked back at him, but her eyes remained hooded and distant. "When it became apparent she would have none of me, I took her by force."

Cassie took a hasty step back. The back of her knee connected with the bed, her leg buckled, but she managed to stay on her feet. "Not like that Cassie," he gushed as he realized how the words had sounded. "I changed her. I thought if she became one of us she would want nothing to do with Liam, she would want *me*. I thought it would be wonderful to shatter her innocence and turn her into a monster.

"It was to be my greatest accomplishment."

"I see," Cassie said dully. "And once she became a monster you grew tired of her?"

Devon ignored the twinge of pain her words caused. He

deserved her contempt, he hated it, but he deserved it. He had been an awful *thing* back then. He'd relished the kill, savored every one of his victims and enjoyed the dying light in their eyes. Though he had tried to make up for his almost six hundred years of murder and mayhem, he knew he could *never* atone for the blood staining his soul. A soul only Cassie had managed to ease the torment of.

"No. Annabelle never became a monster."

"I don't understand."

"I didn't either," he admitted. "I thought once we were changed we all became monsters. I thought the demon took over and we had no choice but to torment and destroy humans before killing them. I never knew how wrong I was. Yes, Annabelle awoke with the same intense thirst all new vampires awake with, but she didn't go for humans.

"Somehow, she managed to keep enough reason through her transition, and enough restraint, to control her hunger, something even I, at my advanced age, had never done. I just took and killed, and took some more. But that night Annabelle did *not* kill, at least not humans anyway. I found her in a field of cows, half the herd had been slaughtered before her thirst was finally quenched. Animals are enough to keep us going, and strong, but it takes more of their blood to fully sate us."

Cassie nodded, but her hands were clenched on her arms so tightly she left bruises upon her fair skin. He yearned to go to her, to stop her from hurting herself, but he remained where he was. She would flee from him now. He was certain of it.

"I was mortified, and so unbelievably staggered to find her there among those *cows*, crying."

One of her eyebrows lifted inquisitively. "Why was she crying?"

Devon closed his eyes. The image of Annabelle, sitting in that field, surrounded by dead cattle with tears running down her blood streaked face had been seared permanently into his brain. Annabelle's delicate shoulders had shook; her hair had been caked with dirt and blood. He'd been so conflicted and confused by what she was doing. He hadn't been able to understand why she would choose such pitiful fare when there were so many delicious humans out there to enjoy. He had especially planned for her to go after Liam; he'd thought it would be great to watch her destroy the person she thought she loved so much. It would have been his crowning achievement in his mission to destroy anything good in the world.

"She was crying because she had killed the cows," he choked out. His voice was hoarse as the tidal wave of memories threatened to consume him. For years, he'd tried not to think about the monster he'd been back then, and especially what he'd done to Annabelle. What he had intended to be his crowning achievement had ended up becoming his ultimate downfall, or at least his downfall from the world of drudgery and murder.

"I didn't know how to react to that. I mean, who would cry over dead cows? And why was she feeding from damn *cows* when there were thousands of humans to destroy? I simply stood there, watching her, listening to her lament about killing them because the farmer wouldn't have enough milk and meat for his children now.

"She confounded me, but I found myself utterly fascinated by her. I had seen many *many* things in my lengthy life, but I'd never seen a vampire cry over their kill. I had never seen a vampire show regret for their actions. We didn't know what regret was, or at least that's what I'd believed.

"When she calmed down enough to actually speak, she looked up at me, not with accusation and hatred, but with a wealth of sadness and compassion. I had done this to her, and she was sad for *me*!" Devon began to pace restlessly as his skin crawled with the memories assaulting him. He hated the monster he'd been, hated the things he'd done. Annabelle had been the worst thing he'd ever done, but without her, he wouldn't be the man he was now. Without Annabelle he would still be a monster, preying on the innocent, and he wouldn't have Cassie.

If he still *did* have her.

"I sat down beside her, unable to move. The realization of what she was now was earth shattering to me. I had afflicted her with the demon, but her goodness had been so pure she was able to fight against the monster. She'd been out of her head with her compulsion for blood, but she still had enough control not to kill humans. I'd never met anyone like her, never met anyone with such a pure heart, until you."

Cassie's gaze blazed into his as tears swam in her eyes. She blinked them back, as a mask of remorselessness settled over her refined features. "I hated myself for what I had done to her, and I suddenly began to rethink my entire existence. I'd never been a good man when I was alive. I had been rich, spoiled, and hadn't cared who I hurt. As a vampire, I was the epitome of a monster, and I had reveled in it, until that moment.

"We sat silently in the field as she grieved the loss of her life, and I grieved for all the souls I'd extinguished, and there were so many of them. I've been trying to do right since that night, but I can never truly wash the blood from my hands, or from my soul."

He grew silent as he paced over to the window. The moon was beginning to set; the night was still except for a small fox creeping across Chris's front lawn. "What became of her?" Cassie inquired.

"She taught me how to control my appetite and showed me there was goodness in the world, something I'd never believed before her. It was easier to justify my actions if I thought everyone was just as evil as I was, whether they were human or vampire. I began to feed on animals, determined to try and change who I was. I had always loved a challenge, and this was the biggest one I'd ever accepted."

"And she grew to love you?"

He laughed shortly as he turned away from the window. "No, Annabelle never loved me in that way, it was always Liam. As I began to change, I realized I'd never loved *her* either. I was incapable of love at that time of my life. If I'd loved her, I never would have done that to her. What she felt for Liam was love. It was real, and it was *true*."

A single tear slid down Cassie's face. "And she lost him."

Devon managed a wry smile as he shook his head and ran a hand through his hair again. "No, I did manage to do one good thing back then. I convinced her to go to him, to approach him gradually so as not to scare him. Liam had never believed she'd just abandoned him and her family; he had always thought her dead. It took a couple years of coaxing, but eventually she went to him. I think, in the end, she went to him because of the grief Liam was still in over losing her. He'd never moved on, never found someone else, and had become a hollow shell of the man he'd once been.

"And when she went to him, when she told him, he didn't run screaming from her. He didn't shun her or turn her away. He accepted her." Cassie's tears rolled freely down her face now, Devon was certain she didn't realize she was crying. "He turned for her."

Her hair fell forward in a golden shield as her head bowed. "That was when I realized what love was. I'd been feeding from animals the whole time to prove to myself I could, I knew then I didn't have to be a monster. I had made the wrong choices when I was changed, but now I could do something to try and make up for it, and that was what I vowed to do.

"I stayed with them for a few more years, until I gained better control of myself. Unlike Annabelle and Liam, I knew the pleasure of human blood, and I knew the rush of power that came with it. It was tougher for me to resist temptation, but when I felt confident enough to go out on my own, I did so. They needed their time together, and I needed to start trying to make amends for my sins. I will continue to do so for as long as I exist."

Her heart was in her eyes as she stared at him. "I never experienced love until I met you Cassie. Annabelle showed me there was nobility in the world, but you brought me back to life. You showed me what it was to put someone ahead of myself, and to be willing to *die* for someone. You showed me what it was to truly love."

A sob escaped, her tears fell more rapidly, but she didn't come to him. No matter how much he wanted her forgiveness and understanding, she still wasn't ready to give it. No matter how difficult it had been to tell her about Annabelle, he knew there were worse atrocities in his past. Atrocities she may insist upon hearing about.

"And Elizabeth and Isla?"

Devon's hands fisted as he resumed pacing. Her questions were wandering closer to areas he didn't want to tell her about. She was getting dangerously close to Robert, the worst secret he harbored, and one he didn't intend for her to have any knowledge of. *Ever.*

"Elizabeth is the woman who changed me."

At Cassie's quick inhalation, he returned to the window and kept his back to her. How did he tell her about the bastard he'd been, before he'd become a vampire, and still look at her? He couldn't.

CHAPTER NINETEEN

CASSIE FOUGHT the urge to go to him as she stared at Devon's rigid back. Her hands itched to touch him to ease the self-loathing he radiated. But if she went to him now he would stop talking, and there would be no other chance for her to learn about him.

Though he may not like to remember these things, he had to talk about them, and he had to be forgiven for them afterward. He needed *her* forgiveness, and although she didn't know what was still to come, she knew he would receive it. This man before her was not the monster that had done these things.

This man was the one who cherished and loved her. With all the women in his past, and she was certain there were far more than these three, it was *her* he loved.

"I was born in Devonshire England, hence the name. I was the second son of a Duke. I was wealthy, spoiled, and without the added burden of being the first born that my brother Robert carried." Cassie frowned as bitterness crept into his tone at his brother's name. "Robert was serious, studious, smart, the apple of my father's eye, his one *true* son. I was a cast off, the one who would only count if something happened to Robert. I prayed everyday nothing ever *did* happen to him, for I wanted nothing to do with my father, or any of his responsibilities. I despised the man for his indifference, and hated him more for his cruelty."

He kept his gaze focused out the window, unwilling to turn back to her. His shoulders were stiff as anguish poured from him. Though she had asked for the truth, it wasn't worth this. These memories were destroying him. "Devon you don't have to do this, you…"

"Yes I do," he interrupted harshly. "You have to know. You have a *right* to know."

Cassie's mouth snapped shut, her stomach clenched as she slid onto the bed. "My father had what you would call anger issues. I cried out once and my mother came to my defense, she was punished for her insolence so I learned to take *every* beating in silence.

"When I turned eighteen I was eager to escape, desperate to be free, even if it was only to the university. Once free, I took refuge in the local taverns, drinking heavily, gambling, and… other things," he mumbled. His shoulders slouched as his head bowed. Cassie didn't have to hear what those other things were to know they were women. "I stopped going to school. I lost myself in every form of drudgery I could find, just hoping it would get back to my father. I didn't care if he disowned me, I'd discovered I had a talent with cards, and I was doing well supporting myself.

"Then I met Elizabeth. She was in one of the gaming halls I often visited. It was amazing to see her there, women weren't allowed into the clubs unless they were working them. Elizabeth was definitely *not* working this club, or at least she wasn't working it as one of the escorts. No one there seemed to know her, but they all fought to get closer to her, and no one asked her to leave.

"What none of us knew was that Elizabeth had discovered the men's gaming halls were a perfect way to make a lot of money. She could take it from anyone at anytime, and of course there was plenty of food for her there."

He rested his arm against the top of the window and leaned forward as he focused on the night. Though the tense quiet was killing her, Cassie remained silent. Devon was no longer with her, but trapped in a past he couldn't escape.

"I lusted after Elizabeth, but I wasn't like the other men, I didn't chase her around. I didn't throw money and jewels at her; I didn’t even buy her a drink. It aggravated her; she simply didn't understand how I was able to resist her. I still don't know how I did. For, although she was a vampire, I didn't feel the lure to her as strongly as other humans did.

"That factor, and that I wasn't a good human being to begin with, made her decide to change me. She enjoyed watching my antics, my drunken brawls, my inane lack of caring or respect for the human race. I was selfish and I was fascinating to her, and she thought I would make a spectacular addition to her race."

His arm dropped away from the sill. "She was right; I was a fine addition to the species. The transition was painful, but once complete I took to my new identity like a fish to water. Elizabeth showed me the way, teaching me to hunt wisely, not to get caught, and how to survive. I loved the death, the blood, the torture, and I relished in the power."

He became silent again. "What happened to her?" Cassie prodded when it appeared he wasn't going to say more.

Devon's back was straight as a rod. "She was killed in Prague by a group of Hunters about a hundred years later." Though he answered her, she sensed something more behind his words, but he was distressed enough without her picking at any more scabs. Elizabeth was dead, that part of his past wouldn't be showing up on her doorstep like Isla had.

Biting on her lower lip, her gaze shifted to the night beyond him. He talked about a couple hundred years as if it were nothing. To her, a couple of *years* were huge. To her, two years was almost a lifetime, never mind a hundred of them. Cassie shivered at the stark reminder of just how different their worlds were, and always would be, if she decided not to join him.

"I stayed alone for years, enjoying my solitude, and my life. When I met Julian I recognized the same kind of cruelty and depravity in him that resided in me. We got along well, destroyed so very many lives, and relished in inflicting as much cruelty as possible. We were always together until I met Annabelle."

"You're not like him," she whispered.

His head swiveled deliberately on his shoulders, his emerald eyes burned with intensity as they finally met hers. "Don't kid yourself Cassie; I was *exactly* like him. No, I was worse. I'm still capable of extreme acts of violence, especially when it involves keeping you safe," he grated.

Her heart kicked over, her eyes closed as pain swept through her. *Worse?* She tried to deny it, but she knew it was true. He'd been the epitome of a monster, there was no changing that and he still could be, she'd witnessed his brutality tonight. Goosebumps broke out on her arms as she shuddered again. "And Isla?" she choked out. She didn't really want to know, she was simply looking to change the subject.

"I met Isla in Rome, and I knew I had to have her. Isla enjoyed toying with men and wrapping them around her little finger before cutting them loose again. She thought she could play with me, but she had a rude awakening instead. As a human she was ruthless, manipulative, and beautiful. As a vampire she was a sight to behold. I changed her, *I* created her, because I wanted to see the amount of cruelty and death she could bestow upon the world. She was outstanding at it, exciting, fascinating."

Cassie was finding it damn near impossible to breathe as his lip curled and the gleam in his became vicious. He was trying to push her away, she realized with a start. He didn't feel as if he deserved her, and the more he relived his past, the more he hated himself. He was trying to push her away before she could take no more, and left him. That was *not* going to happen.

"Isla began to fancy herself in love with me, I didn't return the sentiment, but I did enjoy her company. Often."

Cassie winced, her nails dug into her skin at the bluntness of his words. She bit into her bottom lip in an attempt to keep from crying. "Stop," she whispered.

"Stop what? The truth?" he practically snarled.

Cassie was unable to stop the tremors wracking through her. "No, stop trying to push me away. Please Devon, I can take almost anything, but not that. Please."

"Cassie…"

"I understand about your past, I do," she interrupted. "But please just stop."

She never heard him move, didn't know he had until he was kneeling before her, his beautiful eyes lost and bleak. "I'm sorry Cassie, forgive me. Forgive me for everything."

Tears slid down her cheeks as she cupped his face and ran her thumb over the perfect contours she knew and loved. Pain had etched lines into his face that weren't normally there. He desperately needed her forgiveness, the desire for it burned in his eyes. But she wasn't the one who could give it to him.

"I cannot forgive you," she whispered. "You have done nothing to *me* to warrant my forgiveness. You are not a monster anymore Devon, you haven't been for years…"

"The women."

Cassie winced involuntarily. That was something she would have to work on in her own time, and in her own way. Her confidence had been rattled, her fears confirmed, but everything he was telling her, happened back then. And now… Now he was hers, and she was *not* going to let him go. "Devon I knew there were other women, I'm not a fool. You've been around for a while."

She managed a wry smile she didn't feel, but he needed her reassurance, and he needed her love. For him, she could do anything. "It's you who has to forgive yourself," she whispered.

His eyes were troubled and yet so very hopeful as he searched her face. "I don't deserve you."

"Yes, you do."

He seized hold of her hand and kissed it tenderly. Urgency radiated from him as love poured from his soul. Her breath was stolen from her as the influx of his desire beat against her. Tugging her toward him, he wrapped his hand around the back of her head and pulled her mouth to his.

His intensity overwhelmed her as his tongue swept in to take possession of her mouth. Reasonable thought fled as he invaded all of her senses and shattered her self-doubt and concerns. He rose up over her, pushing her back onto the bed, his firm body came down on top of hers. Cassie's heart hammered, her body tingled with excitement as his hands slid over her, and brought her body to electrified life. She'd never felt anything like this, never knew such exquisite pleasure could exist.

Her fingers dug into his hair as she pulled him more firmly against her. This was right, this was where she belonged, where she would always belong. Since the moment she'd met him, he'd owned her heart, body, and soul. He was her other half, the only one who could ever make her whole.

His kiss became almost painful in his desperation and need. His hands slid her baggy sweatshirt up to stroke over her skin. He caressed her tenderly as his fingers slid down to the waistband of her workout pants. Though she was swept away in a rising wave of passion and pleasure, a bolt of trepidation tore through her. She loved him, she truly did, but she wasn't ready for this. Not after *this* night, and not when she was still so rattled and shaken.

"Stop, Devon, wait," she managed to wheeze out. She tore her mouth from his, if she didn't stop this now, she never would. His body stilled against hers as his eyes became questioning. "I can't, I'm not ready." She shook her head, unable to meet his gaze again as humiliation burned through her. She was sure Isla had never told him no. Cassie shuddered at the thought. She was acting like a silly child, but she simply wasn't ready for this. "I'm sorry."

"Cassie, look at me. *Look* at me," he ordered again when she kept her gaze firmly planted on her bureau. Trying to keep her shaking under control, she met his gaze again. "I don't want to do anything you're not ready for. I've waited over seven hundred years for you, and I'll wait for you forever. When you are ready, I *will* be here Cassie. For you, I can do anything."

Muted sobs wracked through her as relief and love filled her. Rolling off of her, he pulled her against him and cradled her. She didn't doubt his words; she simply hoped she would be enough for him when the time came. That he wouldn't be disappointed in her. That he wouldn't compare her to *them*, and find her lacking. She also wished her doubts about changing for him weren't back, but she was frightened of his world, wary of the cruelty and deprivation filling it.

She rested her hand on his chest and curled her head into the hollow of his shoulder. She frowned when he seized hold of her hand and moved it to the other side of his chest. *This* was what he did every time she rested her hand over the spot where his heart should be beating, she realized. It was one of the reasons she'd never noticed his lack of a heartbeat before. Well, that and she'd been too infatuated with him to notice much of anything else.

But now, she noticed.

Tugging her hand free, she rested it back over his deadened heart. It was a little disturbing not to feel a heartbeat, but she loved him too much to care. "No," she whispered when he grasped for her hand again.

"Cassie," he groaned. "You shouldn't be constantly reminded of what I am."

She lifted her head to meet his gaze. "You're the person I love Devon, and I want to be reminded of that every second of the day."

His hand clenched around hers and pressed it against his silent chest. Cassie smiled as she bent to kiss him. She lost herself to the bliss he offered her.

DESPITE THE AWFUL events of the night, Cassie awoke in a surprisingly good mood. Devon's arm was draped over her; his face was slack and innocent as he slept. She dropped a kiss on his brow, and scooted carefully out of the bed so as not to wake him. Padding toward the bathroom, she pulled her bandages carefully off, glad to find the cuts were healing well.

She took a quick shower and changed into a pair of jeans and a Red Sox shirt, opting for comfy rather than stylish. It was Sunday after all. Her grandmother would already be making pancakes and sausages for them, and an egg white omelet for Melissa. Cassie was pulling out more bandages and antiseptic when a faint knock sounded on the door.

She pulled it open and smiled at the sight of Devon's tussled hair, and sleepy half smile. His green eyes perused her as an eyebrow quirked. "Adorable," he muttered.

Cassie felt her cheeks flush as she ducked her head. Noting the supplies on the sink, he came toward her and tenderly pulled her shirt up. His forehead furrowed, his eyes darkened as he studied the deep scratches on her side. "Almost completely healed," he mumbled, more to himself.

"Why do you sound so upset about? Shouldn't you be happy they're healing well?"

He glanced up at her. "Of course I'm happy, it's just surprising."

She wasn't fooled. His smile didn't make it to his eyes, nor did it ease the lines marring his brow. "I told you I heal fast."

"I know." He kissed her forehead gently. "Let me help you."

Taking hold of the peroxide, he began to work on the gashes. His touch was so wispy she barely felt it. Smoothing the bandages into place, he rose beside her. "How are the ribs?"

Cassie shrugged and prodded at the bruises already fading from her ribcage. The cracks were already healed, but the bone was still bruised, though not badly. "Much better," she assured him.

His eyes were still dark as his hands wrapped around her waist. "I have to go, but I'll be back in a little bit."

Cassie swallowed heavily; she hated to see him leave. "Be safe," she whispered.

"Always," he vowed and kissed her tenderly.

She watched as he slipped out the window and disappeared over the sill. She hummed to herself as she made her way down-stairs, practically skipping down the last set of steps. Chris was still lying on the couch with his arm tossed over his eyes in an attempt to block out the sunlight filtering through the windows.

"Good morning," she greeted cheerfully.

Lowering his arm, he stared skeptically at her. "Ugh," he grunted.

Cassie laughed happily and turned toward the kitchen. "Get up lazy butt!" she called over her shoulder.

The ring of the doorbell stopped her before she made it to the kitchen. She hurried to the door, surprised that Melissa and Luther had rung it, they usually just walked in. Shrugging, Cassie grasped hold of the handle as Chris bolted upright. He leapt to his feet and cleared the back of the couch in one fluid motion.

"Cassie no!" he barked.

But it was too late. She already had the door open, and what was standing on the other side was something far worse than she ever could have imagined.

CHAPTER TWENTY

Why didn't she smell pancakes cooking? And the sausage should be frying by now. She should be able to smell the mushrooms, green peppers, and onions that would be sautéing for Melissa's omelet. But why didn't she smell them? It was pancake Sunday, and next Sunday was Belgium waffles, but for some reason the pancakes weren't cooking right now.

Had her grandmother slept in? No, wait, she never slept in, she was always up early, humming and dancing around the kitchen as she cooked. Cassie's gaze darted to the driveway. Where was the little red Mustang? Her grandmother's baby, her one luxury. It was always parked *right* there, gleaming and shiny because it was waxed and washed at least twice a week. Her grandmother loved to ride around town with the top down, and the wind blowing her strawberry hair back as she blasted the radio.

Where was the car?

There was a thrumming vibe in her eardrums that blocked out all sound, all reason. She turned back to the people before her and the buzz instantly increased in her head. It sounded like a swarm of bees had encircled her, but they would be preferable to the people on her doorstep. They were speaking, or at least the woman was, but she couldn't hear them. She knew the woman was speaking though, because she could see the woman's lips moving, even if there was no sound.

Cassie's gaze returned to the empty driveway again, then back into the house. She inhaled deeply once more, but still no smell drifted to her. She didn't want to look at the people before her again, but she knew she had to. She didn't want to hear what they had to say, because with heart wrenching certainty she already knew what those words would be, and they would *destroy* her.

Chris moved into the doorway of the living room, his broad shoulders were slumped, his sandy blond hair disheveled from sleep. His eyes were filled with a sadness so profound it pierced Cassie's heart, and ripped her from the blanket of denial and shock she had wrapped herself in. Tears already shimmered in the sapphire depths of Chris's eyes as they met hers. Of course he would know what they were saying. He'd known before she'd opened the door, and he didn't have bees buzzing in his head.

He had told her not to open it, why hadn't she listened?

Sluggishly turning back around, her gaze focused on the well built woman before her. Though she looked severe and professional, her brown eyes were sympathetic. The man beside her was young, the freckles on the bridge of his nose stood out starkly against his pallor. He appeared to be new on the job, and it was obvious he was uncomfortable here.

"Are you Cassandra Fairmont?" the woman inquired, probably for the third or fourth time.

A pounding on the stairs momentarily drew all of their attention. Dani froze three feet from the bottom, her mouth dropped as her eyes shot to Cassie, and then around the house. Tears spilled down her cheeks and dropped from her chin.

Cassie shuddered as cold swept through her veins and turned her entire body into a block of ice. She was certain she would never be warm again. Swallowing heavily, she turned back to the police officers on her doorstep. Devon appeared behind them, his shoulders were set as if he were about to receive a blow.

The presence of the officers must have stopped him from leaving as he'd proposed. Though his black hair was still a tumbled mess, he was the most handsome man she had ever seen. For a brief moment, feeling returned to her numbed limbs, but it was promptly doused by the tidal wave of pain coursing through her. She couldn't look at him anymore, she couldn't bear to.

"Yes, I am," she felt like a robot as she choked the words out.

The woman nodded as her hands clenched upon the hat she held before her. "May we come in?"

Cassie looked up at the clear blue, completely out of place sky. It should be gray, stormy, with no hope radiating from its rolling dark clouds. The birds shouldn't be singing. Nothing should be happy today, *everything* should stop. The world simply just had to stop spinning so she could curl up in a ball somewhere and shut out everything around her. How could she be in this much pain and nothing around her was stopping to acknowledge it?

"How?" she managed to croak out through her numbed, raw throat.

"Excuse me?" the woman inquired in surprise.

Cassie's focus sharpened on her, her eyes narrowed as a wash of molten lava began to burn through the pain enshrouding her body. "How did she die?" she grated. The hand clenching on the door handle nearly ripped it free.

The officers exchanged a brief, startled glance. They were

probably used to people breaking down into tears, not glaring at them as if they were Satan himself. They sure as shit weren't used to people asking them how their loved ones had died. "Miss, if we could please come inside," the woman prodded.

"How did my grandmother die?" Cassie demanded.

"Cassie, don't." Chris walked over and rested his hand reassuringly on her shoulder. She glowered at him as she shrugged his hand off. He looked as if she'd slapped him, but he made no move to touch her again as she turned back to the police officers.

The woman nodded briskly. "I'm afraid your grandmother was in an accident. We found her car early this morning. It appears she swerved to avoid hitting something."

Cassie's` mind tripped over the words. A car accident? No, impossible. No accident had taken her grandmother from her. "I want to see her."

"Excuse me?" the younger officer blurted.

"I want to see my grandmother's body," she enunciated clearly.

"Miss, I don't think that's a good idea," he gushed.

His partner shot him a silencing look, but she looked extremely discomfited by Cassie's request also. "Miss, your grandmother has already been identified by dental records and her license; there is no reason for you to…"

"I have a *right* to see her," she interjected stridently.

"Yes, but…"

Cassie turned away and grabbed her shoes from the hall closet. She didn't care what else they had to say, she *was* going. Come hell or high water, she was going to see her grandmother. She didn't care she didn't have socks on as she slipped her feet into her sneakers. Seizing hold of her coat, she turned back to the officers.

"Where is she?"

"Miss…" The woman broke off as Cassie gazed at her fiercely.

There would be no dissuading her, and although the woman officer didn't like it, she wasn't going to argue any further. "We'll take you over," she volunteered.

"Follow me over," she said to Chris, not bothering to look at him as she pounded down the stairs after the officers.

Devon moved to stop her, but she sidestepped him easily, as she shot him a dark look. Keeping her head high, she slid into the backseat of the police car and didn't look back as the cruiser pulled out of the drive. Chris and Devon hurried to their cars and fell in behind the cruiser.

Cassie didn't see anything on the ride, nothing registered past the haze surrounding her. Fury hummed through her veins, pain constricted her chest in a vice grip. She could barely breathe, and she found herself not caring. She would be ok if all movement, all functions of survival simply shut down. She already felt partially shut down, she felt cold, and hollow, and numb. If her grandmother could no longer breathe, no longer see this world, then why should *she* still be able to? Cassie shuddered, her fingers dug into her legs as she tried to think past the anguish consuming her.

The world went by in a blur as they drove to the hospital. Upon arrival, Cassie found herself moving through a thick fog as she followed the officers into the lower level of the building. She barely acknowledged Chris and Devon following behind her as she made her way through the sterile, dimly lit halls.

"Wait here," the woman said briskly and left them standing outside a set of double doors.

Cassie's hands fisted at her sides as she stared at the thick steel doors. Devon and Chris didn't try to approach her again. They seemed to realize she needed her own space right now, she couldn't handle it if they tried to hover. She didn't know how much time passed by the time a young, dark haired man in a lab coat stepped out of the double doors. His dark gaze ran over the three of them before settling on Cassie. "Miss, I…"

"I am going to see my grandmother." She wasn't willing to listen to another person trying to dissuade her from her course.

He licked his lips nervously before nodding. "Ok miss, but I must warn you there is some damage to the body."

Cassie shuddered, her eyes closed as a small moan escaped her. The body? The *body*! The woman in there was not a *body*, she was her *grandmother*! But as the words raced through her mind, she knew they weren't true. What was inside that room wasn't her grandmother; what was in there was only the shell of the person who had taken care of her, and raised her with so much love and tenderness.

Inside that room was the only blood family Cassie had ever known and who had loved her unconditionally. For a moment she wavered, uncertain if she could do this but the sting of her loss dwindled in the face of the thick haze of rage suddenly encompassing her. If she stayed angry, then she didn't have to face anything. If she stayed angry, she could make it through this, and she wouldn't turn into a blubbering mess on the floor.

She owed it to her grandmother to stay strong. She owed it to her grandmother to learn the truth, and to get justice for the atrocity that had been committed last night. She owed it to her grandmother to see her killer was *destroyed.*

"I want to see," Cassie managed to choke out.

The man nodded, but his eyes shot nervously to Chris and Devon. It was more than apparent he hoped they would step in to try and change her mind. "Cassie," Devon said as he touched her arm.

Her lip curled as she jerked back from him. Suffering filled his emerald eyes, as worry and love radiated from him. Again, Cassie felt herself wavering in the face of his love. She opened her mouth to speak as her heart flipped in her chest. Devon could make this a little better, in his arms she could find the shelter she sought, the protection and love she so desperately needed right now.

In his arms, she wouldn't hurt so badly.

She took a small step toward him before fully recalling why she was here. She couldn't continue to hide behind him; she had to face this head on. Her grandmother had sacrificed so much for her, had kept her alive when many others had been killed. Yet Cassie had been curled up in Devon's arms last night, hidden from the world, while her grandmother was being terrorized and murdered.

Hatred swamped her, disgust and self loathing consumed her. Her grandmother deserved far better than what Cassie had given her. Tearing her arm away from Devon, she took a shuddery breath as she tried to get air past the intense pressure in her chest. "Don't," she snarled.

His hand fell away, he looked quickly to Chris, but Chris wisely chose not to try and dissuade her. "Let me see my grandmother now."

The man's dark eyes slid once more to Chris and Devon, but when they showed no signs of helping him, his shoulders slumped in defeat. "Please follow me," he said.

Cassie followed behind him. The stench of the astringent chemicals barely registered in her mind as she slowly moved forward. Her life would never be the same.

The man paused outside another door and slid his keycard through the machine next to the door. The doors opened with a low whoosh. Fluorescent light filtered on in the room, illuminating the tile and cold floor and the sheet covering the table in the middle. Her heart hammered at the realization her grandmother lay under that sheet.

No, not her grandmother, the *body* lay under that sheet.

Her fingers dug into the flesh of her arms as she hugged herself. She thought her bones might fracture from the uncontrollable shaking of her body. The man briefly glanced back at Cassie before he gradually pulled the sheet back. Chris gasped before turning away. Cassie remained unmoving as her gaze became riveted on the side of her grandmothers face. She'd been so pretty, so full of life and cheer and love. Now, her delicate features were marred by bruises, and a large bump had formed in the center of her forehead. Scratches and cuts spoiled what had once been smooth porcelain skin, but that skin was now tinted a bluish gray color. Her lips had been leached of color and were nearly as white as the walls surrounding them.

It was only a body, Cassie told herself repeatedly. Her grandmother was free now; her spirit was keeping company with the ghosts she'd spoken to in life. Though Cassie tried to convince herself of this, she found no comfort in those thoughts. There was no solace to be found in the knowledge her grandmother was free.

Though she dreaded stepping any closer to the body, she knew she must. Moving stiffly forward she paused next to the metal table her grandmother lay upon. For a moment Cassie expected her eyes to open, and a radiant smile to spread across her face as she launched up and yelled surprise. It would scare the crap out of her, but Cassie found she wanted nothing more than exactly that to happen.

But as she stood there, staring down at her grandmother's prone form, she began to realize she would never see her grandmother's sky colored eyes again. Pain blazed forth again as tears burned her eyes and the hard lump in her throat made it difficult to breathe. With trembling fingers, Cassie touched her grandmother's cheek. Her skin was cold and unyielding. Cassie nearly buckled as agony swamped her. It was sheer strength of will keeping her standing and breathing.

With trembling hands, she brushed back her grandmother's strawberry blond hair. Two jagged tears marked her grandmother's neck, they were wounds that could easily be explained by the accident. But Cassie wasn't fooled into thinking the accident had caused them. No, she knew exactly what monster had put those marks upon her grandmother.

Her hands clenched upon the table, rage slid through her with the force of molten lava. It burned away everything she was and left only a pile of smoldering ashes in place of the person she'd once been.

CHAPTER TWENTY-ONE

DEVON STOOD by feeling completely helpless. He wished he could do something for her, but this was something she had to do on her own. Something she had to come to terms with in her own way. Unfortunately, her way seemed to be the most difficult way possible, and there was nothing he could do to stop it.

Cassie's hands shook as she pushed aside her grandmother's hair, her pain and suffering beat against him in rolling waves that made it difficult for him to think. Chris was deathly pale; his lips were white as he watched Cassie. Though Devon could sense Cassie's torment, Chris seemed to be swamped by it, unable to escape from the emotions she emitted. Her mourning was so intense Chris couldn't turn his telepathic ability off to it.

Chris briefly met Devon's gaze, his sapphire eyes shimmered with unshed tears. He'd also lost the woman who had helped to raise him, a woman who had loved him when his own mother couldn't, or wouldn't. Devon slowly turned back to Cassie. Her eyes remained locked on the condemning marks on her grandmother's neck.

Devon's skin prickled as tingling waves of fury and hatred blasted from her. Chris took an involuntary step back, and his head bowed beneath the force of the emotions battering against him. "Cassie," Devon breathed.

This was Cassie, *his* Cassie, sweet, innocent, and so achingly lovely and loving. She didn't know how to hate. Or at least she hadn't before now. But he could feel her hate blazing against him, suffusing her, and leaving her shaken and shattered. Her head bent, her golden hair cascaded forward as her slender back heaved with the force of her breaths.

Though she didn't want his comfort right now, he no longer cared. She was going to get it. He couldn't leave her to face this alone. Striding purposely forward, he rested his hands on her shoulders, as he tried to help ease her pain and anger.

She remained immobile for a moment. Then, she turned suddenly, and pulled free of him as she spun away. "*Don't* touch me!" she snarled. Her hands fisted at her sides as she glared at him with antipathy. Her reaction stunned him, but it was what he'd seen in her eyes that left him immobile and terrified. "Don't you *ever* touch me again! This… this is *your* fault!"

Dismay tore through him as he instinctively took a step toward her again. He ached to console her, to make this a small bit better if he could. He also had to protect her from what he was beginning to fear may lurk inside of her. Something he'd been trying to deny about her, but now realized it was likely true.

"Stay away from me." Her voice broke, her body shuddered. "You helped create that monster. He's here because of *you*! Not us, but *you*! He killed her, and it's *your* fault!"

Devon felt as if he'd been punched in the gut. She'd forgiven him for so many things, loved him through them all, but this…

Well this had been the final straw. She'd been broken; there was no more forgiveness in her. Her beautiful azure, amethyst eyes darkened, her small hands fisted at her sides as her shoulders shook.

Though it didn't beat, he could feel his heart shattering, could feel the darkness swamping up within him as it tried to consume him. Without her, his life meant nothing. He could feel the monster inside of him turning, twisting to break free, trying to use this as its opportunity to take control once more and return to its killing, wanton ways. Return to slaughtering innocents in its quest to satisfy its unending thirst.

Devon shuddered, his eyes closed as he strived to maintain control of his own body. No matter what Cassie felt for him now, he could not return to the *thing* he'd once been. If she didn't love him anymore there was nothing he could do about it. But she did *need* him. He had to protect her, and keep her safe. Julian and Isla were still out there, and they would use any opportunity they could to get at her, to destroy her and her friends. If he lost control, she would be vulnerable to them. No matter what happened, he knew he couldn't exist in a world where Cassie didn't.

He focused on the body in the middle of the room. He should have seen this coming. He'd been so wrapped up in trying to keep Cassie, Chris, and Melissa safe he hadn't thought about Lily. But she'd been a prime target also. Despite her age, she was also a Hunter, and she was Cassie's grandmother.

Julian would try to break Cassie. He would toy with and torment her before killing her, and Lily was the perfect way to do so. Julian had touched Cassie, he would know about Lily, and how much Cassie cared for her. How had he not seen this coming? Self loathing washed over him as his hands fisted.

Cassie spun away from him, her still damp hair whipped out behind her. "Take me home."

Chris gaped at her. "Cassie, don't do this." The words were choked out of him; his voice was hoarse with pleading and sorrow as his eyes focused on Devon.

Cassie was fairly spitting with vehemence. "Take me home!"

"Cassie…"

She stormed out the door, leaving them both gaping after her. Devon was the first to recover. "Go," he said gruffly.

"Devon…"

"Go." It killed him to send another man with her, even if it was Chris, but he couldn't go with her, and she needed protection. If he insisted on trying to get closer to her again, he may very well push her over the edge. He ached to be the one comforting her, but it wasn't to be. Agony twisted through him, but he remained immobile as his gaze clashed with Chris's grief-stricken one. "Go."

Chris shook his head. "She'll come around, she's just…" He broke off as he ran a hand through his already disheveled hair. "Well, I don't know what she is right now. That's not Cassie."

No, it wasn't Cassie, Devon knew that. What he didn't know was whether Cassie would come back to them, or if her heartache and rage would consume her. "You have to go Chris. She needs someone right now."

Chris's gaze flitted to him and then back to the doorway. Not only was Chris dealing with his own pain, but Devon's and Cassie's were beating against him, tearing down his walls, and pulverizing his soul. Finally, he settled on Devon again. "I'll talk to her."

"It won't help, not now." Chris opened his mouth and then closed it again. "Go."

"I'm sorry," he whispered. Ducking his head, Chris moved out the door with his broad shoulders slumped in defeat.

Devon wanted more than anything to follow after him, to follow after her. He turned back to the body, to Lily. Her face was still uncovered, her lips pale, and her skin the color of death. Yet she somehow she still looked refined, elegant.

Moving over to her, he clasped hold of her cold, rigid arm. There had been so much life and love inside of her. She had been so accepting of him. She'd never turned against him, even when the others, including Cassie, had been distrustful of what he was. He'd seen many dead bodies in his life, but this was the first one that truly upset him. Not only because it had caused Cassie so much pain, but also because he had truly liked the woman too.

"I'll take care of her," he promised her.

Lifting the sheet, he placed it smoothly back over her. There was a knot in his chest, an aching loss he wasn't sure he could survive. He'd lost the only thing that mattered to him, the only person he'd ever truly loved.

Yet, he couldn't acknowledge the loss, not now. There was too much he had to deal with. The first of which was what he'd seen in Cassie's eyes just moments ago. There had been something about her he'd been trying to puzzle out for the past few weeks. Something about her abilities, or lack thereof, that had been nagging at him. There were so many things that didn't make sense; he just hadn't known who to turn to in order to help him figure it out.

Now, he did.

Turning from the morgue, Devon made his way outside. The sun's rays did little to warm him as he made his way toward his car. Hitting the alarm button, he threw the driver's side door open and slid inside. He drove unhurriedly through the winding back streets as he tried to puzzle out everything that had just happened. The flash of red he'd seen in Cassie's eyes haunted him as he made his way toward Luther's house.

~

THE HAZY FOG of anger enshrouding Cassie was a welcome relief to the agony threatening to rise up and consume her. She couldn't escape the image of her grandmother's face, so cold and almost unrecognizable. Where was her smile, the light in her eyes? Where was the welcoming, loving hug she gave so easily?

Gone. Forever.

Neither could she forget the haunted, tortured look in Devon's eyes when she'd turned against him. She briefly wavered in her determination, and then the rage snapped back into place. There was no room for regret in this new world of hers, no room for wavering. There was only room for *revenge*, and she wanted that more than anything else right now.

Including Devon.

"Cassie…"

"I'm not going to talk about it." She abruptly cut Chris off. She didn't require any sympathy or reason right now. She didn't want love anymore. It only left her vulnerable, open to loss and pain. It was something she'd known before Devon arrived, something she'd lived by. But he had made her forget about it, for a little while anyway. Today she had been forcefully reminded. Today she had been slapped in the face with it.

Devon had made her love, and hope, and dream again. Those were things she knew were perilous, but she'd been unable to stop herself from doing them in his presence. He had opened her up, left her exposed, and she hated him for that. She *hated* him for making her forget about the pain and death encompassing her life. If he hadn't arrived, then none of this would have happened. Julian wouldn't be here without Devon, and Cassie would have been better prepared for the loss of her loved ones. The loss of her grandmother still would have crippled her, but it wouldn't have devastated her to this degree. It wouldn't have shattered her in this way.

But Devon had come and now she was an empty shell of the person he'd made her. There was no room for hope and love in her anymore. Not when revenge was consuming her. Fisting her hands, Cassie stared unseeingly out the window. She *would* find Julian and she would destroy him or at the very least, she would die trying.

She just had to make sure she took that monster with her when she went. Chris turned into her driveway and parked beside Luther's car. Cassie stared silently at the small cape style house. It had always seemed so welcoming and homey before. Now it was foreign, alien; cold. How could it be a home when the person who had made it such was gone? It couldn't.

It wasn't her home anymore, but that didn't matter as she didn't plan on living here for much longer. Chris turned toward her, his eyes weary and troubled. She didn't meet his gaze, she simply couldn't. He'd always been more like a brother than just her friend, and she didn't want to love him anymore. If something happened to him too…

Cassie shut the thought down. If something happened to him, she would deal with it. She would survive it. It would *not* destroy her.

Although, it would. No matter how much she told herself it wouldn't, Chris's death would level her. Cassie shuddered as her tears nearly choked her. What had she done? What was she becoming?

Her head bowed as her shoulders heaved. Chris tried to touch her but she jerked away from him. His touch would unravel her completely. She couldn't fall apart, not here, not now. There was some*thing* that had to die first.

Chris's hand hung briefly in the air before falling back to his side. Forcing her walls up once more, Cassie shoved the door to his beat up Mustang open. Climbing from the car, she marched up the walkway, climbed the stairs, and pushed the door open. The house was just as wintry inside as it had appeared outside. Melissa, Dani, and Luther were gathered in the living room. Their heads shot up as she stormed into the foyer. Chris dejectedly trudged in behind her.

Dani and Melissa were huddled on the couch; they hastily wiped the tears away from their reddened cheeks when they saw her. Luther was in his customary spot by the fireplace mantel with his arm resting on top of it. Though he wasn't currently crying his eyes were bloodshot and swollen as well. Melissa hurried toward her, strands of hair clung to her face as she held out her arms. Melissa reached for her, but Cassie took a hasty step back.

"Don't," she ordered briskly.

Melissa's hands fell to her sides, as confusion marred her pretty features. Luther and Dani had also started to come forward, but they both stopped only feet behind Melissa. "Cassie…"

"Did you see this coming?" Cassie demanded her voice strained and almost unrecognizable.

Melissa's mouth dropped. She glanced briefly at Chris, who still hung back, looking more like a kicked puppy than the man Cassie knew so well. He gave an almost imperceptible shake of his head that caused the fire inside of Cassie to flame higher. "Did you?" Cassie fairly barked.

"No!" Melissa cried. "No Cassie of course not, if I had I would have stopped it…"

"You couldn't have stopped it, *we* couldn't have stopped it. There was no stopping it. There is no stopping any of it."

The four of them stared at her in disbelief. "We could have helped, somehow," Melissa whispered.

"There *is* no help."

Cassie rested her hand on the banister as she made her way upstairs. She had to take inventory of her weapons, make sure she was well supplied and everything was in condition for a fight. She would need them when she went hunting later.

"Cassie, where is Devon?"

She turned back at Luther's question. "No longer welcome in this house."

The only thing that broke the profound silence was the chiming of her grandmother's cherished grandfather clock. Cassie shuddered as she climbed the stairs, she ignored the eyes she could feel boring into her back as she made her way to her room.

CHAPTER TWENTY-TWO

DEVON SLID down in his seat, and his eyes fixed on the house across the street. He should have known Luther and Melissa wouldn't be here. Of course they would be with Cassie. But that was ok; he was willing to wait for as long as it took. He just hoped Melissa didn't come back with Luther. This wasn't something he wished to discuss in front of her.

Sliding lower in his seat, Devon tried to keep his mind off of Cassie and the events at the mortuary. He didn't think he could stand to lose her, but he had, and though he felt empty and hollow, he couldn't help but question if it was for the best. There was the obvious threat Julian and Isla represented, but *he* was also a danger to her. He could control himself around her, for now, but he wasn't sure for how much longer. It was something he'd realized a few weeks ago, when he'd accepted what she was to him. He'd known they would either have to end it, or eventually she would have to join him. Neither option had appealed to her, but in the end she would have chosen life, a family, and humanity over darkness and death.

Over *him*.

And who could blame her? Certainly not him, but he hadn't been ready to lose her just yet. More time together might have made it easier for him to release her. Even as he thought it, he knew he was lying to himself. It never would have been easy to release her, and more time together would have made it worse.

Neither man nor monster could have let her go without a fight.

When all of this was over, he would have to get as far from her as possible if he was going to avoid changing her by force. He could still take her, he could make her stay with him, and the monster inside of him was very tempted by the notion. The man knew it would be the worst thing he could ever do to her. She would hate him, she would never forgive him. He would lose her forever.

You could keep control of her mind, a little voice inside him whispered. *Keep her as yours, make her love you again.*

Devon shuddered, both excited and appalled by the thought. Yes, he could do that, but she wouldn't be *his* Cassie, and though he could make her love him again, it would never be the same. It would never be the love she'd so easily and trustingly given to him before. It would be a forced love and it would be fake. He would rather live without her than force that upon her.

Shifting uncomfortably, Devon's hands clenched on the wheel as sorrow swelled within him. He had to get his mind off of his thoughts; he would go crazy if he didn't. He may very well break if he continued to sit here and obsess over his misery.

A Toyota Camry rolled by. Relief filled Devon as he was offered the diversion he'd been looking for as Luther swung into his driveway and parked the car. Devon's eyes narrowed as he searched the shadowed interior, he was relieved to discover Melissa wasn't present. Luther sat in the car for a few moments, his hands gripping the wheel as his head bowed in grief. Devon had intended to wait for him to get out of the car first, but he was restless and had waited long enough.

Opening his car door, Devon made his way across the street at an easy lope. Luther's head shot up, and he jumped in his seat when Devon tapped on the driver's side window. Quickly rolling down the window he stared at Devon through bloodshot, swollen eyes. The clear gray of them was emphasized by the glasses perched precariously on the tip of his nose.

"Devon," he greeted gruffly.

"I have to talk to you."

Luther sighed heavily and dropped his head. "I can't change her mind Devon, I wish I could, but I can't. God how I wish I could," he muttered as his gaze drifted to his closed garage doors. From what Cassie had told him that was often where they held their training sessions.

Devon swallowed heavily, his muscles constricted in his chest. "I'm not here for that. Changing her mind won't happen." Devon didn't add he was trying to make himself believe this was for the best.

It took a moment for his words to sink in; Luther's gaze came back to him as his eyebrows drew questioningly together. "I don't understand. Why are you here then?"

"There are some things that have been bothering me, about Cassie. I'd like to discuss them with you."

Luther's eyes darkened as deep lines creased his brow. Devon felt guilty about adding more to the man's troubles, but he was the only one who might have answers for him. "Um, yes, yes of course."

Devon stepped back as Luther pushed his door open and dropped his keys. Instinctively Devon caught them before they hit the ground. Luther's eyes widened, his mouth parted slightly as he met Devon's gaze. Devon was slightly offended by the alarm flitting through Luther's eyes, but he understood it. He *was* frightening, and without Cassie he was highly unstable, and Luther knew that. Luther also had no way of knowing why Devon had arrived on his doorstep. Devon handed the keys back and managed a small reassuring smile in an attempt to ease the man's fears.

"Thanks," Luther murmured.

He slid from the car and walked briskly up the brick walkway to the front door. Balancing the screen door with his hip, Luther unlocked then opened the door. "I hope you don't mind if I pack a few things while we talk. I think it best if Melissa and I stay with Cassie for a bit."

He said all of this as he disappeared inside, and flicked on switches as he hurried down the hall. Devon stopped at the doorway, unable to go further as Luther disappeared around the corner, still talking as if Devon was behind him. Leaning against the door jam, he speculated about just how long it would take the distracted man to realize he was talking to himself now.

Not long as Luther's head reappeared in the hallway, a questioning look on his features. "I can't come in unless I'm invited," Devon reminded him.

Luther looked completely flustered as he hurried back down the hall. "Oh of course, where is my head? Come in, come in."

Devon stepped easily through the doorway as Luther went in the opposite direction he'd gone before. Devon shook his head, faintly amused by the scatterbrained way Luther scurried about. He followed Luther down another hall as he threw on more lights before stepping into a large study stacked floor to ceiling with books. At least twenty bookcases lined the walls, but they weren't enough to hold the vast quantity. The excess tomes had spilled onto the floor, parts of the couch, and the large desk in the middle of the room. Devon couldn't begin to guess at the number of books filling the room.

Most had faded bindings and yellowed pages. A musty scent hung heavily in the air. Other than the lamp on the desk, and the fixture overhead, no other illumination spilled into the room. That was largely due to the thick drapes drawn over the two windows behind the desk.

Seeing the room, Devon knew he'd come to the right place. If Luther didn't know what was happening, then surely one of these books could explain it. "I just have to grab a couple of volumes." Luther was searching the shelves as he spoke, his finger ran rapidly over the bindings. "What's on your mind?"

Devon would have preferred to have Luther's full attention, but it was more than obvious the man was discombobulated and distracted right now. Besides, he didn't think it would be long before he did have Luther's undivided attention. He began to tell Luther about all the bits and pieces he'd picked up about Cassie. The better than normal hearing, the above average eyesight, her exceptional healing ability. The immense speed and strength she possessed that far surpassed Chris and Melissa's, or any other Hunter Devon had ever seen.

All of which had been explained by her not possessing special abilities. Whereas most Hunter's powers had been filtered into extrasensory powers, Cassie's abilities were more centered upon fighting and killing. She hated it, but couldn't deny it. The others were also above human in their strength, speed, and healing, but they weren't nearly as strong in those areas as Cassie was. In fact, Cassie's abilities were so acute, they almost bordered on being as finely honed as his. Something that shouldn't have been possible considering she was very much alive.

Then, finally, he told Luther about the red he'd seen in her eyes at the morgue, the red that had finally brought him here. The color never should have been present in her amazing eyes. Not unless she was a vampire, or unless there was something else going on within her. Something that none of them knew about, maybe even something that had never occurred in the history of the Hunter line before.

The thought scared him more so than living without her for an eternity. He could keep her safe from the hazards of the outside world, but he was greatly afraid there may be something he couldn't keep her safe from. Herself.

"What are you saying?"

Luther had slid onto the corner of his desk, one of the few spots not already occupied. Clutched loosely in his hand, seemingly forgotten, a book dangled from his fingertips. Devon had been right; he *did* have Luther's full attention now. "What happened to the other Hunter's like Cassie, the ones who didn't have any abilities?"

Luther frowned as he slipped off his glasses and rubbed the bridge of his nose. "I don't know. There were only a handful of them over the years. I suppose, like all Hunter's, they met their end while fighting. Do you suspect something different?"

Devon ran his hand through his hair as he began to pace. There was far too much pent up energy inside of him, he didn't know what to do with it all. The more he paced the more restless he felt. "I suspect somewhere along the way something did happen to at least one of them."

Luther pondered his words as he remained unmoving on the edge of the desk. "Like what?"

"Her eyes were *red* Luther."

"The lights maybe."

"I know what I saw," Devon told him. "Something isn't right; she's not like the others."

"No, she's not, but that doesn't mean…"

"*None* of the others," he interrupted harshly. "I've come across many Hunters in my time, but *none* like her. You have to find out what happened to the others without abilities. I suspect there is more to it than just her enhanced speed, healing, and senses."

Luther slid his glasses back on. "You think it's manifested in a different way?"

"I do."

Luther placed the book on the desk and leaned forward as he pinched the bridge of his nose. "I think you may be right."

Devon stopped pacing and turned sharply toward him. He'd hoped Luther believed him, but he now realized he'd fully expected to be turned away. "You do?"

Luther nodded. "Yes, the power inside of Cassie is far stronger than the others. It's much stronger then *she* realizes. I've feared for a while it may be too much for her to handle, though it never occurred to me it might manifest in the way you're suggesting. But we can't be positive your theory is correct either. Not until we find out about the others like her, and then we'll go from there."

"You want my help in this?" Devon was unable to keep the shock from his voice.

Luther managed a wry grin. "I doubt you're going anywhere until Isla and Julian have been taken care of."

"No, I'm not," Devon answered firmly.

"Good. She may not be willing to admit it right now, but Cassie needs you, and hopefully by the time this is all settled she'll come to her senses about that."

Devon folded his arms over his chest as he studied the smaller man. "You don't blame me for bringing Julian and Isla here?"

"No." Luther slid off the desk and pulled his glasses off to clean them again. "I don't blame you; the three of them would have come up against monsters such as these eventually. The only difference is they would have been killed without you. This wasn't your fault, Cassie will realize that soon."

Luther said the words, but he didn't sound convinced of them and neither was Devon. They both knew that she was stubborn, and right now she was also lost and livid and devastated. "Until that happens, I have a feeling you'll require something to keep you busy." Luther gestured around the room. "We'll start here; I know a fair amount of these books, but certainly not all of them. If the answers aren't here, then we'll start to look elsewhere. The others can't know about this right now. There's no reason to concern them when we're not certain if there's anything to find."

"I understand."

Devon glanced around the room; the books would definitely keep him occupied. Even if they didn't keep his mind completely off of Cassie, at least he would have a mission, something to do, something to accomplish. He was frightened that if they didn't find a solution soon, it would only be a matter of time before they ran out of time and the answers slapped them all in the face.

CHAPTER TWENTY-THREE

CHRIS SAT RIGIDLY in the chair with his head bowed and his hands clasped firmly before him. His knuckles were white, he wasn't sure he could open his fingers he'd been clenching them for so long. But he was worried if he unclasped them, he might just fall apart. His head was throbbing with the pulsating emotions pounding against him.

The worst of which was Cassie and Devon. Cassie remained immobile beside him; her head held high, and her chin tilted up. The large, dark sunglasses she'd taken to wearing were firmly in place. He would like to think they were hiding her tears, but he knew better. She hadn't cried yet. Not in front of them, and he was fairly certain not at all.

The solid wall of hate she had erected around herself didn't allow room for tears. It didn't allow room for anything, especially not grief. He turned his head slightly toward her. He desperately longed to reach out to her, but knew he would only be rebuked again, just like he had been a hundred times over the past few days.

She didn't want comfort, she didn't want love. She simply desired not to feel anymore, not to care, and *revenge*. Fortunately, at heart, Cassie was a caring, giving person. That was part of what was destroying her now. She didn't know how to deal with her fury, her loathing. It was eating away at her, driving her deeper into her hole, and causing her to hide from the world once more.

It was destroying him that he couldn't do anything to help her. This wasn't the Cassie who had hidden from the world before. That Cassie may have kept people at arm's length, but she had *never* radiated this *hate*. Chris couldn't tune out her emotions, he'd tried, but the force of her rage broke through all of his barriers to beat him down.

Chris shuddered. He was losing his best friend, and there was nothing he could do about it. She wouldn't let him, or anyone else, help her.

Devon wasn't helping him either. He could feel Devon, somewhere nearby, probably in the woods, watching. Chris could feel his distress and heartbreak as he was also impossible to block out now. Between Devon and Cassie they were killing him, and there was nothing he could do to stop it. He didn't know what he was going to do if something didn't change soon. He couldn't sleep at night anymore.

He shuddered again, his hands clenched to the point it was painful. His sorrow over the loss of Lily was being overshadowed by their emotions. He had loved Lily; she'd been like a grandmother to him too. She had raised him, loved him, and sheltered him when his own mother had been unable to handle the life handed to her, unable to love her son anymore, and retreated into an alcohol induced stupor.

A tear slid down his face as his own grief momentarily overwhelmed Cassie and Devon's, allowing him a brief reprieve. He lifted his head as the minister's prayer ended. His attention immediately focused upon the gleaming mahogany casket draped with wreaths of flowers. It hovered above the hole, Lily's permanent resting place.

He shuddered again at the harsh reminder that Lily would never again walk amongst them, loving them, caring for them. A sob choked his throat; he could barely breathe through the pressure in his chest.

It was chilly for November, but he couldn't feel the cold through the emotions swamping him. Heartache enshrouded the people surrounding him, some were openly crying, others stood and remained stoic. Even his mother had come, and though her breath reeked of booze and cigarettes, she appeared to be only hung over and not intoxicated. She stood on the other side of the coffin, her head bowed, and her sandy blond hair spilling across her shoulders. At one time she'd been a beautiful woman, but years of rough living had aged her far too early.

Seeming to feel his gaze, she lifted her head. Sapphire eyes, identical to his, momentarily met his. Though there was loss in her gaze, there was little else. She'd checked out of the brutal reality of their lives years ago. She wasn't capable of handling much anymore; she sure wasn't capable of dealing with what her son was, or handling the loss of his life.

Chris swallowed heavily, not only had Cassie been orphaned by Lily's death, so had he. He hadn't been close to his mother in years, and he'd always known he never would be again. But for the first time he realized that in his mother's eyes, he was already dead. To her, he was simply still breathing for now; still walking for a brief period of time, but it was only a matter of time before he wasn't. She had already dealt with the loss of her son; she was simply just waiting for it to come true.

Chris tore his gaze away from her, unable to handle the look in her eyes. Unable to handle the realization she already thought him dead when he was still very much alive, and planned to stay that way for a *lot* longer. Dani and Melissa sniffled beside him; Cassie stiffened as her head rotated a little to look at them. Though her eyes were completely hidden, he could feel the full force of her gaze on him.

Her jaw clenched, her face was unreadable as her mouth pursed into a thin line. God, he missed *his* Cassie. This girl sitting beside him was a stranger, someone he didn't recognize. This girl was so unyielding. All things Cassie never had been. It was as if the real Cassie had been abducted by aliens, and this was the thing they'd replaced her with. He hated to think of her as a *thing*, but that was what she was now. There was no trace of humanity in her anymore, no love. He'd felt many atrocious emotions from people over the years, but this was the biggest void he'd ever felt from another soul.

If she would just let someone touch her, and hold her, he knew she could come back. She wanted nothing to do with any of them anymore, and he knew all she craved was revenge, and death. He was beginning to fear she'd been lost to him forever.

She didn't even want Devon, the one person (well vampire) who had been able to bring her to life before. If she'd shut Devon out, when Chris knew exactly how in love with him she was, then what hope did he have of getting through to her? He'd thought Cassie and Devon's love could survive anything. He hated being wrong.

He still held out hope Devon would finally be able to reach her. The only problem was she wouldn't let him get close enough to do so.

Cassie suddenly stood, drawing Chris's attention back to her.

He was surprised to realize the funeral was over. Cassie dropped a single red rose onto the coffin as it began its final descent into the ground. He followed behind her and dropped another rose down as the first shovel of dirt was tossed into the deep grave.

Cassie flinched as the dirt thudded against the coffin. For a brief moment he felt a flicker in her walls as anguish rushed forth to clash against the hatred. Hope sprang forth in him as he stretched his hand out to her, but he felt her walls slam back into place. Though he couldn't see her eyes, he felt her gaze disdainfully rake over him. His hand wavered in midair before falling limply back to his side. Cassie lifted her chin as she marched forward, her head was held high as she gracefully slipped through the departing crowd.

Though some people tried to approach her, she easily sidestepped them as she continued toward the waiting limo. Most fell back from her and didn't bother to approach as they headed for their cars. He didn't know if they would bother to come to the house. Cassie had been accepting of their condolences, but aloof and abrupt.

Luther stayed close to Cassie's side, but stopped briefly to speak with a woman before hurrying to catch up with Cassie. None of them were willing to let her out of their sight for any length of time. Chris didn't put it past her to take off on her own in search of Julian and Isla. No, they couldn't leave her alone; if they did it was likely she would get herself killed.

Mrs. Manz picked her way carefully around the headstones as she approached them. Cassie slid into the darkened interior of the limo. "Christopher, Melissa, Danielle," Mrs. Manz greeted as she nodded to each of them.

"Mrs. Manz," Chris said. Though many teachers, and the principal, had come to offer their support, none of the student body had arrived. Cassie had become the social leper of the school, but Chris had still expected at least a few of her old friends to come. He'd been wrong, and he despised them for it.

"How is Cassandra doing?" Mrs. Manz inquired as she glanced at the limo.

"As well as can be expected," Melissa assured her, though it wasn't true.

"What an awful tragedy," Mrs. Manz murmured as she tugged on the sleeve of her black jacket. "Will you let Cassandra know she doesn't have to worry about her assignments until she returns?"

"We will," Melissa told her.

Mrs. Manz squeezed Chris and Melissa's arms. Apparently if she couldn't console Cassie, she was going to settle for consoling them. "Take care."

They nodded as she hurried away, leaving them alone at the edge of the gravesite. Dark clouds were starting to roll in, a breeze tickled the back of his neck, and he detected the hint of snow in the crisp air. It was fitting a storm was rolling in as it seemed to fit the moods of the people gathered around him. "We should go," Chris said.

"Yes," Melissa murmured.

Chris shuddered as he huddled deeper into his coat; it wasn't the chill in the air that bothered him, but the one in his soul. The sound of more dirt hitting the coffin spurred him into movement. He didn't want to be here anymore, but he also didn't want to be near Cassie at the moment. He wasn't sure he could handle her anger anymore.

Unfortunately, he didn't have a choice. She was his best friend, and she needed him, even if she refused to acknowledge it.

~

Cassie stood rigidly in her living room, unwilling to sit down, unwilling to move. Though not everyone from the funeral had come here, there were still enough of them to make her edgy and unsettled. Most of the people were from her grandmother's church. They were her grandmother's friends, but she wanted them out of her house.

They milled about, eating the food they'd brought, and conversing amongst themselves. They avoided her now, apparently having decided she was beyond their reach, which she was. Melissa and Dani were standing by the dining room table, talking with a few members of the church. Chris stood by the fireplace, casting her looks that aggravated her more and more.

She simply didn't want his worry, or his concern. She understood it, but she didn't want it. Turning to the window, she stared out at the darkening night as snow fell in spiraling flakes. It had just started, but it was already beginning to build on the lawns and trees that still hadn't completely shed their colorful leaves.

Headlights swung into the driveway as Luther pulled in. He'd left shortly after the funeral, citing that he had a few things to take care of. He'd been disappearing for brief periods of time ever since her grandmother's death. Cassie didn't know what he was doing, and she didn't particularly care. There was nothing she did care about anymore.

She watched as he blew on his hands in an attempt to keep them warm as hurried up the walkway. "Cassie, maybe you should eat." She glanced back at Chris and shook her head. She had no appetite anymore. "You should eat," he pressed.

"I'm fine."

He sighed reluctantly before moving away from her. She didn't like causing him anymore suffering, he was grieving for her grandmother too, but it was best for him if there was distance between them now. It would upset him less when she was gone.

Her eyes scanned the dark night, though nothing moved she knew Devon was out there. She knew that as well as she knew the sun would rise tomorrow, the earth would turn, and she would still be dead inside. Cassie rested her palms against the cool glass, yearning to go to him.

She wouldn't feel so lifeless in his arms.

She couldn't allow herself to do that. He was the reason her grandmother was dead after all, to forgive him would be a betrayal of her grandmother's memory. To allow herself to love him again would only make what she had to do much more difficult. Her hand slid away from the glass. No, there was no room for forgiveness inside her anymore. She wasn't sure there was room for *her* inside of her anymore.

She almost welcomed the certainty of her death, almost welcomed the release it would bring her. She just hoped by the time it happened Chris and Melissa would have distanced themselves from her. She didn't want them to be *this* devastated, this hopeless and enraged after she was gone. Though she wanted a release from this frozen existence, she wanted even more for them not to have to feel this way too.

"Cassie." She turned toward Luther but ignored the plate he held out to her. Shaking his head, he lowered the plate. "Cassie, your guests are leaving."

She focused on the line of people standing by the door. The only thing that got her moving was the thought her grandmother would be disappointed in her if she was rude to them. She clasped hands, exchanged hugs, and murmurs and was greatly relieved when the last person filtered out. Closing the door behind them, she leaned against it.

"Melissa and I are going to stay again tonight," Luther said.

It took her a moment to focus on him; her vision was becoming blurry from exhaustion. "If you feel you must."

"We don't want you to be alone," Melissa told her.

"I'll be fine. Dani still lives here."

Dani shifted nervously. "Would you like me to leave?" she blurted.

Cassie shook her head as she stepped away from the door. There may be little left of her, but she wasn't going to throw the girl out on the street. "No, you can stay for as long as you have to."

Dani glanced at the other three, unsure how to take Cassie's answer. It hadn't been inviting, but she hadn't been booted to the curb either. "I think it's best if we stay," Luther stated firmly.

They were worried about what she would do if they weren't watching over her but they couldn't watch her all the time. They would have to go home at some point, and eventually Devon would have to feed. Now that the funeral was over, Cassie had much more time on her hands to think about how she would get away. How she would carry out her revenge.

"I'm going to sleep."

Though she uttered the words, she knew they weren't true. She hadn't slept in three days; she didn't expect to sleep tonight. She ignored them as she wearily climbed the stairs. She had become a bitch, a miserable cold bitch; she knew that, she just couldn't bring herself to care.

But then all of her caring, her love, her *life* had all been burnt away by the rage festering within her. It was best if she stayed alone, best if she kept every one away from her. It was better if they didn't know how little there was left to her. Better they didn't know all that was left of her were smoldering ashes of the person she'd once been.

A person she would *never* be again.

The End

~

Book 3, *Kindled*, is now available!
***Kindled* on Amazon: ericastevensauthor.com/Kdlwb**

Stay in touch on updates and new releases from the author by joining the mailing list!
Mailing list for Erica Stevens & Brenda K. Davies Updates:
ericastevensauthor.com/ESBKDNews

FIND THE AUTHOR

Erica Stevens/Brenda K. Davies Mailing List:
ericastevensauthor.com/ESBKDNews

Facebook page: ericastevensauthor.com/ESfb

Erica Stevens/Brenda K. Davies Book Club:
ericastevensauthor.com/ESBKDBookClub

Instagram: ericastevensauthor.com/ESinsta
Twitter: ericastevensauthor.com/EStw
Website: ericastevensauthor.com
Blog: ericastevensauthor.com/ESblog
BookBub: ericastevensauthor.com/ESbkbb

ABOUT THE AUTHOR

Erica Stevens is the author of the Captive Series, Coven Series, Kindred Series, Fire & Ice Series, Ravening Series, and the Survivor Chronicles. She enjoys writing young adult, new adult, romance, horror, and science fiction. She also writes adult paranormal romance and historical romance under the pen name, Brenda K. Davies. When not out with friends and family, she is at home with her husband, son, dog, cat, and horse.

ALSO FROM THE AUTHOR

Books written under the pen name

Erica Stevens

The Coven Series

Nightmares (Book 1)

The Maze (Book 2)

Dream Walker (Book 3)

The Captive Series

Captured (Book 1)

Renegade (Book 2)

Refugee (Book 3)

Salvation (Book 4)

Redemption (Book 5)

Broken (The Captive Series Prequel)

Vengeance (Book 6)

Unbound (Book 7)

The Kindred Series

Kindred (Book 1)

Ashes (Book 2)

Kindled (Book 3)

Inferno (Book 4)

Phoenix Rising (Book 5)

The Fire & Ice Series

Frost Burn (Book 1)

Arctic Fire (Book 2)

Scorched Ice (Book 3)

The Ravening Series

The Ravening (Book 1)

Taken Over (Book 2)

Reclamation (Book 3)

The Survivor Chronicles

The Upheaval (Book 1)

The Divide (Book 2)

The Forsaken (Book 3)

The Risen (Book 4)

Books written under the pen name

Brenda K. Davies

The Vampire Awakenings Series

Awakened (Book 1)

Destined (Book 2)

Untamed (Book 3)

Enraptured (Book 4)

Undone (Book 5)

Fractured (Book 6)

Ravaged (Book 7)

Consumed (Book 8)

Unforeseen (Book 9)

Forsaken (Book 10)

Relentless (Book 11)

Coming Fall 2020

The Alliance Series

Eternally Bound (Book 1)

Bound by Vengeance (Book 2)

Bound by Darkness (Book 3)

Bound by Passion (Book 4)

Bound by Torment (Book 5)

Coming Spring 2020

The Road to Hell Series

Good Intentions (Book 1)

Carved (Book 2)

The Road (Book 3)

Into Hell (Book 4)

Hell on Earth Series

Hell on Earth (Book 1)

Into the Abyss (Book 2)

Kiss of Death (Book 3)

The Edge of the Darkness

Coming Summer 2020

Historical Romance

A Stolen Heart

Made in United States
North Haven, CT
26 June 2022